Who Was Killed?

Cher Bonfis:- Born into a rich elegant world where copious amounts of money cushioned every breath…No, sorry, that was a lie. Let us begin again… Born into absolute poverty in a cheap, ugly, bed and breakfast, which was on the backside of Blackpool, during the off season, to a single parent mother, who was on benefits…. Sorry that was another lie… Is it worth beginning again? Probably not, for the words written here, or in some newspaper, would not really allow you to access the mind of this author. If you want to know about this person best you read the things this person writes. Trivia over details of this life are irrelevant. What you should know is that there is much gratitude for your interest and there is hope that you have found something rewarding. If you believe in love and kindness. If you believe everyone deserves a chance to live a happy life then you and Cher Bonfis have a lot in common. Word by word we will strive to make things better. So thank you for stopping by, and may all good things be yours.

Who Was Killed?

Cher Bonfis

Arena Books

First published by Arena Books in 2021

Arena Books
6 Southgate Green
Bury St. Edmunds
IP33 2BL.

www.arenabooks.co.uk

Cher Bonfis
Who Was Killed?

British Library cataloguing in Publication Data. A Catalogue record
for this book is available from the British Library.

ISBN 978-1-914390-07-4

BIC categories:- FA, FHP.

Cover design
by Jason Anscomb

Typeset in
Times New Roman

A CORUPT POLICEMAN

A DISLOYAL ADULTERESS SPOUSE

CONSPIRE TO RUIN THE LIFE

OF

A LOYAL AND LOVING MAN

"There are things which must cause
you to lose your reason, or you have none."

Viktor Frankl

CHAPTER 1
The End

A carving knife. A lunge. The knife plunged through the white cotton fabric and into the chest, just left of centre. There was no moment for defence; the knife plummeted into the pasty, white, skin, between two ribs, and tore the left ventricle of the heart, and severely damaged the left lung. Blood gushed as the blade was pulled back through the flesh. The wound was neat. Disquietude in the victim's eye's. The sting of the steel blade. Tears to the eyes. Skin of the cheeks vacuumed into the mouth. Outline of the cheek bones in the skin. Silver white glint came upon the face. This event had not featured on their list of expectations. The finale exhale the noise of mule being branded. The legs folded beneath the corpse. The form crumbled. The body was motionless.

The Murderer wondered, for a second, if the noise of the last breath had been overheard, two ears scanned the night air for the sound of neighbour response. There was none. The hand, which had plunged the knife into skin, was motionless, whilst the ears listened, then the murderer's other hand reached across to the tea towel, so conveniently placed, on the hook by the sink, and it was used to wipe the blood from the knife, and then from the right hand. These actions were slow and considered, in contrast to the lunge, which had just missed the rib; the serendipity that had brought this life to it's end.

Then, silently, the murderer returned the cloth to the hook. The light was dim but the cloth was clearly red with the evidence of the demise. The murderer looked down at the executed corpse, and watched to make sure that it was really, and truly, no longer breathing. The watching continued for a few minutes, and then, when the murderer had reorganised their thoughts, and had decided what next to do, the murderer reached down to the body; the wiped hand hesitated a moment, for fear that the victim might come back to life. Then the wiped hand pushed into a pocket, and it's fingers gripped on to what was in there.

It was murder, the premeditation was but a moment, but there was no doubt in the murderer's mind. The stabbing was a deliberate act. There was no hiding that, but the relief, now that the murdered was no longer was ecstasy.

It only took a moment to murder but it had taken forty-three years to get to this point. So, although this chapter is marked 'The End' the story was far from over, even with this death. This story would reverberate many 'Blood Moons' into the future.

One might think that there should be a lot of 'background' music to this tale, for one of our main protagonists is a musician. Thinking back, now, there are memories of pubs with 'Juke Boxes', but that was certainly not every pub, in 1973, when this story began, and recollection would have it that 'Muzak' was not a constant feature of everyday life. The sound systems, and the way music was stored, was not so conducive to it. 'The Musicians Union' used the slogan 'Keep Music Live', as music storage systems developed bringing insecurity to musician's families. There were places where the radio was always on, but young women going to buy clothes were not, in those times, entering disco's which also sold garments. Generally pubs did not have televisions on every other wall, around their premises either. Televisions had not long been able to produce colour pictures, and the size of the sets, and the difficulty with getting a good signal, conspired against them. Of course some pubs installed them for the novelty value, it was progress, after all, colour television only twenty years after the Coronation of Queen Elizabeth II, wow; well people had walked on the moon so why not? Not every car had a radio either so, may be, the world was less noisy than in the days of writing down the events of this story. Of course things started to change with the introduction of the cassette tape, but it took a while, evolution. Evolution is what a good part of this story is about.

"Evolution?" Questioned Harry, looking over the shoulder of his best pal Bill. Harry had his back to the wall and he could see the barmaid, Jill, pulling another pint.

Then Bill said. "Concentrate Harry, even though my back is to the bar I know that you are looking at the lovely Jill. You are married Harry, stop it, and tell me what you were going to say about evolution. You start going on about women evolving, and you sit there ogling Jill, as she leans forward to pull a pint, you are like some caveman Harry, I seriously do not believe you have evolved much since your Great, Great, Great, Great, Great Granddaddy was running away from some sabre toothed tiger." His voice was tinged with the sound of South London.

"Well that is my point Bill, boys will be boys, and men well, we are men. It takes ages for things to change. It says so in this book *On the Origins of Species.* Said Harry

"Did you buy that book Harry?" Asked Bill.

"No Bill I got it from the library. I saw a copy in a geezer's house a few days ago and wondered what it was all about. Written by a feller called Charles Darwin. There is no harm in looking, in looking at Jill. Bill she is a beautiful young woman, and I love the cut of that dress she is almost wearing! See how she pulls that pint, well I wouldn't mind her pulling me Bill." Harry paused and then said "A pint, Bill!"

"I know you wouldn't Harry, everyone else in here can see that too. Seeing as we have gone all educational, Charles Darwin and the like, I read in the paper that Pablo Picasso, the artist bloke, died a few days ago. Now he had no trouble pulling the birds. Easy for a Painter. 'Hey darling I want to paint your picture, just get your kit off will ya.'" Both men sniggered,

"Well that's what the French are like Harry." Mused Bill.

"I don't think Picasso was French, Bill." Said Harry.

"I read in the paper he died in France." Said Bill.

"He may have died there but I am sure he was born in Italy, I may be wrong Bill, may be it was Spain." Said Harry. "I cannot understand what people see in those funny paintings, of his. Don't get me started about the French."

"Where have you seen a painting by Picasso?" Asked Bill. "I have never even seen a photograph of one, actually I have never met a French person either. Have you Harry?"

Harry put his book on the table and lit an Embassy cigarette, with his lighter. Bill did not smoke, he watched the blue haze rise out of Harry's mouth and listened.

"There was this posh gezeer, he bought a colour tele from me, I took the tele up to his house, great big place out in the country, he bought the most expensive tele, well he could afford it, you should see the aerial I put up on his roof, I'll bet he has the best reception anywhere in the country. Anyway that geezer had two of Picasso's paintings, hanging in the room where I put his tele. The geezer had to tell me the pictures were by Picasso. I said to the geezer why don't this Picasso bloke just paint pictures of what he sees, so we could all know what he's painted. The posh geezer asked me a question." Said Harry.

"What did he ask?" said Bill.

"He asked how did I know that was not exactly what Picasso saw? He said how does anyone know what anybody else sees? He said how does anyone know that the colour green is not the colour red inside some other person's head? Well it makes you think, don't it Bill? When you think about it how do you know that anything you do, or say, is seen or heard, by another person, in the way you meant it?" Questioned Harry.

"Blimey Harry, this is some conversation." Said a confused Bill.

"Anyway, as I was trying to say them French, they don't have so much bother with Sex like we English. They don't mind a bit of staring at a pretty girl. I think the girls there like it too. From what I could make out sex is written into the constitution of the French along with *liberté, égalité, fraternité.*" Continued Harry.

"Which of those words is French for sex Harry?" Asked Bill.

"I am not sure but probably égalité. Anyway I know this; the indiscretions of French politicians are matters for their private life, and conscience, not for your every day French proletariat geezer to gork at, in their newspaper, over petit déjeuner." Spoke Harry.

"Blimey Harry you know a lot of them French words." admired Bill.

"I picked up a few phrases in Paris at the end of the war Bill, I wasn't there for long, that's not all I picked up Bill I got crabs off a French girl in one of them bordello's. Sex is different there. The English, we are so screwed up by sex, that is part of the reason I am still staring over your shoulder at Jill, Bill."

"Well what about the Welsh, the Irish, and the Scots. Harry are they screwed up too?" asked Bill.

"Sex is sex, no matter what society surrounds it, but different societies employ different methods to try and hem it in; your Mormon's, and your Sultan's they take on load's of wives. In the Hymala's there are women who take on two husbands. Them out in India and Pakistan arrange marriages for their kids. Some of them Muslim folks hide their women away under black dresses that cover them from head to foot, with just a gap so the woman can see where she's going. The English control sex by making it dirty, and something to be ashamed of. You should have heard the fuss about my crabs, I tell you what though, she was worth it! I ain't never seen a woman as sexy looking as Michelle, in that Paris brothel. I'd swim the channel for another night with Michelle."

"Well why don't you Harry? Apart from having a wife here in England of course." Asked Bill. "I was in the Desert in North Africa in the war, there were no brothels where I was, just tons and tons of sand."

"Well Bill she died, she was killed at the end of the war Bill, terrible loss Bill, terrible."

Harry was away in a dream at that moment. Then someone put a coin in the juke box and Alvin Star Dust was singing *'My Coo-Ca-Choo'*. It was the first time he had heard this song, it was new. Harry walked over to the bar just as Jill moved to the other end of the bar to serve another customer, so instead of Jill Harry was now facing the manager of the pub, Norman.

"Harry, nice to see you. I have decided to go for it, my answer is yes, we will buy one of them new colooor televisions from you. I'm going to

get Bill to build me a platform for it over in that corner to stand it on."
Said Norman, who had been the manager of the Rose and Crown for ten
years. Then Norman called out "Bill."

In 1973 Norman wondered how he could make space for a huge, new,
colour television set, and how he could afford to buy one. He had no idea
that forty three years later many people would own a device, small
enough to keep in a pocket, which could be a phone, a camera, a torch,
and a zillion other things, as well as being a colour television, on which,
not only programmes could be conjured up, but a persons favourite song
hit complete with a pretty video, with no wires attached, including *'My
Coo-Ca-Choo'.*

Harry, Bill or Norman had no idea that in less than half a century
scientists would be able to produce babies in test tubes, and that scientists
would produce mice using materials only from the females. Is it any
wonder that some people get left behind, and confused, as changes
happen faster, and faster. Many of the changes having nothing to do with
evolution.

Remembering Harry's words, all these years later, it is obvious that
many English people still have problems with sex, or should we write
'IT? It is still a mystery to some. More jokes where made about 'it' than
there were serious discussions about 'it'. Why discussions should be
'serious'? That is yet another mystery. Despite millions of years of
reproduction, and huge increases in populations, the questions 'who',
'what', 'when', 'where', 'why' and 'how' to teach of 'it'. How to deal
with 'it', and how to regulate   'it', and so much more, was unresolved.
People are confused. Many have never understood that 'sex' is hard wired
into humans in their DNA. Even if nobody gives instruction, people work
it out, it is like walking, there comes a time in a person's life when they
find they can, then they do. May be they fumble and tumble a bit, but
with a little practice most get the hang of it, even if they don't discover
the finesse.

Sex produces laughter or an over-serious, clinical response, like those
of presenters of a radio programmes called 'Woman's Hour'. By contrast
television comedy shows, produced by the 'new generation', in England,
are peppered with innuendo and double entendre, no differently from
when Harry Champion was king of the Music Hall singing *'The End of
Me Old Cigar'* to sniggering Music Hall audiences. Young women, of the
twenty first century generation, have begun the 'Me Too Movement' It
has called out many men, some deservedly so. However, many other men
have been left confused, to say the least, and vast numbers of ordinary
men, who would never dream of performing any sexual misdemeanour,
have felt tainted by all the horrid, torrid, publicity, even though they are
innocent. Others have run to the cover of, what they claim to be, an

addiction to sex and have pleaded to be treated with leniency and have asked to be given another chance.

Some young men, on hearing that there fellows have been accused of rape, have been left wondering if they should get a written contract signed before they dare hold the hand of a girl, let alone kiss one.

Then there are a few women, as in the Janis Ian Song 'Seventeen'. *'I learned the truth at seventeen, this world is meant for beauty queens, and high school girls with clear skin smiles who married young and then retired'*. Who wonder what on earth is going on, for no man ever 'came on' to them, some wonder what would be so bad about that? They ask what makes men shy away from them?

"No Bill." Said Harry, as they resumed their seats, with fresh pints of 'Watney's Pale Ale', in pint beer jugs. "'The Great English Public' may never be liberated from their embarrassment with sex, for if they were what would the tabloid newspapers do? How would comedians make a living? Arguments will always abound over what sex is allowed, or not allowed, to be shown in cinema or on Norman's new colour television. Why does he pronounce colooor like that, I wonder?"

Well at least Harry, Bill or Norman had no 'World Wide Web' to deal with, for in 1973 Tim Bernards Lee was just at the end of his time at his Grammar School, Emanuel, by Wandsworth Common, South London, not so far from the Rose and Crown. The Rose and Crown that was also just a few streets away from the Nursing Home, where in some forty years, in 2018, Harry would celebrate his 95th birthday. Even as a resident of that Nursing Home Harry had no idea that there were issues amongst staff members regarding the behaviour of two male staff members towards several female staff members. Issues of how far a man is allowed to encroach upon a women's space and the 'Mine-Fields' of sexual relationships in a workspace. In 1973 these were concepts Harry, Bill or Norman had never had to battle with.

*

In 2016 Harry's Grandson Craig, and Bill's Grandson Dave, were best friends. They were having a drink in The Rose and Crown, now Managed by Norman's Grandson, Norman. Craig said.

"Well it's the evolving cultural acceptability of things. Things once accepted, but now, considered heinous, and visa versa. We men are grappling with millions of years of evolutionary pressures, trying to conform to what would have been alien in our Granddad's time, back in the war."

"I agree." Said Dave. "I read this book."

"What? You read a book!" Exclaimed Craig. "I can hardly believe it, you are such a snowflake."

Dave continued. "It went on about the cultural super highway which has allowed mankind to progress ideas at speed that evolution cannot keep up with. So your body, and deep parts of our psyche, are still roaming the savannah, hunting and gathering, whilst our lives today have been revolutionised by our clever ideas, and fantasy, and technology. Life has always been full of change, and life has always been a roller coaster. The twenty first century has supplied such abundance of food, water, and creature comforts. Comforts beyond the dreams of Midas, to some people, in some parts of the world. That people are released from the toil's, which for centuries, ate up most of their waking hours."

Craig chortled. "This book is not about us then Dave! Seems to me I work more hours a week than God gave us and I have never touched anything that turned to gold!"

Dave continued. "Don't interrupt me Craig, I will loose the plot. The point is that now people have some spare time and some of them use it to think up 'new problems', things previous generations would never have considered to be problems at all. They expose these new problems, and discuss them, and, maybe, sometimes they try to solve these problems. Maybe sometimes they succeed. More often than not, people simply enjoy wallowing in them, like a happy hippopotamus in a watery marsh, people like to have something to moan about. They like to have something they can get cross about. After all; things are only problems when they are perceived to be. Look at the world today people can choose to be Vegetarian, or even Vegan. They can even choose the sex which they would prefer to be. There are more and more choices confronting people these days, it's mind boggling. Some times people think up evil things to do."

Dave put his book on the table. It was about human history. A man from the other side of the pub stood up from his chair. He had a cigarette and a lighter in his hand. He went out of the pub, through the door to smoke it outside.

Norman came over, from his normal place, behind the bar.

"Craig, Dave. I'm putting on a special night, in three weeks time. 'Colooor Tele Night'. It will be the anniversary of the first colour television in this street. My Granddad, Norman, bought it from your Granddad Craig, and your Granddad Dave built that shelf, over there, for it to stand on. People packed this pub out, night after night to get a look at it, my Granddad had been so worried about buying the set, it was a small fortune, but within a week, or two, the investment had turned into a profit. So Craig I want you to see if you can get Harry down here, to be the guest of honour. I am sorry Dave, that your Granddad, Bill, has passed on, but I have had this blue plaque made."

Norman held up a circular blue plaque, a bit like the ones which are put on the outside of buildings where famous people have lived. In silver the names Norman, Harry and Bill shone upon it.

"It will be put up on that wall, above the shelf and Harry can unveil it on the night. Jill, Harry's favourite barmaid, will be here with her husband and children and grand children. She will switch on the, brand new, tele, which will hang on the wall above it. I have been reading about the history of television. Did you know that the first publicly televised, silhouette, images transmitted by John Logie Baird in 1925, in Selfridges, on Oxford Street, in London? Unbelievable that now most people carry a television in their pocket. Look at the size of that shelf your Granddad built Dave."

The television on the opposite wall of the pub lit up, it was very thin, but it had a fifty five inch screen, the familiar music of 'Coronation Street' could be heard. An actor walked across the screen.

Dave said. "Look! Oh, what is his real name?"

Norman said. "Oh, I can't remember."

Dave said. "Well he was a man who had 'evil' done to him, poor man. All these changing attitudes towards sexual conduct, we were speaking about, well they provide opportunity for some people, to use sexual conduct as a weapon, against some completely innocent men. The way many people have learned to react towards sexual misconduct means that, even, suggested sexual misconduct is sufficient to ruin a person's life, even if they are guilty of nothing. Look at that poor singer. The 'Me Too' women are right, but the other side of the equation has provided the easiest way to smash somebody's life to smithereens. It is not just a way to damage, it is the way to annihilate, it is a banana republic firing squad. Anything to do with sex, even putting a hand on a woman's knee."

Craig said. "Well of course there have been a lot of bad eggs too."

Dave said. "True but there are men and women who have turned this stuff into weapons and have wreaked lives out of malice, to get their own back for whatever reason they may have."

Craig said. "I can tell you a story, it is a true story, of a good man, and a good woman, and a man called Raymond and a murder that was done because of the kinds of things we have been speaking of.

Dave said. "Go on then."

Norman said. "Hold on, there is no one in the pub, it is almost closing time, wait while I shut the doors and I'll get us another drink then tell us the story Craig. Is it about someone you know?"

"Oh yes, I knew them, but I have never spoken of this to anyone before. I was doing some renovations on a house just by Cheltenham, back up past the racecourse, a few years ago. It is quite a long tale. I know most of it, some because I saw things with my own eyes, some because I became friends with one of the men involved, some because I read reports in the newspaper, and saw things on the television. I also was called as a witness at the inquest."

"I'll be back in a jiffy." Said Norman. Once Norman had returned Craig began his story:

*

One of the characters of this tale will have their life smashed to pieces by another as they give in to carnal desires, and they cause catastrophic harm. This, however, is not a tale of 'Adam and Eve' or some sordid love triangle where adultery does the harm. It is more a tale of wanting more, or wanting something different, from that which was already possessed. It is a search for excitement, or possibly an escape from boredom. It is a search for lust and quivering, juddering sexual relief. It is certainly a tale of an unquenchable desire for an experience, as yet unknown. It is also a wider story of twenty first century women throwing off the shackles of thousands of previous years, realising that they cannot only expect more, but also get more from their lives, even if they are not sure of what is available.

Just think of how things have changed, and changed so quickly. Until 1975 French criminal law provided lighter sentences for *Crime Passionnel.* English law considered adultery as the *highest invasion of property.* Not so long ago women were the property of their fathers or their husbands. An aggrieved husband *'could not receive a higher provocation'* than his wife's adultery, until English laws were updated in 2010.

Aborigines in Australia have their 'Dream Time Myths', in one they describe the way that people had to go about on their bellies, until one day one reached up and touched the sky, others, following the example, reached up too and as they all pushed together, of a sudden, the sky ripped apart and the people found they could stand up on two legs and there was a beautiful new blue back drop to their lives. Later on in this tale one of the characters discovers this 'Dream Time Story', and it becomes an obsession. It fills them with a power to push on, and up, for something more than they already had. Stories are powerful things. Never mess with stories, they often come true and remember where there is sexual desire there can also be, and often is, evil.

CHAPTER 2
Forty-Three Years Before

Raymond was at school, he was an adolescent, and he hated the spots which came to his face so he rubbed Clearasil onto them, night and morning, using cotton wool buds he pinched from his mother's makeup draw. He was unsure if the treatment made a lot of difference, the spots did little for his self-image. He was not the most comfortable of students and he found it difficult to deal with many of his classmates. In fact, on the day this story began, the last day of term before Christmas, he found himself in a huge fight in the school playground. A boy called Milton had made fun of him, over a particularly big spot, which was right on the middle of Raymond's chin. The morning lessons of Maths, logarithms and more logarithms, and then English where the teacher kept on and on about the glottal stop, all Raymond could think about was Milton's nose and Raymond smashing it with his fist. So, as soon as the class had decanter-ed into the sharp, December, air of the school playground, the fight ensued. Raymond pulled on Milton's shoulder and as he turned Raymond's fist smashed into Milton's cheek. It caught him by surprise and in an instant Milton started a counter-attack. The punches were hard from all four fists. Milton's supporters were many, and vocal, their chanting alerted the duty teacher, who had to get help from three other teachers to separate the protagonists, and restore peace. Both Raymond and Milton were caned, by the head master, for the affray, and Raymond received a suspension from school for the first week of the term which was to follow the holiday. Raymond thus received further, ferocious, punishment from his father, who felt more embarrassed by his son's behaviour, than anything else.

The same day, in 1973 Arwyn met Douglas. They were both a couple of years older than Raymond, at this stage in the story neither of them knew of Raymond's existence, and Raymond had never heard of either of them.

Douglas had long black hair and wore 'moleskin' trousers, in a light tan colour; some would say 'khaki'. Several, unkind persons, suggested that they were left over from the desert war in North Africa, circa 1940. He also had a Parker Jacket, which he had because he liked the one Paul Simon wore on the cover of his first solo album after Simon and Garfunkel had split up. Douglas came from a loving, caring, family. His parents gave him responsibilities, for example, his mother told him:-

"Here is the money you can have, you can use it as you wish, but you must get yourself to and from college, have enough for your lunch and your clothes. There will be no top up's so use this money carefully."

In 'British Home Stores', in the Regent Arcade, Douglas found a pile of these khaki, moleskin, trousers, he knew the colour was garish, yes he knew that, but the trousers were also very cheap, only ninety nine pence a pair, in the, quiet, new decimalised coins of the realm, and that would leave him money to spare for other things.

Douglas saved the money by walking to college, until he had enough money to buy a second hand bicycle. It had drop handle bars, it was gold in colour and had a useful rack, for his bag, at the back. There was a dynamo to run the lights, Douglas was very happy with his purchase.

Arwyn had long, red, hair back then, which fell right down her back, She, by contrast, to Douglas's loose appearance, wore a brown, suede, Gucci coat, of a fashion very popular in those times, and Arwyn gave elegance to that style. Douglas loved her long, red, hair and anything she wore. He often told her how he liked to see her in this dress or that skirt and blouse. Arwyn's family were good, like Douglas's, but they were different from his. The politics in Arwyn's family led to the right. Arwyn's father thought that hanging was way to good for wrong doers. Douglas's father really wanted to understand why someone would do something atrocious, and see if he could help that person to do better things. Arwyn was studying to become a cook; Douglas was taking classes in electronics.

Douglas first saw Arwyn as she was waiting for the bus, near the college, one evening when he rode by on his bike, but it was not until the end of term, the last day before the Christmas holidays, that he found the opportunity to properly meet her. Most of the students headed to the local pubs at lunchtime, as the college term ended.

Everyone was under the legal drinking age, but everyone was drinking anyway. Things were different then. Everyone was kissing everyone. Some of the young men had gone out of their way to bring sprigs of mistletoe with them. Not Douglas he just strode over to Arwyn and declaimed:-

"If I profane with my un-worthiest hand this holy shrine, the gentler sin is this: My lips, two blushing pilgrims, ready stand to smooth that rough touch with a tender kiss."

Arwyn looked at him with a cheeky, disbelieving grin. Her response "You're drunk!"

Douglas smiled back and continued. "Not too drunk to recite from Romeo and Juliet. Wendy." He pointed. "Said she thought you needed a Christmas kiss."

"Oh did she?" Arwyn did not believe for a moment that Wendy had said anything, but a moment later Douglas was kissing Arwyn.

Douglas was a good looking young man, who stood out from the crowd, Arwyn thought that he would be quiet a catch.

Things were different then. Some might say that those days were 'Halcyon'. There was no Internet, there were no mobile phones, and there was no 'Facebook'. People, especially young people, enjoyed great freedoms, may be greater freedoms than those available when this book was being written. For it was possible to keep secrets, and to be private.

Many of the parents of these young adults had run the gauntlet of war, and later had been liberated by the contraceptive pill, but they were still bound by millennia of sexual repression, instilled by religious zealots, or for fear of illegitimacy. Many were happy that their sons and daughters could enjoy freedoms denied to them, although they might not have said the words out loud, but in that very 'English Way', they were able to turn a blind eye to it. So if you think it strange that just a few words could be followed by a kiss on the lips, things were different then. Besides it was Christmas and Arwyn had seen other girls getting kissed, and she had been wondering if anyone would want to kiss her, and then this thin guy with long black hair, and khaki trousers wanted to, and she wanted to be kissed and she thought, 'why not?' It was her first 'romantic' kiss and she drank it down and she liked it.

Douglas asked Arwyn if she would like a drink. "Port and Lemon would be nice."

Douglas had a weekend job, working in a café so the Port and Lemon, although he did think 'wow', as she said it, was possible. He came back from the bar and they sat at a table and talked until the pub shut at three.

So their relationship had begun. That afternoon, they walked the long lane, over the river, to wait for the bus, which would take them to where Douglas lived. It was very cold that December Day, but they both were warmed by the excitement of new feelings surging within them.

Douglas gave money to the bus conductor; Douglas felt it was the job of a man to pay. Arwyn did not even think about it. The conductor took Douglas's money and slipped it into his over the shoulder moneybag, and then he handed over the tickets from his ticket machine. Douglas took the two from the conductor's fingers, fingers that protruded through gloves, which covered only the lower part of the fingers and hands. He wore a matching scarf.

Douglas said to the conductor. "Nice scarf and gloves."

The conductor smiled a huge West Indian smile and replied. "Why thank you Sir, my wife made them for me. It is a cold, cold night. You two young love birds cuddle you up tight." Arwyn blushed.

Christmas came and Christmas went. As the New Year began Douglas walked the three miles from his house off the Gloucester Road to Arwyn's house in Prestbury. He walked this walk, there and back, so many times. He always walked Arwyn home, sometimes Arwyn's Father would drive him back home by the race course and through the west end of Pittville Park.

Like a chauffer Arwyn's father would be in the front and Arwyn and Douglas would sit on the back seat holding hands, half in conversation with their chauffer, but more in communication with each other, a glance here, a squeeze of the hand there. Douglas never wondered why her father didn't just come and pick her up, he did not want him to, because Douglas wanted to be with Arwyn as much as he could, every moment was special, any moment was good.

When Douglas arrived at Arwyn's house he found that Arwyn was not feeling so well, her mother had ordered her into her bed. Arwyn's mother welcomed Douglas into the house and after some pleasantries she showed Douglas up to Arwyn's bedroom.

It was a pleasant house, Arwyn's mother was proud of the things she owned. Arwyn's father took the attitude that he would go without until he could afford to buy something of high quality, something that would last. IKEA had yet to be heard of, and the throw away society had yet to be born.

The telephone sat on a glass table by the door. There was a framed mirror on the wall above the table and a vase of artificial flowers, a little dusty. The walls were papered with a garish orange flavour, with deep brown oval and circle pattern; it would not have been Douglas's choice. The carpet was thick, robust and green beneath his feet.

Arwyn was watching a tiny black and white television. It rested on a wooden locker, to the left of the bed. This was the smallest television that Douglas had ever seen. It was like a transistor radio with a screen, it even had a telescopic aerial, he noted the make Casio, TV-400, he would have liked one for himself.

Douglas had the feeling that this household was somewhat less poor than the one his parents could provide.

The room was really big, much bigger than the one Douglas had. Douglas had to share with three younger brothers. The light was off; there was a chair by the double bed, in which Arwyn lay in the centre.

Douglas sat down, Dorothy left the room, and conversation began. The young couple talked for a long time, Douglas held Arwyn's hand, his arm stretched out resting on the eiderdown. Douglas discovered that Arwyn had felt a bit unwell that morning. Arwyn told him that her mother was always hypersensitive to any minor ailment. Arwyn continued saying that her mother had often been sick when she had been a child, so anything that came to Arwyn, or her sister, or her brother, was treated with the greatest consideration, just in case it was something bad. Arwyn's mother, Dorothy, had also lost a brother to a childhood illness, and a sister, who was only twenty when she died. Dorothy came into the world before antibiotics, and before Doctor Salk had cured polio. So, may be, it is not so difficult to understand her concern.

It was a long time before Arwyn patted the bed and pulled back the cover, to indicate that Douglas should lay on the bed beside her. Arwyn rolled on her side with her head on the pillows. Douglas moved, their faces were now close and they could see properly into each other's eyes then, as the static electricity on a balloon sticks it to the ceiling, their lips were drawn together and they were kissing. The idea of feeling ill completely vanished from Arwyn's mind, for now there was something infinitely better to fill her senses. They kissed for a long time. It was lovely, it was light, and it was delicate. The kissing was not the sort that squashed the lips against the teeth, it was the type that had no weight and that tingled.

Then a conversation, that Arwyn had had with a friend, came to her mind, and she thought she would try, she felt her tongue move forward into Douglas's mouth, and another new sensation was upon her, and Douglas was surprised by it too, and as her tongue withdrew his advanced and the sensations they had just experienced came in reverse to them both, and they melted together as copper and gold, twelve karat Russian, red, gold dripping in the furnace of new love.

The French kissing continued. They were as children and it was still Christmas, there were other gifts to open and his hand, in hesitation, moved towards her breast. She knew it was coming, for other, more experienced, girls had told her of the sensations that they had liked. In the dark, by the light of the little television, with her eyes closed and her mouth gently touching his. She wanted to tell him to do it, she could feel that he wanted too; she was desperate for it to happen, for it had never happened before in her life.

Arwyn made no complaint as his trembling fingers came to rest on her breast. As Douglas's fingers landed as the Eagle. No one had been here before and the excitement gushed through everything that was him. He lingered feeling the softness and the warmth. His fingers felt the softness and he discovered the gentle elasticity that can be found only in such a place.

There was no rush, there was no panic to move on to yet another stage, there was no desperation to strike out for an orgasm. This was a journey of new discoveries; a delightful journey that Arwyn did not want to end and Douglas had no desire to cut short. His fingers advanced and came to her nipple; she clenched her body as his fingers, as the lunar rover, explored further this new, heavenly, tranquillity. She liked it so much. Then, gently he squeezed it.

After a while she pulled her lips from his and whispered. "Do that again," she paused, "please."

He did, and she liked what he did, and she asked him to touch her other breast at the same time. She rolled on to her back and pulled the chord that kept the collar of her chemise together, she undid the buttons and Douglas was able to see her breasts for the first time. Being careful not to make a noise Douglas adjusted his position, he need not have worried about noise, the thick carpet absorbed all of that. When he was comfortable both his hands reached forward to caress both of Arwyn's breasts. Douglas was learning this new terrain, learning how his beautiful partner enjoyed the different rambling's of his different fingers, his nails and his hands. Oh how he wished to please. Oh how she enjoyed his pleasing.

These moments, in the relationship of Arwyn and Douglas, were not unique to them; other couples had enjoyed such times. What may have been unusual was the slow and gentle nature of it all.

The caresses seemed to go on, and on, forever; velvet was the word in Douglas's thoughts, she felt like velvet. Arwyn liked it.

For Douglas it was as the first beam of heat and light as the sun arose in the lunar sky, he had felt the softest warmth his fingers had touched in his journey through life so far.

It was later, and it was Arwyn, who whispered to Douglas. "Let me lie on my back with my head on the pillow, you do the same."

It was Arwyn who took, gently, hold of Douglas's hand and slid it down, beneath the bed covers. The covers seemed to have been released from most of gravity, and for a few moments her hand rested a top of his fingers, and his fingers rested on the soft skin of her tummy, and like a great explorer, who had climbed to a high ridge, he was looking down from the escapement to a fabulous plain below. Full of colours and vegetation, and animals, and Flamingos flying off the, huge, Lake Naivasha, and the Kenyan sun beat down on his head and filled with desire so hot the whole of what life had been was melting away in the sunshine of the exquisitely new.

Douglas felt like a new, and superior, version of Homo Erectus, a species of greater stature than Homo Sapiens, marching down the escarpment to the plain of Eden on the eve of what they both wanted to come.

So her hand guided his hand until his fingers were resting gently amongst the hairs between her legs. Paralysed, for a few glorious, delicious, moments he felt beneath his fingers tropical, virgin territory. She tensed as she felt his hand; no one had touched her there before. She wanted him to hold her there as she breathed in this new, dry equator air. They had crossed the line, and as much as she wanted to absorb this new and exotic experience for longer, her hunger for the next new tingle pressed her to manipulate his fingers into the soft moistness, deeper between her legs. She had done this to herself frequently but this was the first time a man had touched her there. Gently his fingers caressed the delicate folds sliding his finger to and fro, and then she was quivering and her legs squeezed tight around his hand and her head pushed back into the pillow she had laid on, as an adolescent, only a couple of hours before. Now as the Flamingos took flight, their childhoods flew away into a pink cloud of circling Flamingos and they came into land somewhere far away beyond the moon. Two childhood's headed off into to the universe to attach themselves to some, as yet unborn soul, for the cycle to go on.

Arwyn knew what she had just experienced, for friends had told her, but still she was wondering what she had just experienced, and she was wishing she could experience it again as soon as possible. Each nerve ending was screeching for more and she wished that it was possible straight away, but she thought that something so seismic could not be experienced straight way again.

Just for now she felt like an angel in the glow of a warming hallo. Douglas was now the intrepid Neil, and he was buzzing, he could see the hallo framing her beautiful face, in his visor, or, may be, it was that sunbeam, or was it a ray from the tiny television? Whatever his mind was engulfed by the most intense emotions he had experienced, and he climbed up the ladder into the landing craft. She lay motionless, exhausted by 'the' physical sensation of her life, to that moment. All to soon mission control was counting and they had to leave the lunar surface, knowing that life could never be the same as it had been only a couple of hours before.

It may have been half an hour before she opened her eyes. The little television still squeaking out its programmes. They both felt the bond between them joining, as the ring of red gold about them, as the equator, and now they basked in the tropics, and could see the stars in the southern hemisphere and it was new and they wondered if it was all to good to be true.

Arwyn whispered, with worry in her voice. "You don't think I'm easy do you?"

Douglas paused, "No…I love you, and I will always." He whispered in response.

"I really like it." Arwyn whispered back.

Douglas did not seek an orgasm for himself, although his penis was stiff, and as hard as he had known it. He was engrossed in love, not sex, the happiness of having helped Arwyn in this first erotic act that was a sufficiency for him that evening. Besides he knew if he had cum it would have to go somewhere, tissue would be needed, and then the smell might have been difficult. Until now he had only theory, things he had read, things told to him by other boys and snatches of ideas from television, or an X rated movie he and his pals had sneaked, illegally, into. Now he had some first hand experience. He was happy because she was happy. That was how Douglas was with sex, from that moment on his greatest pleasure was to give pleasure.

From then on Arwyn was a part of all Douglass major events, she was at his eighteenth birthday, she was there at his gigs, she was there in the recording studio, she helped the sound engineer push faders up and down as the musicians were conducted, and as Douglas stood on the threshold of his career. He was equally the prime focus of Arwyn's life.

Arwyn was there when a famous record producer called him on the telephone to say that he was very impressed by Douglas's audition for a television programme.

The Producer invited Douglas to his house. It was a new kind of world for Douglas, thick pile carpet on the floor and gold taps in the bathroom. Douglas's house had lino on the floor, and until a short while before the privy was outside in a shed in the garden. Later the Producer took Douglas to a dinner in a fancy fish restaurant on Baker Street, in London. This was not like the fish and chip shop, which, in those days, could be smelt all the way down the road. The Producer ate oysters! Douglas watched, he had never seen an oyster before, although he had heard of them and could not believe that this man, this famous record producer, would put something into his mouth which seemed to be still alive. Then Douglas was asked to choose which fish he would like, from those swimming in the tank before him.

"You could be a big star, you need to tell your girl friend because she may not want to be involved." enthused the producer.

In the clumsiest manor Douglas told Arwyn what The Producer had said; strangely she did not leave.

Douglas loved to be buried in Arwyn's red hair as she lay on top of him on his bedroom floor. Kissing and holding. He loved the looks she gave him and the fun in her smile. They never ran out of conversation. She would sit on his lap, in the armchair, in his bedroom, and recall all the tales of her schooldays, her teachers and friends. She was good with accents and would add them to the voices of the characters of her stories. She told him of her friends and family and how much her sister had spent, of her mother's money, buying make-up. Arwyn adopted a Welsh accent to mimic her mother.

"Oh you little wretch Susan you are. You are nothing but a little thief, all the money from my purse on stuff that makes you look like Jezebel. You wait until your father is home." Arwyn started to talk like Arwyn again. "Well it would not matter if she waited for her grandfather, and his grandfather it will make no difference to Susan, she is Daddy's pet, he would never raise his voice to her, little queen of Cheltenham." Arwyn returned to her Welsh voice. "So she is." Arwyn's voice again. "Brother Gwyn gets away with murder too, he could rob the bank and my mother would not hear a word against him. Me if I put one toe half way out of line, I never hear the end of it. Gwyn ate a great chunk of a birthday cake Mum had made for Dad's birthday, before it had been iced or presented, or candles had had the chance to be blown out on it. Mum simply iced what cake was left; it was a round cake and had a slice missing! It was the talk of the party! Everyone felt it novel."

Arwyn did not need makeup she was as pretty and as beautiful as can be, and she was not so keen on cake, but she loved Douglas and Douglas loved Arwyn.

Arwyn and Douglas liked to go to the seaside, they would go to Western-Super-Mare. Sometimes to Portishead. They liked to explore. They liked to walk around Cheltenham Race Course. It was about halfway from where each of them lived. Sometimes they went to pick Strawberries at the Pick Your Own farm. Arwyn would make the same joke about 'Picking Your Own' each time they went, with suitable variations on the theme.

What Arwyn, really, loved was to play Tennis. If she could not play, watching it being played was the next best thing. Looking back at those days, many years later, Neither Arwyn or Douglas could think what else they did apart from seeing one another during this part of their lives. Douglas knew that, however much, he practiced he would never beat Arwyn in tennis match.

Soon after they had met Arwyn and Douglas had been integrated into each other's families. They would sleep over at each others houses, but in separate beds, as already written it was different then, but it did not stop them loving, and kissing, and petting at every un-witnessed moment. For, some might think, strangely, although actually sleeping in the same bed at night was not allowed, full access of bedrooms was uninhibited at any other time. Parents seldom visited.

Arwyn's father, Robert, was the sixth of eight siblings and had been left as the youngest. He had inherited the family business from his Father, he would have preferred to be an electrician, or something of the sort, but his brother and he were all that were left of the eight. Death and emigration had put the others out of reach. His brother drank and gambled. The chain of five grocery shops made it possible for Robert to provide handsomely for his wife, and Arwyn, and her sister Susan, and their brother Gwyn. The shops were scattered about the town, one very near to the 'Posh Promenade' and one in Gloucester.

Robert worked hard and was a proud man. "Nothing but the best for my customers, that will mean I can give nothing but the best to my family," was what Robert chanted to himself day in and day out.

Robert paid for the care of his mother, who spent the latter part of her life in a nursing home. He paid his brothers gambling debts. Robert had fought in the Second World War, he always protested that he did not speak of it, but in reality, he often spoke of his involvement with ships, and the action he was involved in.

Robert was a member of 'The Order of Buffaloes'; he wore the lapel pin with pride, and believed *'No man is at all hours wise'*.

Robert's great passion was tennis. The one thing he had been able to pass on to his eldest daughter. Pancho Gozales and Rod Laver were two of the stars he particularly had respect for. Robert was born a few years before Pancho. Pancho was an American, which Robert felt was not the best of nationalities to be, no, in Robert's mind being English was the only thing to be, not British, certainly not American, he was not even sure about the Welsh, although he was married to one.

Pancho exonerated himself by the sheer magnificence's of his game; Robert also liked Pancho's temper tantrums. One of Roberts's greatest moments was to see Pancho at Wimbledon in 1969. He was twelfth seed that year. Arthur Ashe beat him in the forth round. Robert tried, not always with success, to mimic Pancho's temper, he tried to be fierce but could never do it for long, it always left him feeling empty and exhausted.

Robert's wife, Dorothy, Arwyn's mother, was always in charge; she could be really fierce, it took very little to ignite her. It never exhausted her, but if she felt she was not in charge, at any given moment, she would scream until everyone stepped back and let her be in charge. She had a kind spirit, but it was hard, if anyone slipped to the wrong side of her, misdemeanours received strong punishments. A stern look, that could halt a tennis ball in flight, well that is how Robert called it. If Dorothy was unhappy everyone would have to be unhappy about it; and the wrong doer would be felled without mercy.

Dorothy was two years older than Robert and from a mining family, her father had worked in the Bersham Colliery in Wrexham, and so had three of her five brothers. Two of them worked in a lime quarry. When the Second World War came along Dorothy was recruited to the Inland

Waterways, shipping coal by barge. She met Robert in a London Pub, he was not keen on an involvement with a foreigner but he fell for her accent, and they were married just a short while afterwards.

Dorothy was an extremely intelligent woman, her intelligence quotient would have been recorded in the top two percent of the population, Robert would have scored at around thirty four percent. This discrepancy meant that Robert could never really get the better of his wife.

Dorothy carried some heavy-duty emotional issues. She became so emotional on one occasion, in tears; she told Douglas that she had been conceived before her parent's marriage, something she considered had discoloured her whole life. Her father and mother had had to move away from their families, and live a hundred miles, and more, away. It was years before they could return and only by some careless talk, she overheard one day, did she come by the truth. The phrase 'born the wrong side of the sheets' was one that caused her great grief, if ever she heard it. Douglas took that as a gentle hint that he should not cause Arwyn to be pregnant.

Susan was Arwyn's sister, different in colouring, darker than Arwyn, different in temperament from Arwyn, much more like her mother. Susan was fun, vivacious and very much her own person. She adored make-up, and fashionable clothes and new hairstyles.

Their brother, Gwyn, was somewhat younger, a happy, but late, addition to the family, something of a surprise, but Dorothy's pride and joy, her little prince, and her daughters knew it. He was the type who got into the detail of things, a serious young man with the brains of his mother and the fussiness of his father.

*

Douglas's family were kind and supportive too, they were religious people, his Father, John was named after John Wesley. John trained to be a Methodist Minister, his wife, Joan, wanted him to do that, and was so very pleased when he was ordained. She had a singing voice, which could belt out the hymns, from the Methodist hymnbook, any, and every Sunday morning, afternoon or evening.

Douglas's parents worked where the family lived, so home life was a lot different for Douglas's family than many other families. Douglas's parents were always there but on the other hand they were not always there, for although they were somewhere about, they were often dealing with other people, who needed their help. Douglas's parents always made time for him, and his five siblings, but the life led Douglas to early independence.

Douglas had to share a bedroom with his three brothers. Wesley, eighteen months his junior. Luke, a little over four years younger. Then there was Matthew, nine years of age at this moment in the story. Their sisters were twins and were just coming up for six years old, Mary and Margaret. It was a large Methodist family. Full of love and joy, and poor in financial terms as they could be, and still keep up some suitable appearance.

Douglas had been in the Boy's Brigade; he became 'Sure and Steadfast'. Actually he had been born 'Sure and Steadfast'. He liked the 'sailors hat' and the 'blue jumper'. He liked the fun with the other lads. The pacifist values, which anchored the organisation, were those that Douglas upheld for all of his life.

Sometimes other boys at school would egg him on. "So what if someone came with a gun and wanted to shoot your Mum, would you just stand there offering the other cheek?" They would goad him relentlessly. That was school in the nineteen sixties.

1974

Douglas had had a good weekend job since he had been sixteen; he kept that job going for several years. He worked in a café washing up, and sometimes cooking and serving. The money he earned meant that he always had money to take Arwyn out.

Arwyn and Douglas were always doing something. Some evenings they would go to a Café, long before MacDonald's were a force in Britain, Mario was an Italian man who offered 'Thick Milk Shakes', in a mind-boggling number of different flavours. In a café near the 'Posh Prom'. Each time they would try a different flavour. Sometimes they went to the Wimpy hamburger restaurant, sometimes to a pizza restaurant where they could get half a pizza with salad and potato at a very realistic price. In later years they both looked back to the time in their lives when they could eat what they pleased, when they pleased, and chocolate biscuits, and cake, and milk shake made not one jot of difference to their waistlines.

The couple often went to the cinema; The Odeon in Gloucester was one venue. They went to any film that was on, some good, some not. Some daring for their time, *'Emanuel'* and the *'Last Tango in Paris'*. Arwyn was amused by the soft porn movies with Robin Askwith, *'Confessions of a Window Cleaner'* etc.... For Douglas it was just a chance to be somewhere warm with his girl, as it says in the Drifters song *'Saturday Night at the Movies'* *'Who cares what picture you see?'* Arwyn liked it when Douglas slipped his hand inside her suede coat and caressed her breast during the movie. She always got a thrill out of being a little risky, the thought of being caught added to the sensations. They saw a *'Clockwork Orange'* and Disney's *'Robin Hood'*.

The day that Douglas passed his driving test he picked Arwyn up, in his Father's car, and took her to a concert in Birmingham, it was November. Rod Stewart and The Faces were on. *'Pool Hall Richard', '"You Can Make Me Dance, Sing or Anything (Even Take the Dog for a Walk, Mend a Fuse, Fold Away the Ironing Board, or Any Other Domestic Shortcomings)"*.

Arwyn often made groups of people smile as she regaled the story of how Douglas had whizzed into the car park and screeched to a halt.

Arwyn was a big Rod Stewart fan. She even had a poster of him on her wall. Douglas did not care for him in the least, that kind of music set Douglas's teeth on edge, but he loved Arwyn, so despite the din, and the ringing it left in his ears, he paid for the tickets and he put up with the concert.

Douglas's first car was a Vauxhall Van. There were seats in the back that a previous owner had installed; they could fold down so the space was usable for other things. Like the cinema the Vauxhall gave Arwyn and Douglas a place to be, a place where they could kiss and pet, it also gave them a freedom to visit different places that they could not by public transport. One funny thing was that it was almost the same colour as the trousers Douglas had worn back in college days. Arwyn ribbed him about that more often that he could count.

Arwyn and Douglas knew lots of the dark and lonely places; there were plenty of lonely spots around the Cotswolds. Even some streets nearer her home. They would sometimes have some fun where it was not so dark, and not so lonely, and that was exciting. Once in a multi-story car park!

Arwyn liked Douglas to tell her stories, as they petted, he told her of times in the future when he would make love to her on tropical beaches and she would cum. Douglas would cum on her breasts and he would massage the semen over them until it was dry. They would kiss, and they would kiss.

Every Sunday evening Arwyn and he would travel by train to a jazz club, in Gloucester. Douglas had to play piano as people came into the club, and whist they drank before the main guest artists took over. After the show they would get the train back to Cheltenham. In those days it was still possible to get a single compartment where they could not be disturbed, there were few travellers on Sunday nights.

A man called Paul manned the bar for the club. Arwyn and Douglas's drinks were all free from him. They drank quite a bit back then, Port and

Lemon, Gin and Tonic. After Arwyn would sleep over at Douglas's house on the 'put up sofa bed', and the following morning they would travel to college together. In this was a message that Douglas never really grasped, but thirty and more years later he would remember it with the sensation, one might have, if a frozen shard of ice had pierced a beating heart, and stopped it dead, in one cold, and brutal moment. Once near to the college Arwyn did not want to be with Douglas, or to let her college friends know about their relationship.

Before their bus journey, however, each Monday morning Douglas would sneak down early, before the rest of the household woke. He would tiptoe into the living room, wedge a chair at the door and climb into the bed with Arwyn. One morning his mother got up early to and tried to open the door. She later asked him why she could not open it. Douglas looked embarrassed but Arwyn had an answer.

"Oh I am sorry Mrs. Tellam, my bag was trapped between the sofa and the door." Nothing more was spoken of about this, much to Douglas's relief. Then he caught sight of Matthew, Douglas's brother, who was about to open his mouth, and Arwyn took Matthew's hand. "Matthew there is something I wanted to show you."

Arwyn and Douglas's first holiday, away together was in August. They went to Wales to stay with some of Arwyn's relatives. Three Aunts, and an Uncle and his wife. The young couple were, certainly, not allowed to stay in the same house; the memory of Arwyn's Grandmother had not completely faded. So Arwyn stayed with the Aunts and Douglas stayed with the Uncle and his wife. It did not restrict their physical encounters in the slightest. They shared a shower and fondled each other, beneath the blanket, which kept them warm whilst watching the Aunts television. Their house had no central heating so they watched by the light of the coal fire.

The trip to Wales was wonderful. They went on coach trips, once to Snowdonia. Arwyn bought Douglas an ornament of a Dragon on this trip;

Douglas made a joke about Arwyn giving him a statuette of Dorothy. There was a short row about this joke and Douglas bought Arwyn some perfume to smooth things over. If Arwyn had made the joke it would have been different of course, Arwyn made the jokes, especially if the jokes were about her family. Arwyn wore some ruby red lipstick, and Douglas loved her.

They went swimming in at the baths under a sign, which had written on it 'No Petting',

They went to Rhyl and Colwyn Bay and Liandudno and ate Laverbread, neither were that keen on it.

Snowdonia Arwyn described as her perfect place. "If we were to marry this would be the place I would want to have the ceremony." She smiled.

Douglas laughed at her. "There is no Chapel or Registry Office."

Arwyn said. "Well we could pretend that the train is a ship, the driver can be the captain, and he can marry us."

Douglas thought 'yes I would like to marry you Arwyn.'

They went right to the top on the steam railway. They spent a glorious day, in the sun and a few moments in the rain. Llanberis Station, Llyn Du'r Arddu, Clogwyn, the summit, Glaslyn the scenery took their breathe away.

Later they walked over a little bridge over a stream, and they saw an interesting sight, hundreds of tiny baby frogs coming up out of the stream and crossing the path, they were all about two centimetres in length and there was not enough time to count them all.

Uncle told Douglas that he had hated every minute of his working life. Douglas determined to become a truly professional jazz pianist so that he would never have to say such a thing to any children, to whom, he might one day be father.

There were so many things that were interesting and moving. The light was new, the air was new, and people spoke with a lilt in their voices, which was very attractive.

Arwyn's Uncle Ivor took them to see where he worked in the lime quarry. Ivor joked that his brothers came home from the pit covered in coal whilst he came home from the quarry covered in lime.

"Hard to be more opposite that that." Joked Ivor "Are you the opposite of your brother Douglas? Arwyn is certainly the opposite of her sister Susan. Anyway they always make fun down in the pub saying we should be on the tele, but I don't know what they are on about, we haven't got a tele."

All too soon it was time to go home. Douglas composed and composed.

Arwyn and Douglas went to stay with Douglas's Grandmother. They drove in the Vauxhall Van and had another super time. Browsing the shops, visiting the beech and taking the bus to Skegness. Douglas's Grandmother in tow. She lived in Wainfleet All Saints.

Arwyn's Christmas Present to Douglas in 1974 had been a Polaroid Camera. A camera that could produce a finished picture instantly. It was a revolutionary item of new technology. In 1975 Douglas found it created a splendid business opportunity.

Meanwhile Raymond had spent another unsatisfactory year at school, most days all he could think was that soon it would all be over and he could get out into the world and get a job. Raymond was intelligent, the actual school work he did, he did well, and he passed examinations. It may not have been recognised by those responsible for his education, that Raymond was mostly bored, for most of what the teachers put before him put no stress upon his capacity. That is where all the problems came from, and went back to. All the issues teachers had with him where that Raymond saw through them, and needed to learn things beyond the simple. The devil makes work for idle hands and so Raymond amused himself by working out deceptions and by lying. He set himself goals, and he set himself targets. Just how big a lie could he tell a particular person for them to believe it. Then how many lies could he tell, and the best part of it was could he remember all the lies he had told, and to whom he had told them, without getting mixed up. If he could make someone look stupid at the same time that was just a bonus. The more he did the better he became. Reality and fantasy swirled in and around each other like the pretend smoke on a film set. Raymond wrote all his deceptions down in an hard back note book, like those policemen used.

1975

Douglas was booked for his first Summer Season at an hotel in York. This meant that he and Arwyn had to be apart for six months. They wrote letters just about every day, Arwyn always starting with 'Dear Joppy.'

Remember, back then, no one had email, no one had a mobile phone, no one knew what a text message was. If you wanted to speak to someone you had to find a public telephone, and have a pocket full of coins, and of course the person you wanted to speak to had to have a phone in their house to receive the call. Only half the households in Britain had a telephone then. They had to be near the phone when you called, for there were no answer machines, or voice mail. In those days, especially if you had a limited income, the distance from Cheltenham to York might as well have been as far as to Melbourne in Australia.

Several times during the season Douglas travelled down to London to see Arwyn, sometimes he went by train, the stopping train could take all night.

One trip was necessitated by a call from the team who ran a television programme. They wanted to introduce Douglas to a man who managed several top acts of the time. For this trip Douglas purchased a Record Player for Arwyn. It was the only item he could cram into his suitcase. Luckily the suitcase had expandable hinges and fasteners, allowing the case to be thicker or thinner depending on the load. So the lid of the case was at the maximum and just fitted around the player with it's speakers. It was a Stereo Player, an innovation back then. They did not have so many stereo records for sale, for few people had stereo players. Douglas had a birthday card ready to go with the record player, in it he wrote, 'I do not think this will play records by Jeff Beck, The Faces, The Dimensions and certainly not....Rod Stewart! I Will Always Love You. Any of Dolly Parton's will spin with ease.' It was July 10th the week had been cloudy.

Arwyn had become a cook in a London Hospital and she had begun to think about becoming a Teacher. She still had her long red hair and Douglas was still totally mesmerised by her.

One time Douglas drove the distance in his Vauxhall Van, Arwyn drove back to Yorkshire with him. The journey to Yorkshire was a long one back then, no A1(M), not much fancy dual carriageway, and having reached Peterborough they stopped to have lunch. When they returned to the van it would not move into gear, the car was stuck. Already on the journey the accelerator cable had broken, luckily it was fixed by a friendly mechanic. The gears were not such a happy story, the car was towed away and Arwyn and Douglas had to finish their journey by train. They had to return to fetch the car a week later, the garage did a very poor job, and the car had to be repaired a second time the following week.

Arwyn's holiday at the hotel with Douglas was a little like setting up home together. Douglas had a static caravan, in the trees, behind the hotel, as did the other band members, and some of the other hotel staff. It was his little house in the woods, so for the first time they were a couple with their own little home.

Douglas's pleasure was to wake up beside Arwyn. It was one blustery night, in the middle of her stay, with the caravan rocking and rolling in the wind that they, at last, made love properly, for up until now they had never had actually had sex, they had been sexy and petted a lot. They took this new adventure seriously and discussed it.

There was lots of talk about contraception because there was great fear of pregnancy instilled into both their minds. The sex education that they had received would not have filled a post card had Arwyn sent one to one of her friends. Douglas told Arwyn of the embarrassed biology master, when he had been at school, turning absolutely puce as he described the mating habits of frogs, adding the caveat that sexual intercourse between men and women was vaguely similar! So with ignorance, a bit of fear, and a lot of excitement Arwyn helped Douglas roll three, Durex, Condoms, one on top of the other, on to his erect penis and 'just in case' they inserted Rendells Spermicidal Contraceptive Pessarie into Arwyn's vagina. It may not sound that romantic, but if you think again it was very caring, and very considerate, and it meant that when that actually did make love they felt that there was no worry, of unwanted consequences, so when it finally came to it they were both relaxed. Sex is, in some ways, like seeing, smelling, or touching, one's brain takes in the external stimuli and converts and interprets.

Douglas had wrestled for years with the teachings of the Bible, obviously the Methodist way was strongly imprinted within him, but he had come to a place in his life that rejected such ideas. He was trying no longer to be bound by them. Of course this was not easy when his father had been named after John Wesley.

Arwyn had no such notions in her head, she was keen to try proper sex and so long as she was not going to find that she was pregnant afterwards she was eager to try it, she had been eager for sometime.

They were naked in the bed with the covers warm around them. It was anything but the movies. It was warm and tender, with, surprisingly, no fumbling. They knew each other very well, of course. They were both totally aware of everything they were doing, the kissing the touching; it was, really, real excitement.

They kissed, and caressed, and touched, and they hugged, and held and after this, when it all felt right, Douglas rolled between Arwyn's, soft, and shapely legs and is pelvis moved towards her. The wind howled around the caravan and it shook.

Arwyn was ready, and open, for 'her' Douglas and she wanted him as he wanted her. His, clothed, penis touched the opening of her vagina and he gently and slowly started to enter her body for the first time. He felt the resistance and she felt it too, her virginity gave way, then he felt that he was one with her, and she felt she was a part of him. They were still for a moment or two. He then started to move inside her, he felt that before that moment he had never truly been alive. In her imagination she had never realised that these wonderful intense feelings, physical and emotional, were something that existed.

Arwyn's arms were around Douglas's back as he moved within her, and she panted, and he poured his love into her, and she gratefully received all that he was willing to give. He could feel the semen gathering in is testicles. She could feel the inside of her vagina beginning to contract, to suck his penis deep inside of her she wanted to cum, and she wanted him to cum. Her body moved, without her permission, adding to the movements of his penis entering and pulling out of her. It was not violent, it was not fast but they came to a rhythm together that became more, and more, intense, and more, and more warm, until she could hold it off no more. Her body convulsed and sucked him into her, and at the same moment he felt the lava of semen pumping up through is stiff penis, and they came together with an intensity that neither had experienced in all their petting. For the first time Arwyn came from the inside.

They held tight to each other as the semen pumped up from inside Douglas. They both knew that with all that they had felt in these moments that she would have been instantly pregnant, for with such love it would have been impossible for new life to hold itself back.

She wanted every drop. She liked to feel the pump and wanted it as many times as was possible. He wanted to give her all he could, and when it had all gone from his testicles she wondered what it would feel like to have had all that sperm inside her vagina. They were tingling, like chill blains, she held him inside her, not wanting him to leave, and he wanted to go no where, and deep inside her was where he wanted to be, for the rest of his life. Then, exhausted, they cuddled and slept a deep sleep that night.

Douglas composed new music the next day.

It was sunny and they took a walk into the town centre, down the tiny streets, of The Shambles, the old walls and the peacocks. They had tea in Betty's, then over to the Minster.

The people who came to the hotel then did not, by and large, own cameras. Film was expensive, and cameras were not cheap, and that was before the cost of developing, and then waiting for the snaps. Having a Polaroid camera, that would produce instant pictures, was a novelty. After any event, or competition at the hotel Douglas would, for a small charge, take a photograph, using the Polaroid Camera Arwyn have given him the previous Christmas. Douglas earned more money from the camera than he did in fees for his work. He was lucky because during most of the season a chemist shop in the town had a special offer on the films, which made them super cheap. Douglas often wondered why chemist shops sold film and offered film developing services, why the chemist? Why not the Green Grocer or the Butcher?

Arwyn's holiday came to an end and she had to catch the train home. Douglas wanted her to stay, of course he did. He would not see her again until the season's end. He really had not considered how long a summer season was when he started it and he had not realised that then the summer season, and earning a living, were totally linked. He knew already that in the following year he would again have to go away.

Arwyn returned to her digs in Camberwell, where she shared with two other girls who cooked at the hospital. They were eager to hear all about York and 'if she had', they wanted to know if Douglas had proposed. Arwyn told them not to be daft, but the following weekend, under the influence of a bottle of 'Blue Nun' wine, Arwyn did share some of the story of losing her virginity. Next morning she almost wished that she had not, but then she realised that both her friends were quiet jealous of her, and neither had, yet, found a man to take theirs.

1976

One weekend, in 1976, they went on an outing to Stratford-upon-Avon. They visited the shops and saw the Church where, some think, William Shakespeare was buried. They took a turn around the museum, and booked tickets for Romeo and Juliet, which starred the fabulous Francesca Annis and Ian McKellen in the leading roles, for that evening's performance.

Then, to fill a part of the gap between then and the performance, they hired a rowing boat on the Avon. It was lovely weather. They were proceeding, in a good fashion, Arwyn lazying and Douglas rowing. Douglas got some romantic notion in his head about rowing to a quiet bank and lying in the grass with Arwyn. Somehow one of the oars seemed to get tangled in some reeds, near the bank. In trying to free the oar Douglas fell back, lost his balance and both Arwyn and he fell into the river, fully clothed. They panicked a lot of swishing about in the river. Douglas trying to remember his Gold Swimming Safety Award, and his life saving certificates, gained so many years before, and never used until now. Did their lives flashed before them? Well up until the moment when Arwyn realised that the water was so shallow that she could stand up. She started to laugh and they spent most of the rest of that afternoon, in a launderette. Sitting with towels about him, trying to get dry before the Theatre. The lady who ran the launderette was most helpful, and accommodating, and she did laughed too.

Douglas dripped. "You know I am not sure that this is a laughing matter!"

Arwyn and the launderette lady laughed at Douglas and he was laughing too.

Douglas's father asked Arwyn, a few days later: "Who pushed who in the river? Oh I see you both ended up in the water, hilarious. I wish I had been there and if I owned a camera I wish that I had it with me."

Douglas got an eye infection and found them very sore for more than a week.

*

"...but soft what light through yonder window breaks? It is the east and Arwyn is the sun. Arise fair sun and kill the envious moon who is even now sick and pale with grief." Chanted Douglas as they drove home.

Arwyn cried. "Give it a rest Bill!"

Douglas recited. "Do'st thou bite thy thumb at me mistress?"

Arwyn started singing. "*My old man's a dustman...*" The song by Lonnie Donegan.

Douglas switched on the radio, as he did so Arwyn shouted. "What's the matter with my singing?" then she paused. "Oh shut up it's Rod!" Sure enough it was Rod Stewart singing the 'Isely Brothers' hit *This Old Heart of Mine.*'

Arwyn continued to work as a cook in the hospital. She was an excellent cook, young bright and very intelligent. She worked hard and her boss appreciated what she did. Always punctual, always well dressed and always wishing to please. Whilst there she decided that she actually would train to be a teacher. She made an application and started her training. Arwyn's Father, Mother, Gwyn and Douglas helped move her possessions into the halls of residence, a narrow room with a window and a kettle opposite Wimbledon Common.

Arwyn enthusiastically embraced her new career. She regaled stories of her lecturers and her fellow students. How one of the lecturers had hosted a fun competition in the pub one Saturday afternoon where all the students had to take it in turns to throw a piece of chalk across the room at a target.

Whilst not on summer season Douglas and his band performed in venues all about, there were television and radio shows and records to record. Any spare time he had, that Arwyn did not have duties, he would spend with her. They went out to dinner; he loved to watch her face through the candlelight. They went to many restaurants.

One December Douglas asked. "Shall we go out to dinner?"

Arwyn said to Douglas. "Can we afford to?"

Douglas told her, "I have earned four thousand pounds this month, I think we can."

Four thousand pounds was a lot of money then. The average wage was seventy-two pounds a week. A mini car could be purchased for six hundred pounds. It was a really hot summer. 'Ying', Denis Howell became minister of drought and as a very cold winter followed Denis Howell, 'yang', became minister of snow.

Arwyn had made a good friend of another student teacher, Barbara, who had a boyfriend who was training to be a doctor. Barbara and Mark became 'best friends'. Barbara lived in a flat in London and Mark had a flat in Lewisham. There were dinner parties and outings to pubs and there were pizzas and a host of other excitements.

Arwyn and Douglas had a very normal relationship, sometimes they disagreed, some times they argued, sometimes Arwyn draw back and sometimes she came forward, a pattern which was to have serious consequences much later in the story.

Birthdays were important, in 1975; Douglas brought Arwyn the record player. Other years he got her a gold pendent and a beautiful leather writing case. She gave him shirts and socks and ornaments. Aftershave was another gift she gave. Douglas treasured all. Any time they were out, shopping in town or a market Douglas would find little things to buy for Arwyn.

Arwyn's teaching career had begun and she was living in a flat not far from the school in which she was a student teacher. Arwyn and Douglas had been going through a difficult patch in their relationship, probably the strain of beginning a new career, love making became less easy and Douglas knew that he had to back off and he did, the consequences were that for a brief time impotence came upon him. When Arwyn was ready again for intimacy Douglas found it difficult but as the relationship mended he was able once more, and then there was a disaster, for the condom broke and for the first time Douglas's semen entered Arwyn's body and there was panic.

Neither he or she was ready to contemplate a family; neither was ready for a child. They waited for what seemed like an age, they spent many edgy days, Arwyn stressed by the prospect of becoming a mother, she had never been pleased about period pain, until she felt it on this cycle. She did not tell Douglas immediately, they had a nice, but tense, day shopping then, as the darkness of the evening drew in, she stopped his worry and told him to relax, her period had started. They were in a very nice shop when she gave him the news, he was looking at a pile of bobble hats, so he brought her one it was fun and made them both laugh.

Arwyn loved looking around the shops, choosing clothes from the hundreds of items on offer. Douglas liked to be with Arwyn so he tagged along whenever she invited him, watching, approving of this garment, telling her that that garment was slightly less fine than another. Telling her that she could make anything look good. He tried so hard not to show his boredom, he tried not to yawn, he found a seat and started practicing piano, in his head.

Douglas's next summer season was in a very posh hotel in the South West of England. Arwyn came for a holiday and one evening he told the crowd that the following music was inspired by Arwyn. Arwyn was so mad at Douglas for bringing her to the attention of the crowd, and she was really angry with him for quite some time.

"How dare you bring me to the attention of all those people?" She screamed at him.

Later the couple drove through the rhododendron lined road and then they headed off into the countryside. Arwyn was still angry but eventually she forgave him.

That evening Arwyn lay on top of Douglas, he was deep inside her, and they were lying still enjoying their togetherness. Arwyn had forgiven

Douglas and he whispered to her that he loved to feel so close to her; his eyes were full of tears.

One wonderful afternoon they spent in a glorious garden, the gardener, who was the guide, gave a running commentary pointing out interesting things as they followed the group up and down the garden paths, everything he said, in his special, country type accent, was prefaced by the words,

"Look at these sumptuous blooms." It became something of a catch phrase between them.

Douglas took Arwyn to a smart restaurant, they ordered Gammon steaks with pineapple, it was the fashion. It was so warm that on some nights it was possible to drive down to and swim in the sea at midnight.

Most Tuesday evenings, during this season, Douglas drove to London, it was a bit of a drive back then, but Wednesday was his day off, and he could see Arwyn, for a few hours, and have some fun before returning early on Thursday morning.

At the end of the summer two of the band members decided to marry. There was a big celebration and a big day out for all in London, they all went to Carnaby Street and pretended it was still the 'Swinging Sixties'. Kaftan's and Cheese Cloth shirts.

1976 was all Romeo and Juliet without the tragedy.

CHAPTER 3
Add Five Years and the French

Arwyn never had she seen a Frenchman eating breakfast before. She could see the French man over Douglas's shoulder. The Frenchman plunged his croissant into a huge cup of hot chocolate, and then into his mouth. To Arwyn this was very amusing; here she was on holiday, her first trip to France, and the man she was watching had a cup, which was huge.

She whispered to Douglas, who started to turn and look. "No don't look!"

Too late, he had already turned and was staring at the Man who was dressed in a business suit and chewing.

Everything was different, and everything new.

At that moment Le Garçon, brought them their hot chocolate and croissant.

Arwyn joked. "Last one in's a sissy! Make sure you take your snorkel! What do you think French people make of a Full English Breakfast when they stay in London?"

Douglas said. "Well they probably try it for the novelty value and are glad to be back home. Taste the croissant, it is wonderful, and the hot chocolate wow."

The hotel, in Rouen, was plush, modern, the grandest Arwyn, or Douglas, had ever been in. When they arrived, the afternoon before, and signed in with different surnames, the hotel concierge provide keys for two adjoining rooms, even though Douglas had booked, and paid for, only one room, that is how it was in 1978. The couple made love in the same bed that night, and never did open the door to the second room. The room was elegant, modern with a bed which was one of those which could never be cosy. The bed was hard, designer, and a little cold.

Douglas had a brand new car, Rover SD1, smart executive car, black, two-litre engine, European car of the year in 1977. Douglas was proud of this car; it's square headlights and a dashboard, the flash of blue from the heater control that caught his eye in the night. A car was, of course, necessary for his work, but it also reflected the success, which Douglas had already achieved in his profession. Arwyn felt good about the car too, she could not drive then but it was a good car to be a passenger in. Most of her friend's boyfriends had second hand cars. Douglas's car was smart, and this smart young couple, twenty-two years old, looked smart. They journeyed via Paris where they climbed the Eiffel Tower. Arwyn stood with her back to Paris, her curled, red, hair framing her beautiful face, as

Douglas took her photograph. She never spoke many words about liking or disliking but she was enjoying this. It was new, it was different, and it was exciting.

Arwyn, to Douglas was the perfect woman, he thought she had the kind of face that many a French parfumerie would have been happy to have adorn their advertising posters. Her red hair, like the hair of a maid in some Irish legend, framed her ivory skin, dimpled cheeks and green, green, eyes. Not so much the colours of those of Welsh heritage.

They went down to the park, beneath the tower, and then drove around Paris for a while. Douglas parked and they wandered up a boulevard to a café for coffee, and something from the pâtisserie. It was not cold in the sunshine and they sat at a small table outside. Arwyn noted the French fashion. They took in sounds, and the smells, and the tastes. The Seine sparkled and Notre Dame chimed. The artists displayed their paintings, smoked Gitanes, and drank Pastis, a perfect cliché.

It was autumn, late in October, and this was an adventure. For, as with sleeping arrangements, the world was other then. A journey, by car, through France, was exotic, and exciting, and all was so different from drab old England. Arwyn watched the road for the differences between France and home. She wound down the window and shouted into the breeze in an excited, schoolgirl like, fashion.

"Rapell, rapell." she had a smile, larger than the Mona Lisa's, painted between her cheeks. "S'il vous plaît. Avez vous un chambre pour mon bel amant et moi? Je m'appelle? Goddess! Pourquoi tu ne savais pas déja?"

("Attention, Attention." "Please have you a room for my lover and I. My name? Goddess! Why did you not already know?" The above being Arwyn's version of French.)

A similar French couple may have felt the same of England. It being different from being French. Sometimes all it takes is to be 'other' and 'exotic-sium' is ladled upon whatever it is.

The English never really understood much beyond the little island of their universe. At least that is what Douglas thought to himself. Why would you want to eat that English, cardboard, bread once French Baggett has caressed your lips? What on earth would convince you that instant coffee was a good idea once you had tasted coffee in a French Café, as you eased down another beautiful item from the pâtisserie, so delicately crafted and topped off with a strawberry?

Rouen was lovely. Arwyn and Douglas wandered the streets and saw the French, and the way the French did what they did. The air was crisp and the sounds of French tongues lapped at their ears as the pair strained to recall distant, schoolroom, French classes. Douglas noted, for the first time, that on the corner of most streets was a Frenchman with a flat cap, leaning against the wall, one foot up and held on the wall, his knee bent, cigarette hanging down on the bottom lip of his open mouth and a baguette under his arm.

They found the Cathedral and marvelled at its Gothic majesty. The fine stonework, wonderful figurines and heavenly windows. Douglas thought of the famous paintings by Claude Monet. He wondered how long Monet had gazed at the building to see it in varying light. At this moment it was in full sunlight. Crisp were the lines and sharp were the shadows.

"This used to be the tallest building in the world." Douglas told Arwyn. "It is the place where they tried Joan of Arc. Nearly five hundred and fifty years ago. That is amazing, to be remembered five hundred and fifty years after your death."

Douglas thought of Joan of Arch, and heresy. About Joan being something others thought she should not be. Douglas often felt that he was often not what others thought he should be. For he did not really conform to the norm. He did not have a 'proper job', but to be a jazz pianist one could not really be 'normal', and there were few jobs on offer for a jazz musician anyway."

Douglas speculated. "The real trouble with the world is that one group of people, with a narrow vision, of what they consider to be right and wrong, imposing their vision on the rest of the population."

They walked the cobbled shopping areas, the City captured them and they had fun in the, cool, autumn sun.

Arwyn questioned. "Is the whole day going to be a philosophical dissection, or could we take a look in the shops now?"

"Sorry." Douglas smiled.

Arwyn liked shops and shopping, Douglas did not much care for it, but he cared for Arwyn, and if that is want she wanted to do, he would try not to yawn when she was watching him.

Often Douglas would look for somewhere to sit whilst Arwyn safarised the shop floor hunting bargains, and sophistication, amongst the myriad choices of garments on display. If he could find somewhere, and see Arwyn, so much the better, once settled he would start practising his piano by playing in his head. First the scales, up and down, slow and fast and, if there were time, he might breakout a tune or two, sometimes the tune became audible to all those who were in the shop, as Douglas, oblivious, delved deeper into his repertoire.

On this fine day in Rouen, in this beautiful store, Arwyn tried on some dresses and she bought one in a shimmering satin, which was a dark blue, with a round neck, and three silver buttons to the right.

Douglas thought that Arwyn was the most beautiful woman in the world and he loved her. Douglas had heard about sexy French women, but although he had walked through French streets all the morning he had seen none. To Douglas Arwyn was the prettiest, sexiest, woman who had ever been, or would be. He had no desire for any other women, unlike some other men; he looked only at Arwyn and was completely happy in his choice. He delighted in her company. The pang of excitement as she arrived and the sigh of disappointment when they had to part.

Douglas had absolutely no desire to change Arwyn in any way. He would never have dreamed of trying to restrict her by saying that he wanted her to wear this or that, or telling she had to do this or that. He would never have told her that he did not like her friends, or family, even if, at times, he found, one or two of them, shall we say, tedious?

Arwyn also was not a 'clingy soul', anyway she knew that Douglas had desire only for her, so she never experienced jealousy, and she knew if she called Douglas would be by her side in an instant. At this stage in her life she did not need someone to make her safe through their power, Her relationship with Douglas was one of equals, they both gave and took in equal measure. Later in her life her security needs were to become somewhat different, but for now, in her twenty's life was smooth and sweet.

When Arwyn and Douglas first met she wanted to be with Douglas, he was stable and she felt secure when she sat on his lap and when they kissed he made her feel safe. Arwyn liked physical contact. She squeezed Douglas's chin and called him 'Joppy', derived from Scott Joplin, the King of Jazz pianists and one of Douglas's favourites.

"I just wish I could be one thousandth as good as he one day," sang Douglas.

With her teeth clenched and her smiling, round, and dimple cheeks, she loved it when they touched their chins together. She liked it when they kissed.

Arwyn did not always understand Douglas. He read a lot of books. Arwyn was very intelligent, but she did not read much, except for the things she had to for school, and she did not wish to analyse everything and compare it to the history of mankind. So, as in much else, Arwyn and Douglas were quite the opposite ends of the tree. So they should be, just like billions of other couples, all over the world, opposites attract because people need what they lack. Many couples misunderstand that and spend their time trying to change their partner. No one can change anyone. You accept and enjoy your partner for what they are, and what they are able to do in your relationship. If you decide not to, the only outcome that can be is a disaster.

The following day they drove to Le Havre, it seemed to be so far. They followed the river Seine on the D51. Driving on the 'wrong' side of the road was not a problem Douglas had driven across Europe before; his work had already had the privilege of visiting several countries. Douglas thought that the roads in France went on forever, it was sixty miles or so - one hundred kilometres or so, but it seemed like two hundred. They went down to the grey, sand covered beach and let the waves chase them for a while. They endured the cold, French, drizzly, rain until they were soaked through. Then kilometre after kilometre of tree line roads.

Douglas explained that the story was that. "Napoleon had planted the trees to give his soldiers shade as they marched."

Arwyn laughed. "You really think he had time to plant all these trees! How long did it take these trees to grow? No sorry I just don't believe that!" Arwyn liked to take the 'Douglas' out of Douglas, she liked to be facetious, and she laughed again.

Under the trees, through the rain, back to Rouen and dinner French style. Restaurant La Couronne, some say the oldest restaurant in France. Magnific. Arwyn wore her new dress.

Summers and winters followed on one another and both Arwyn and Douglas grow in their professions and their lives. Douglas's life took him to various countries and through television and radio studios his career was rich and diverse and fun.

Arwyn worked hard as a teacher; there was celebration when she got promotion. She learned the ins and outs of each 'nook and cranny' of her profession. She found it exciting and she knew that although she had learned much there was so much more to learn.

Of a sudden they realised they were older. The British Government were found guilty of mistreating prisoners in Northern Ireland, by the European Court of Human Rights. Roman Polanski skipped bail and fled to France after having sex with a thirteen-year-old girl. Charlie Chaplin's remains were stolen in Switzerland. Jimmy Carter was President of America. It was the year of the film 'Grease' with John Tarvolta and Olivia Newton John and James Callaghan was Prime Minister of the United Kingdom.

CHAPTER 4
Raymond is Twenty

R aymond had managed to get to twenty years old, but he was not too sure how; it was his birthday and some family members had shown up and there was something of a party. They had a cake and his grandmother told him what a good boy he had been, and how proud she was of him. There were presents, and then some of his friends and he left to go to the pub. They drank a lot and then someone said they should go for an Indian meal. One of his friends owned a Ford Anglia car. A small car but somehow all six of them got in, three crammed into the back with the forth laid across their laps, with his feet out of the wound down window. They set out on the two mile journey, their driver, Seth, assured them than he was sober enough to drive.

It was a bit wet and the yellow street lights glared up in reflections from the dark tarmac. That may have been the distraction; Seth completely misjudged the distance and drove the Anglia into the back of a large, dark blue truck. Seth must have realised, just before the car hit he had turned the steering wheel to the left, the Anglia skidded and Seth took the full impact, Gary, who's feet had protruded through the back offside window, was seriously injured, his feet were crushed in between the two vehicles. As the Anglia spun it mounted the pavement and hit the brick-wall of a factory. Gary lost a lot of blood, doctors had to amputate both legs at the knee. Gary's body held the three, who had been sitting in the back, in place. There were no seat belts. All three were injured by the flying glass and whiplash.

Raymond who had been in the front passenger seat, spent over two months in hospital recovering from his injuries. How he had survived this, the firemen who cut him from the wreckage, agreed was simply a miracle. Raymond felt terrible about his friends and he carried the guilt of this accident with him for the rest of his life, his best friend, Seth, had nearly killed him. The accident bought emotions to his mind, in a way that nothing else had ever done or would do. It knotted his stomach and played on his mind. To cope he put the memory in a box in a compartment in his brain and locked a door on it, hoping that it would never more escape, but in reality it often bashed the door so hard the door was almost smashed from it's hinges. Raymond was not one to celebrate birthdays after that.

CHAPTER 5
Moving with the Times

Arwyn was five years older than the girl who had been at college looking for her first kiss. Her confidence, suppressed by a domineering mother, had grown and had been trying to burst out, a bit like when one squeezes a balloon that has not been completely inflated. Squeeze it here and the balloon escapes through the fingers and bulges out through the finger and thumb. She had enjoyed the trip to France and she liked to be with Douglas but, she felt, 'if only I could get to the other side of this balloon what would it be like? What are other boys/men like? What would it be to have sex with someone who was not Douglas?' The questions would not go away, and curiosity could be suppressed only for a while. It was easy enough to get a date; there were few days that went by without someone asking. In the end the temptation became more enticing, then the thoughts of loyalty were subsumed by a passion for unknown territories, and when the young man asked her she just nodded her head. It was easy, and Douglas did not need to know, how would he find out? She soon realised that she could keep Douglas and see other men, it was easy and there were plenty and it was different, and it was the same and she felt absolutely no shame—but should she?

Douglas was here and there and around the world and where he went he carried his girl in his heart, and wherever he was he composed, and when he returned he had no idea that Arwyn was no longer exclusive to him, and he wanted to marry her. He had plenty of opportunities to fall into bed with many different women, but he did not want to.

He took Arwyn to a beautiful restaurant and he had with him a shining engagement ring. He remembered their trip to Snowdonia.

The meal eaten he took her hand, he smiled. "Will you marry me?"

He had not foreseen the possibility of rejection. He had not contemplated that there were two opposing answers to his question. So as the scalding flowed over his self-esteem, he crumpled inside and felt himself burning up.

How he drove her back to her flat he did not know. He did not go in. He had just never thought she would say no. All that time ago in Snowdonia it had been her idea.

So shocked was he by her rejection he sat in his car, once she had left him, and he could not move. He fell in to some sort of unconscious space. He stayed still for an hour or two, may be more. When finally he did set off he had not driven more that a mile or two when he found his car being pursued by a police car. He pulled over and a scruffy looking, plain clothes, policeman climbed into the passenger seat of his car, several uniformed officers surrounded the car. The plain-clothes man addressed Douglas by his name.

Douglas queried. "How do you know my name?"

The policeman looked surprised. "If this is your car, and you are the registered keeper, it is easy for me to know who you are Douglas Tellam, all I have to do is radio to the police station."

Douglas went cold with fear, during the conversation Douglas explained what had happened and how the shock of Arwyn's rejection had stopped him in his tracks, and that for quite a time he had been paralysed, unable to drive.

When the policeman was satisfied with Douglas's explanation he explained that the police had been looking out for a gang who had been committing robberies, it had been noticed that Douglas was sitting in the car, and the police had suspected that Douglas was the 'get-a-way driver'! First the shock of his life with Arwyn and then a bizarre occurrence with the police. It was a strange and unusual time for Douglas.

It was not over between Arwyn and Douglas, no, no for what was now happening had been happening for a long time, but Douglas had only just begun to be aware of it, it was an evil act of treachery and torture. Arwyn pushing him away and then pulling him back.

Arwyn telephoned to Douglas and they met up and they spent an evening together and they made love and Douglas thought there was hope, even then. Then he arrived to see her and saw her arm in arm with another man. He did know how to respond. He found an earthquake of jealousy within himself now and instead of being buried to death by it he was enraged and great clouds of dust escaped from deep within him and he wanted to strike down the man with whom Arwyn walked, he wanted to fight for her and he leaped from his car shouting in a rage he had never felt before and the man dropped Arwyn's arm and he ran.

So began a 'Push-Me-Pull-You' relationship, sometimes she wanted him, sometimes she did not. Only later did Douglas remember the college days when Arwyn was nothing to do with him during college hours. He always wanted Arwyn so anytime she called he would go running until, one terrible Sunday, he turned up to see her and was confronted by Colin, a muscular young man, who erected scaffolding for his living. Arwyn shouted down the stairs at Douglas to leave and not come back, and then came Colin, with belligerence tattooed on his forearm, with the final warning and parting shot.

So that was the end of that.

Although it was not, for Douglas could not forget, Douglas could not come to grips with what had happened. He slipped into an half twilight.

He felt lost and abandoned. He could not grab the part that she invited him to her place and had then sent this roughcast man to end her relationship for her. Months of 'Push-Me-Pull-You' and Douglas never turning up without an invitation had ended in a cruel and evil way.

Colin did not last so long in Arwyn's life, he had the body but the intellect was lacking. She had had enough of him after a violent car crash, caused by his erratic driving. She walked away from the accident, found a public telephone and was taxied away from Colin, never to see him again.

The there was David, Peter; Paul followed closely by another Paul and another David. A couple of years down the track and she found herself on the back of Geoff's motorbike, she liked that.

Then James took her, in his open topped sports car, on holiday. They sailed on a Ferry and then rode down through Spain, right down to Málaga; they stayed in various Paradores along the way. General Franco had not been long dead and his ghost was still singing in the trees. Or so Arwyn believed. She was full of dirt and dust each evening but she liked James and James liked Arwyn. He did not mind how dirty she was, the dirtier the better, joked with her.

Somehow Arwyn managed to move on from James to another man called Simon and then to a chap called Cuthbert.

Cuthbert was from a different class background, which Arwyn found intriguing for a while. Cuthbert asked Arwyn to leave some of her clothes at his house. So she did, quite innocently, until one day she went to see him and found he dressed up in her clothes, he claimed it was the smell he liked, but Arwyn found this to be beyond her comfort zone and she left Cuthbert still wearing her knickers and did not see him again.

For Douglas it took a long while to adjust, he could not get his mind into the new spot from which it now had to operate. At this time he was living alone. He found some of the evenings very lonely, and depressions came and went from him in a slow and unkind manor.

Then Douglas had a phone call from a theatrical agent. The women was full of praise and very complimentary about Douglas's physical appearance. For Douglas it was that moment, as when pushing a car that has failed to start, and, suddenly, as the driver jerks his foot from the clutch and the engine catches, and the cars motor is running again. It splutters a bit but with a revving of the engine, a bit of blue smoke from the exhaust and the road again beckons.

Douglas did not go out looking for girls to date for quiet a few months. Then, on a whim, one Friday evening, he drove into the town centre, and paid to go into a disco. As he handed over his money, and the bouncers looked him up and down, he knew that it was a mistake. The music was loud the lights flashy, it was smoky and smelt of booze. Actually this was what his nightmares could have been made of and he wondered what had possessed him. Then he remembered. Female company, may be sex, he had not had that in a while. Not since several days before he had had to meet that awful Colin the 'Scaffold Man'. He looked about and asked several girls if they would like to dance, none of them did.

Douglas had no intention of ever returning to such a disco place again. Then Tom came around, a neighbour from down the street, Tom also had his bother finding women so they decided, together, to give the Disco one last chance. It sort of paid off as two girls did come back to Douglas's house with them, but they turned out to be sisters, and in the cold light of the kitchen they were not as alluring as they had been in the flashing darkness of the nightclub. It would seem, just as the sun rises in the east, that the two girls felt much the same about Tom and Douglas. All in all it was decided that Douglas would drive them home and he did and that was that.

Over the next year or two Douglas did meet up with and became friendly with a number of young women, some with whom he just had friendships and some that he also had sex with.

Elaine worked at the opticians. She was a member of a local Church of England Church. She had contacted Douglas and asked if he and his colleagues would perform a Jazz concert at her church to raise funds for repairs to the building. One night Elaine and Douglas were in his bed and she naked was sitting astride him and they both felt good.

Douglas looked up at her pretty face. "Elaine I think this is good and I would like to make things a bit more serious between us."

Elaine's reaction was. "Well I like you too, and I think that we would be good together, but I do not think my boy friend would like that, he took me on holiday to Italy two months ago, he paid for the whole trip."

That shocked Douglas, he felt very naïve, he did not realise that girls did that, but then that is exactly what Arwyn had done. Would he ever learn? How could he? People told their story and there were two courses of action, believe it or believe it not. How could you ever know if the woman you were with was just with you?

Then there was Beverly, pretty in her way, it was the way the sunlight would catch her cheekbone, and she would turn a smile. They had been out quite a few times but Douglas had not thought that Beverly had become attached to him. That evening he told her that he was off on a tour around Europe and would be away for six months. He was genuinely surprised by the gush of tears and the wailing that followed. He was lost for a response and then blurted out. "Well you could come and meet me and come around with me for a week."

The sunshine returned to Beverly's face whilst Douglas felt a lead weight in his stomach, he liked Beverly but not quite that much.

Next day she called him, "I cannot come unless I can get a new passport, and the passport people are on strike."

Douglas felt relived. He went on his tour and once in a while he called Beverly. He lied that he was sorry about the Passport Office and the strike etc. etc. but he was actually relieved that she could not come.

Until the day that she announced. "My mum went to Newport, and went to the Passport Office, and she got me a new Passport so I am coming."

To say that this was a disaster would be an understatement. Maybe she was nervous, may be she was scared, or may be she was simply awful. Douglas met Beverly at Düsseldorf Airport. He took her to his hotel in Krefeld, in Germany; there were some performances to give in the area.

Of course during the era of Adolf Hitler, Jazz had been outlawed, some unfortunate musicians, and also fans, were incarcerated. There had been loopholes in the laws and so Jazz survived and was played during that dark time. Now, in the 1980's, it was once again flourishing and indeed well enough supported for it to be heading in several directions at a time. There were those who venerated traditional Jazz forms, and those who preferred free Jazz.

Douglas said to Beverly that during one performance, in Köln, the great Torsten de Winkel had played on stage with Douglas's band. "Would you believe that, the great Torsten de Winkel? Played with my band."

Beverley tried to make a joke. "So you played with this guy's winkle! I have never heard of him, what has he had in the top ten?"

Douglas knew exactly why he had not wanted Beverley on this trip and why things had not, nor ever would be serious between them.

"If you translate 'Winkel from German into English the word means 'Corner'." Douglas was trying not to lose his patience."

He changed the subject, for he knew that Beverley had very limited enthusiasm for Jazz. So he switched the conversation to Abba and Beverley went along with the conversation for she had all their records and was a member of their 'Official Fan Club'. She had seen them in concert in the New Bingley Hall in Stafford, 11 November 1979. "I went with Simon Jones," Beverly said. "He was the best snogger I ever snogged."

She looked wistfully over Douglas's shoulder and saw a man pushing a bratwüst into his face. 'That' she had never seen before. Douglas felt quite bemused by Beverley's forthright statement, he wondered how he could become a better kisser, and then thought better of the idea. Beverley spoke again. "*Chiquitita*, that's my favourite."

The hotel was very comfortable, but the night, for Douglas, was very uncomfortable. Beverley wanted to have sex; Douglas did his best but had the feeling that his best was nowhere near good enough.

They travelled up to Berlin by car. It was not an easy thing to do back then. East Germany was a 'walled state' to get to Berlin one travelled the autobahn from Helmstadt at fifty miles an hour-eighty kilometres per hour, after paying for a visa and being thoroughly searched by the border guards. Along the road they saw the cars of the East Germans, the Trabant, chugging with their 'sewing machine engines' along the open road through the acres of farmland to either side.

Once in Berlin Douglas tried to point out some of the interesting sites. "If you go down there you will find the Olympic Stadium from 1936 where Adolf Hitler was embarrassed by Jess Owens."

Beverly was already exasperated. "I have no idea who either of these people are, or what you are talking about?" There was anger in her tone and her voice modulated into an East End of London lilt.

They arrived to stay with friends of Douglas and then Beverly did something that was never forgotten, she sat on their sofa a let out the most enormous belch, if she were ever mentioned, years after this event was always called 'Burp-y Beverly'.

The performance was to be at the Waldbühne. 'The Forest Stage.'

He explained to Beverley. "I saw the great Joan Baez here, she was truly magnificent." Said Douglas.

Beverley scoffed. "Who's she another of your boring Jazz trumpeter's? Or something?"

It was a really special thing for Douglas to play in the Waldbühne, he wished that Beverley had been else where for he knew that such a gig would not be an automatically regularly recurring event.

Douglas was glad when they finally arrived in Calais but they missed the ferry and Beverly took out her frustration on a complete stranger who had not held the terminal door open for her. She shouted after him in coarse English.

Douglas admonished her saying. "You do not even know if he speaks English."

Beverly replied "Don't treat me like a child."

Douglas's reaction was. "Why not? You behave like one most of the time. Your interest in the world about you is minimal, your manors in most situations are sorely lacking, the only thing you really know about is ABBA."

Beverley was revving up now, she was mightily angry, her face turned puce, and then she let rip with a tirade of obscenity and swearing which finished off with. "....and sex, I suppose the only reason you do that is for relief. Well I can tell you, you gave me no relief whatsoever. So thank you for nothing mister jazz man."

Douglas did not see her again once he had driven her back to her house, he was happy not too. As he drove away he switched on the car radio and instantly the car was full of Benny, Anni-Frid, Agntha and Björn and they were performing *Chiquitita*. Douglas allowed the song to die away, and he turned into Gloucester Road, it was time to see his Mum and Dad, he had been away for quiet a while, and he missed them.

Then came Jane, Douglas liked her a lot she was fun and interesting and great company. As a friend she was just great, but Douglas had absolutely no sexual feelings towards her. Then one evening she called at his house, he had not been expecting her, he had been working hard and was so very tired. He invited her in, gave her a cup of tea and they started to watch a television programme. Douglas closed his eyes and fell asleep. When Douglas woke Jane had snuggled up to him on the sofa. Douglas was quite shocked.

Then Jane asked. "Can I have sex with you?"

This was not what Douglas wanted and Jane saw it in his face. When she did she became emotional and started to cry, Douglas could not stand that, he did not want her to be upset. So after drying of tears they climbed the stairs to his bedroom and sat on the bed. Then Jane threw another awkwardness into the situation. Something that Douglas had never heard of before.

Earnestly Jane took his hand. "Before we do this there is something I must tell you." She paused and then blurted it out "I have only one breast."

This was a lot for Douglas to cope with, he was not ready for this and he did not want Jane to feel any worse than she had, down stairs a few minutes earlier.

Douglas liked Jane, but he did not wanted to have sex with her, and now he felt that he had to have sex with her. It was a difficult thing for him, not because of Jane's breast, but because he knew that a good friendship was over. Jane realised it too, but was happy to have 'made love', as she later wrote in her dairy.

There were other relationships, for both Arwyn and for Douglas. They were of similar disappointment for both of them. However, they both moved on to what might be called more 'Serious Relationships.'

CHAPTER 6
Arwyn found someone to be serious with

It was a wedding and although she was older now, than when this story began, Arwyn was the bridesmaid. Her best friend, Barbara, was to marry, not to Mark, Barbara and Mark had parted company a long while back. Today Barbara was to marry Simon. The day made Arwyn feel more on the shelf than she had felt before. Although she could not but be happy for her dearest, closest, friend. Simon was a champion of men, anything and everything that Arwyn thought should be a man. He had a fine looking face, he was slim but with a muscular physic and he was sexy.

The years had rolled on, Arwyn's job was fine, she was head of her department. She had good friends, not many, but those she had were all intimate, and knew all there was to know about her. At least that is what they thought, and it was what she wanted them to think.

An outsider, looking in, might have been inclined to think that there was not much of substance to know. However, if they had bothered to scrape down through the layers of Arwyn's life, both the outsider, and her closest friends, could have seen a different Arwyn, because actually Arwyn never reviled the real Arwyn, certainly not to her friends and absolutely not to strangers. Not since the early days with Douglas had she reveal her real self to anybody.

To those with whom she worked, colleagues and students, she was an exemplary teacher, caring and with time to deal with all that came her way. Difficult students and their parents were calmed by her knowledge, and experience. Student teachers were enthralled by her innovative techniques for keeping 'control' of her classroom. She would tell them.

"It is more common sense than anything, to attend to the fine details. Simple things like who sits next to who, and making sure everyone had a sharp pencil before the lesson started."

To her friends she was ever the generous, never forgetting a birthday, always there to help. Aunty to their children and confidant of their secrets.

Beneath the facade there was another. A frightened little girl who trembled before a domineering mother, now be careful how you read that, for her mother, Dorothy, loved Arwyn, she loved her so tightly with all the anxiety in her own heart. So terrified and full of fear was Dorothy that anything should harm her daughter, or that her daughter would stray from the correct path. Arwyn was actually smothered in love. Like an 'Ice Storm', when rain freezes on trees and cars and makes it look as if they have been covered in the same toffee as a toffee apple. Arwyn was so smothered that she was allergic to just about everything. Like a National Service Man haunted by a loud Sergeant Major, Arwyn's early life was all to do with not upsetting her mother.

The result of this, of course, was that Arwyn developed several 'Arwyn's' each with a different face for the world and each totally separate from the other. Lies and deceit were not really lies and deceit, in her mind they were simply the tools she used to make her life bearable, or may be liveable.

There was so much that Arwyn's mother did not know about her daughter's life, For example she knew nothing of Margaret, Arwyn's best school friend, nor the antics of their journeys to and from school, the day they tried smoking, the time they knocked the door of the grumpy old man and ran away, the many days they skipped off games afternoons and went to town. Dorothy had no idea that her, angel, Arwyn would even dream of such things when she was a child.

Even that evening, when Arwyn and Douglas had their first petting session, Arwyn's mother had no idea that such would happen under her roof, as far as she was concerned Arwyn knew nothing about 'that sort of thing' and would not need to know until shortly before her wedding night.

Yet even that was a sort of lie, because Arwyn's mother kept that secret in her heart, it dominated her life, conceived 'Out of Wedlock', as it was then known. Her father and mother had had to leave home, and marry, and make a life far from all they had known. So to keep her daughter safe from such calamity Arwyn's mother kept the secret of sex locked away from Arwyn, thinking that she was the only person on planet earth who could, or would, convey such information to her precious child. She never thought that it would be something which could be self-discovered, and self taught, besides there being many other people in the world who could, and would, fill in the knowledge vacuum; that was a naivety more common that one might think. There was a notion 'We will not mention that and it will go away'.

You might say that that was the sand on which Arwyn's castle was built, certainly lying was as easy as the tide coming in and out, and there were but few pebbles on her beach, let alone any rocks. Then she bumped into one.

They were sitting across the table from one another, at the wedding reception. Still in the bridesmaid's dress, and Arwyn, looking really rather sexy, in her make up and special hair do.

Gavin was not the sort of man she would have expected to be drawn to. He was not in the same physical realm that she had been seeking.

Short with a mop of curly, light brown, hair and he wore glasses upon the, boxer's nose, of his round face, and slightly large and protruding ears. That which shone through to Arwyn was not physical, it was sexual, and Gavin was up for that, without a doubt.

He did not ask her to leave with him she simply followed. She climbed into his car without asking where they were going. She had know idea where he lived, they only thing she had for security was that he was a guest at the wedding of her best friend.

Not many miles along the road he turned left and drove down a track and into a clearing in the trees. In moments he was between her thighs and she was tearing had the belt on his trousers. There was a frenzy of mouth-to-mouth contact and at last she had his penis in her hand. She had not felt one this hard or big before and she wanted to see it.

She said. "Hold on."

Gavin leaned back; Arwyn pulled herself up pulled up her dress and let Gavin pull down her underwear.

She glanced at the penis and pulled him to her saying. "Put it in."

He did. She squeezed him between her legs as hard as she could, willing them to cum together and they did.

She had not had an orgasm like that before.

Other men made her cum because they rubbed her clitoris, but this man made her cum from the inside. She remembered the first time she had made love with Douglas, she came from the inside that time, but the memory of that had been lost for a long time. The intensity produced 'fair ground big dipper rides' in her head, and convulsions throughout her body. She wanted to do it again.

They drove to his flat and they did do it again, it was not as intense, of course, she thought, but it beat every other sexual experience to date, and at that time she thought she would never find something better.

This made life easy for Gavin, for whatever went wrong he could always cure the problem with sex. He only had to touch her and she would remember that first time and long for it again. Longing for something and not quite getting it though, can become tiresome, and wearisome. It took quite a bit of time, of course, she was patient, well at least she felt she was. To an observer it was obvious, that the unspoken pressure she foisted upon Gavin, like a Chinese water torture, drip, drip, drip would send him mad one day. Yes she always came from the inside, and she loved his ability to make her body shake every time they had sex, but she wanted that first time again, and it did not come, and still it did not come.

They bought a house, cheap, and in a mess, in Bishops Cleeve, and Gavin started to renovate it, but it seemed to take forever. Arwyn complained and Gavin tried to mend things with sex, but after a while that failed to put things right. She moaned and he went into his shell. He started staying over at his mother's house. He became distant and started drinking vodka in the evening and falling asleep in front of the television after the sport. So it became regular for Arwyn to sleep alone and there came a barrier between them. Gavin forgot to bring chocolates and flowers. Arwyn moaned and complained that the kitchen was still unfinished and would the bathroom ever be started?

Even so she became pregnant, it was a shock for them both. She was on the pill, later she blamed it on some antibiotics that she had taken, those who knew thought she must just have forgotten to take the pill and then they watched as chaos unfolded.

The house had never been that clean, or that tidy. Gavin's ability to start a job and then not finish it had been a joke for a long time. Arwyn's house care skills were at best intermittent and most of the time slovenly. The on coming baby just made all of that worse. Gavin and Arwyn saw each other for fewer and fewer hours each week. Gavin always working, somewhere, but she knew not where. She felt sick most of the time and depressed like she had never felt before. Deep, and pounding, migraine sometimes got her too. Gavin was very fortunate if he turned up and Arwyn was actually smiling.

There was no intimacy between them now, Arwyn was no longer fit to work and the messy world she was living in was that which made matters worse. She seemed to have completely lost her sense of humour.

By the time of the child's birth Arwyn did not want Gavin in the delivery room, he went in anyway. She screamed at him to come away from her feet and to stand by her head, so he could not see the birth. He reached out to touch her but she spat hot coals of abuse at him and he retreated burnt.

Fortunately for the child, Mother Nature then took control of the hormones within Arwyn, they pulled her mind and body together. For in her arms was something new, something precious, and as the little mite sucked her breast a calm came over her and for the first time in her life, she felt, that she was in a peaceful place.

Order came to her, and she was clearly able to list all that had been done to her in her own childhood. She would not do the same things to her child; and in her mind she built a steel cage about her infant, with strong chain and heavy locks, and 'woe betide any who come close to harming my child, for if you so much as think a word that is critical of him I will laser you to death, in an instant, by the flickering of my eye'.

So daughter became mother and Arwyn and Dorothy were almost one in the same.

The birth had not been easy, the pain was intense and it had required the doctor's help. He had to make an incision to free the foetuses head, as it had tried to enter the world. So Arwyn was obliged to remain in the hospital for several days whilst the wound healed.

Arwyn had thought the Gavin would have made a bit of effort to tidy up the house. She even thought that maybe he might have got to work to finish the kitchen, or the bathroom, or in one wild dream, both. He had not and the thought 'what more should I really have expected?' Came across her.

Gavin was made up with his new son. Arwyn's parents arrived and her mother got to work to clean up the house. Gavin's parents came to see the new prince too, although Gavin's mother would never roll up her sleeves to do, even, the washing up.

Then they were all gone again, the house was tidy but she and her new offspring could do nothing but echo about the place. The depression was deeper still, the baby's crying did not help and the anxiety slowed the lactation and caused her, oversized breasts to be sore as her infant tried to suckle.

Then there was a rap on the door; Gavin had not got around to fixing the doorbell. Arwyn answered, the baby was crying, and the man told her that he was a bailiff and that he had come to repossess car, as the hire purchase payments had been in arrears for some months, and as the finance company had had no response to their missives they had applied to the court for an order, which the bailiff held up to the light.

There was pandemonium in her skull. This cannot be. Gavin has for paid this. There must be a mistake.

"No mistake madam" said the bailiff, all but sympathetically, "the amount owed is some eight hundred and seventy five pounds fifty eight pence, that includes the various court costs etc. madam. Of course if you are able to provide me with this sum of money now I can leave the car here and all will be well."

Arwyn, with help from her neighbour, who went to the bank for her, was able to provide the sum required.

She then telephoned her headmaster and told him she would be returning to work on Monday. She called Gavin's mother and her own mother, she did not tell them why she was returning to work so soon, but she felt lucky that they had agreed to help look after her baby. She needed a full time salary and she determined to take on some private students to increase her income.

Jenny and Thomas

Jenny and Thomas were two of Arwyn's students.

"I am really happy she is back. I didn't like that man who has been teaching us these past weeks. He's so boring." Said Jenny.

Thomas replied. "Yeh, I think he was an idiot. Anyway Mrs. Blake *(Arwyn) is* funny."

Jenny mused. "I do not think she is married, she does not wear a ring."

Thomas replied. "I think she has a child."

"Oh." Said Jenny. "I wonder how she got a baby if she isn't married?" puzzled Thomas.

"I don't know." Puzzled Jenny. "My mum said you have to be married to get a baby."

*

When Gavin came home he felt fury from Arwyn, the like of which he could never have imagined, any anger that he had witnessed from her, or any one, before were as nothing compared to the hurricane he now found himself apart of. The anger did not do anything for their relationship they moved further apart.

That being so, Gavin still loved her, and although she was full of anger at him, she still loved him. To that end when one of her colleagues gave an invitation to them both for a party, about six moths later, Arwyn enthusiastically promoted the idea to Gavin, who made some excuses and told her he could not go. Arwyn went alone.

Jealousy is an ugly thing, it burns and rages and sometimes it brings madness to the human mind. So Gavin was full of anger when Arwyn 'tart-ted herself up'. Layers of make up, tight mini skirt over suspenders and stockings and a blouse, which left little, covered. So Arwyn in her high heals changed in Gavin's mind, from something he found constantly sexy, to something he found vaguely repugnant. At the same time the jealousy consumed him and she did not come home that night.

You would be right in thinking that she flirted with several men at the party, and you would be right to think that she danced with one, who, in the dark, caressed the cheeks of her behind. You would be right to think that she felt his erect penis, as he pulled her close to him, and you would be right to think she enjoyed every minute of it. To the extent that she lead him into the garden unzipped his trousers and made him cum.

Then she stopped. She was drunk she found a bed pushed the coats off a part of it and curled up as a foetus and slept.

It was now Gavin's turn to rage, but unlike Arwyn, his rage was slow, and long, and cold. He never found out about the intimacy Arwyn had had with the stranger at the party, but he knew something had gone on. He suspected the worst, that she had actually slept with someone, and it harmed him viciously. One day Arwyn went into their bedroom and was astonished to find that her wonderfully comfortable, King Sized, bed had been replaced by two single beds. These beds were set against opposite walls and a row of wardrobes had been place to divide the room, effectively making one room into two. This arrangement continued for the next three years.

Cheltenham was, as ever, full of people, and horses, and gold cups. There was a glacier between Arwyn and Gavin now, a chasm so wide neither knew any way to traverse the gulf, which day by day felt wider between them. A limbo of nowhere else either could go, so they stayed, and the house sometimes improved, the kitchen was finished and the bathroom too. Sometimes the house was tidy, usually when Arwyn's mother came to stay.

Then there was an event at the tennis club. Arwyn was still fixated by tennis; she loved it as her father had taught her. Whenever she could find an opponent, and she could find the time, she would play. Of course children and tennis, well most things really, do not necessarily mix, so tennis was not so easily woven into her weekly schedule now she was a mother.

Gavin left the notice on the kitchen table and Arwyn's friend Maurine had asked Arwyn if they could go along together. So Arwyn left her son to be cared for by Maurine's mother, at Maurine's house, and Arwyn and Maurine went together to the Tennis Club event. Gavin arrived on his own. The evening was fine enough until Arwyn noticed Gavin talking, and laughing, with a woman who was called Sandra. Arwyn had known Sandra for a while, and in the descriptions folder, of people that Arwyn kept in her head, it was written 'Tart'. Jealousy now came upon Arwyn.

She stood up and went straight across the room, she glared at Gavin. "We are going home. Now."

He stood up, and they went to the car, they drove home.

In the dark of their front room they tore at each other's clothes and to Arwyn it felt like the first time with Gavin. The frustration in them was gone and they lay exhausted on the wooden floor.

Arwyn was now expecting her second child, like the first unplanned, and like the first not truly something that Gavin would have wished for. In a little while things became what they had been between Arwyn and Gavin. He off to work she balancing a child, a pregnancy, looking after the house, which despite some improvement, was shabby, and her job.

Sometime around about now the bedroom was returned to the way it had been three years before. Arwyn wondered where Gavin had kept their bed during this time. She noticed it had a brand new mattress on it.

Her job was the space within which she felt she had some control. The rest, she often felt, was like hurtling down a helter-skelter in the pitch black.

She felt she was never in control. Any time she did think she was in control Gavin would get messed up in the story, and then he would be in control, and the frustration of this is what got to her most. On top of which there seemed never to be any money. There was the mortgage on the house, and she had two credit cards with twenty thousand pounds of debt accrued upon them.

It just seemed to go on, and on the fights with depression, the fights with Gavin, the fight to keep the household, and her job together. Then as the children grow, the fights with them too. There were three children by now, may be it should have been mentioned that Arwyn's second pregnancy had produced twins, a girl and a boy, it was an awkward affair from beginning to end. Somehow Arwyn got blood poisoning and was hospitalised, with heavy-duty antibiotics, for the apart of the third trimester. Then there were complications during the birth and so a caesarean section had to be performed. Arwyn and her new children were almost lost during the fraught proceedings. The children had to spend a bit of time in incubators. If the truth were known the bond between the twins and Arwyn was never really established. Unlike Darren, who could do no wrong, Justin and Tracy seemed to have wronged Arwyn in some way. Their relationships were ever difficult.

Barbara came by to see the new babies. She said. "You like your new brother and sister Darren, I can see you do. That's right give them a kiss."

Arwyn said to Barbara, watch this. She pressed the button on a cassette tape machine and the machine started to sing.

"*Underground, over ground, Wombling free the Wombles of Wimbeldon Common are we.*"

Darren ran to the corner of the room and picked up a tennis racket, he whirled it around above his head and danced in time to the music.

"I will make a tennis champion out of that boy Barbara." Said Arwyn.

The next thing was that Gavin wanted to take a second mortgage on the house. His bate, to get Arwyn to agree to his plan, was to offer a family holiday to Australia. So Arwyn and the children could meet her Uncle and the children could see Kangaroos. She went along with it.

She really could not care much about the financial situation anymore, she felt run ragged and the thought of a holiday, away from all of it, was worth the cost, whatever the cost it was.

Apart from the amazing time, of course the weather was perfect, and the sea glorious, and the fun Arwyn had with Gavin was so different from the life they had back in bleak, grey, old England.

They took millions of photos. Loads of pictures of Robert's brother, Arwyn's Uncle Malcolm, they, Robert and Malcolm were as peas in the pod, Arwyn actually wondered if her Uncle and Father were twins, maybe, she thought that's where my twins came from.

The children were of a perfect age to enjoy the trip, yes the aeroplane journey had been a challenge, but once in Australia they slept well in the evenings, and so Gavin and Arwyn could relax knowing that their children were dreaming.

They did see Kangaroos, and Koala Bears, they even saw a Crocodile. It was the sparkle in the sun and the blue skies that Arwyn kept in her heart. She wondered if Gavin and she were to up root, and take their children to grow up under southern skies, would they all be better off? They would be warmer and she liked Christmas day on the beach. Although this trip was only for one month, both Arwyn and Gavin felt that this is how it had always been, and how it should always be.

The holiday over, whenever a dispute arose between Gavin and Arwyn, he would remind her of the holiday to shut her up. The holiday was really over, England was as gloomy as ever when they touched down at Heathrow. Arwyn eked out the experience by creating lessons centred about the trip. Geography, of course, was easy, but during the trip Arwyn had found herself wrapped up in the Aboriginal myths of the 'Dream Time'. She liked, especially, a story about a magician who desired a simple girl, who was always dancing, when she refused his seduction he turned her into a bird. Then there was the story about how men used to crawl because, what they thought was the sky, was so low they could not stand on two legs, until one day, one of the crawling men reached up and pushed at the sky, others joined in, and they pushed and the sky ripped apart and then they could stand up right and there was a beautiful new blue back drop in their lives. (You know that story for it was relayed earlier in this tale.)

Before the end of term her class were singing '*True Blue*', Arwyn did not play the guitar as well as John Williams, but there was passion in the performance at the end of term concert. Gavin returned with a pair of Budgie Smugglers, Arwyn felt her sense of humour return when she found them in his suitcase.

A couple more years down the road from their Australian adventure and the house, where Arwyn and Gavin lived, was so dilapidated a passer by might have thought the place abandoned. Gavin was paying interest only on the mortgage and that was on the months he actually paid. Arwyn was the one who opened the letters, and she was the one who would make up the difference from her wages, although the agreement they had was for her to pay the household bills whilst he took care of the mortgage.

She felt piled in debt, lonely, except when she visited her friends, and frustrated for, it seemed that most nights Gavin slept in a drunken a stupor, with a bottle of vodka by his side; he snored in front of the television. He seemed to have lost all interest in sex.

 From Gavin's point of view the years of argument and struggle with Arwyn and her constant demands for this, that and all things else had switched off his supply of testosterone. Frankly the way Arwyn presented herself at home was such that a football game, on the television, was far more arousing than she. He saw her leave for work smart and presentable, whenever she went off out with her friends she made the effort. Whenever she was at home she seemed not to bother, nor care what she wore, how she wore it, or what she looked like. She had put on weight and never had a good word to say about anything.

It would be easy to repeat the above paragraph and simply swap Arwyn's name for Gavin for he was equally as bad. There was simply no 'bother' involved at all, neither bothered about anything.

So that is, roughly, the story of Arwyn over thirty years. Not mentioned were the stories of her relationships with her own parents, her sister and her sister's family. Her brother and his family. The relationship Arwyn had with her parents in law. Or Gavin's part in all that. There of course are all the stories surrounding Arwyn and her friends, and Arwyn and her work.

Anywhere away from the mess of her house, her sloth like man, and demanding children, Arwyn was a completely different person. On 'nights out with the girls' she was the life and soul, she knew the best music, and she could drink the rest under the table, but even she was thinking that the years were having an adverse effect on the idea of 'A Girls Night Out.'

"My god" she thought one night, "I am over fifty, I want something better than this before I die."

What she would have liked to have done was to turn back the clock, to the first time she had had sex with Gavin, and to have repeated that experience a couple of times a week, every week. She did not want to allow for the fact that all bodies move on, and what was once easy, progressively gets less easy. She did not want to grasp, that intensity, within any experience, is difficult to sustain.

Some of the story of Arwyn and her three children is something that space needs to be made for. Despite what was stated earlier about the bonding of Arwyn and Justin and Tracy. Arwyn was the lioness and these were her cubs. No matter what hole those cubs dug for themselves, woe betide any person who were to make the slightest criticism of any of them.

As they grow into their teenage all three were easy at times, and difficult at other times. The elder boy, Darren, was on many occasions the subject of police interest. On one occasion Darren was there when one of his mates smashed a car window, reached in and stole a camera from the back seat, after which he spent the night in a police cell, fortunately for Darren the Magistrate believed him when he said he was just there, and had nothing to do with the theft. The second occasion caused him to be arrested after a fight in a nightclub, but to be fair he had nothing to do with starting it. He was Cautioned, something that had a profound effect on him for many subsequent years. There were problems with his driving, speeding, over taking on double white lines and parking fines to make eyes water. The twins were less of a bother, but still there were moments. Rows with schoolteachers and an abortion for Justin's girl friend, who was not quite sixteen. Two fifteen year olds, and very lucky that there was no involvement of the police in that saga, no one who knew could understand how not. The girl's father was rich and he was able to use his money to cure the problem and so all considered themselves fortunate, all expect the girl who never really got over it and Justin never saw her again.

Tracy could get really ratty when she wanted to, and Arwyn found that she was smoking, not just tobacco, again luckily, for them, no police involvement.

They were Arwyn's children, and they could do no wrong, in Arwyn's eyes or ears, no matter what they did.

Arwyn and her kids did have some fun though, she and other mums would have birthday parties and there were trips to the zoo and paint balling. Her children were the floats that kept her from submergence.

*

All this time Raymond's life had been progressing, nothing wildly exciting but he did see a recruiting poster, for a job he thought would not be too bad. The interview went ok, Raymond had no idea how desperate the employers were to find people, so he thought he had met the challenge and passed on merit. The truth may have been more that they needed people, not many people had applied, and Raymond was almost a fit for the position.

Raymond also met a woman whom he liked well enough and they set up home together. Margaret was really sexy and Raymond liked that. So the first part of their time living together, in a two bed roomed flat, above a shop, in Montpellier was fun. That is Montpellier, Cheltenham, England. They were able to enjoy life, they did not have vast fortunes of disposable income, but there was enough to eat in restaurants, and to go to pubs and the cinema.

Things bounced along nicely until Margaret became pregnant. Raymond's applecart was up ended by the birth of his daughter. He felt that he was now number two in Margaret's affections, and he did not appreciate the demotion to the second division. It probably was not like that at all. Margaret was simply trying to be a good mother, she did not feel that she was neglecting Raymond in any way, but for all his bravado Raymond was a sensitive soul and easily damaged by the slightest of knocks. He did stick by Margaret and they continued on together for a good few years before the marriage disintegrated, and Margaret and their daughter disappeared from his life. Attempts, later, by his daughter, to build a relationship with Raymond never got to far. For by the time she had grown, and sorted herself out, and found him, he had become more, and more, wise to the under belly of human existence. His job had taken him to the depths of human depravity and the little amount of trust he had had in his fellows had been sapped.

CHAPTER 7
Seven: Douglas and failed relationships

Douglas had tried to move on and it had now been years since he had seen Arwyn. He was disappointed by subsequent relationships and wondered if he had been left on the shelf. He longed for a partner with whom he could share the good times and who would smooth the bad times. He wanted someone to whom he could give gifts and make breakfast for. He wanted someone who was his life and he was hers. It was nothing to do with sex, he knew sex would be a part of it, but that was not the motivation, no the goal was to find a sole mate. Someone to trust and to be trusted by.

So Douglas came to Holland, he had a beautiful new Nissan Laurel car. Painted red, sunroof, and leather seats and automatic gearbox, and two point four litre engine, so comfortable it was like sitting in a really comfy armchair. His career had been progressing, television appearances and tours worldwide. There were shows to do in Holland and there was a meeting to look forward to. Douglas's best friend was living there with his wife, Douglas had introduced them to each other and they married and had had a baby boy.

Douglas found the house of Peter and Janet, and was welcomed in, and there was much to talk about. Their house was in a part of Utrecht, where many Turkish people lived. The house was a small, ground floor, part of an old building. It had been a shop in former times now there was a living room, a small toilet room, kitchen and one bedroom. The toilet had the characteristic odour of many another in the poorer quarters of various cities. The house was small, dark but homely and it had a piano. They sang some Joni Mitchell songs about *Carey* and *Bows and Flows of Angel Hair* and then Janet told Douglas that they had an invitation to dinner with one of their friends. She was a nurse and she lived in a nurse's home at the hospital. Before they went off to dinner Douglas and Peter got into some serious talk about some major seventh chords. Peter owned a simply magnificent, hand made guitar, and he played it in magical ways. Douglas on Piano and Peter on Guitar, it rocked the street, neighbours stopped outside the door.

Douglas said to Peter. "You should have kept your professional career going Peter, you are simply brilliant."

Peter looked at Janet and then he looked at their son.

"Janet is expecting our second child. Thank you for the compliment, but I could not do what you do, I tried, but the insecurity, I know our life here is humble, but it is good. How you keep up with the pressure, the travel, and the demands of record company, television, fans and just keeping your band together, and on the road. I really admire you Douglas. I always knew that you would be the one of us who would make it, and just look what you have achieved."

Douglas said. "Well thanks for all of that, but I have to say too that I am jealous of you two, your family and your sweet home in Holland, It is also a triumph, and a triumph which I have simply failed to grasp for myself. I just cannot seem to find the right woman."

Clare was a paediatric nurse. She had prepared a very nice meal. There was something interesting about her, in Douglas's estimation. She did not strike him as beautiful but she had a lot of conversation and a sexy smile. Clare found Douglas extremely attractive.

It was not possible to begin a relationship there and then for Douglas was due in Hanover and could not stay in Holland, but he wanted to see Clare again, and told her that he was free of work the following weekend and that he would return, if she would like him too. So the following weekend, and it was quite a long drive, Douglas was back in Utrecht. He made love, multiple times, with a woman that he would marry just six months, to the day, later.

Utrecht, a fine city, Douglas liked the Dutch push-bikes, and the canals, and the Pancake Houses. The autumn had stripped the trees and their clothes, which were now all over the floor. The sky was grey, with that early winter grey, that Dutch people know, just before Saint Nicholas arrives, on his boat, from Spain, so that Zwarte Piet's can fling their candy at the darkness, to brighten the beginning of winter. The children put their shoes, by the door to their bedrooms, and hope for some sweeties on three nights. Again that is something of the past, or that is at least changing, when these words were written. In 1981 they were still alive and kicking along with Haagse Hopjes, and Drop. (Caramel flavoured sweets and liquorice.)

Three hundred people came to the wedding; six of those were invited by Clare, actually only four, because Peter and Janet were invited by Douglas and Clare together. If Douglas had not been so besotted may be he would have seen the discrepancy, and may be he would have pulled back from the brink.

On the day of the wedding the Parliament, in Westminster, was in session. It was Saturday; the Parliamentarians were discussing the Argentinean invasion of the Falklands. Little did Douglas expect that not only the United Kingdom would be entering a war on that day but he too was heading into his own war with Clare.

The wedding went off well. Peter sang with his guitar and there was much ceremony.

Douglas and Clare had become members of the congregation of that pretty Church of England church. Even though Douglas had given up on religion, many years before, Clare liked the idea of being a church member. She, somehow, thought that she would be thought better of, if people knew she went to church. It was something to do with her aspiration to be counted as middle class.

So there were more than just the invited guests. The subsequent wedding breakfast entertainment included a magician who cut the bride into two with an electric saw, a troop of lady Morris Dancers and a barn dance. People would remember that party for years.

Eventually it was time for the Bride and Groom to leave, their car had been filled with balloons, and there were tin cans tied to the bumper and 'Just Married' painted in shaving foam across the back wind screen.

Clare and Douglas drove to the house, which Douglas had owned for several years by then. Clare had moved in, about two months before, and things had gone well.

Douglas parked the car. Then he shuddered for he felt that something had changed. Clare was different; he felt an anger about her. He opened the door and asked if he could carry her over the threshold. She pushed passed him telling him not to be stupid, and that she would be going straight to bed, and that he should not disturb her.

Douglas felt that he had been hit about the cheeks with a large wet salmon.

Things were then a roller coaster, sometimes up most times down. As the months rolled by Clare's general dissatisfaction with anything, and everything, became more and more amplified. If that, was not wrong, there would surely be something that was, not right. Douglas had no idea of what to do, and spent much time just trying to keep the boat afloat.

It was a huge dilemma for Douglas, he had entered into a marriage in good faith, two hundred and ninety four of his friends and relations had been to a wedding ceremony and heard him agree to marry Clare, and a few hours later Clare seemed to have changed her mind about the whole thing.

Douglas questioned himself, he wondered what it was within him that bought out the worst in the women he chose to be with. Arwyn came to his mind, and Elaine, now Clare and he was now married to Clare.

When she was a child Clare had lived in Hong Kong. Coincidence had it, that shortly before Clare's arrival into Douglas's life, Douglas had agreed to a tour of concerts in Hong Kong. Clare had been thrilled to hear this and suggested that they could use the tour as their honeymoon.

Indeed it turned out to be a good thing, as Clare's frosty attitude seemed to melt as they travelled towards the equator, and to the airport, and indeed they had a good time in Hong Kong. The familiar smell of sewage, sweat and excitement, as their plane taxied the run way at Ki Tak. There was always the extra little bit of 'flight horror' to land over the skyscrapers and down on to the thin, short strip of tarmac, with the 'will we stop before we reach the end?' Douglas told a story.

"I was in an apartment at Causeway Bay, one time, I was looking through binoculars down to Ki Tak and I actually saw a Lufthansa plane fall into the water off the run way, it failed to stop!"

Clare's jaw had dropped and she looked at her husband and said.

"Are you seriously telling me a story like that just as we come into land at one of the trickiest landings in the world? I can't believe you!" Then they laughed. The plane landed.

Douglas said. "That story was true."

Clare and Douglas spent the first couple of nights at the Hong Kong Hotel. It was luxury, curiosity of Clare's Uncle, who had offered to pay the bill as his wedding present to them.

Clare and Douglas sat up in the their king sized bed, the Hong Kong television news spluttering into the curtains and the carpet. Clare purred.

"I cannot get over the story you told as we were landing. That man in the next seat was truly shocked. So was I."

"I am sorry, but let's face it everybody was thinking it anyway. We are all so attached to our little lives, none of us know what will happen tomorrow, none of us know how long we will live, none of us know when we will die. We waste so much time worrying about that sometimes I think we fail to live. It is great to be in this fancy hotel, I have never tasted such great orange juice. I just wonder how much Hong Kong we get in this international environment."

They then moved to the YMCA, not so luxurious but perfectly clean and tidy and it was full of really interesting people. It was not that they could not afford to stay the entire time in the Hong Kong Hotel, Douglas just did not want to.

Douglas said. "See what I mean?"

There were a bunch of Middle Eastern gentlemen, who had occupied several rooms on the same corridor. Both Douglas and Clare commented upon the atmosphere they created about their rooms, Clare thought that there was something homosexual about them, remember that this was a time before the liberated societies of later times. Although it should also be noted that homosexual activity was absolutely outlawed in much of the Middle East. Douglas told Clare that he thought it was simply a different culture and that he thought it was nice to see men who obviously cared about one another.

On one evening Douglas and Clare dined in the YMCA restaurant. The food was good. At one table sat an American couple; Clare said she thought she had also seen staying at the Hong Kong Hotel. The American couple were loud, and were ordering the Chinese waiter about. The waiter was doing his best to keep his cool, then the American man ordered him to bring water with ice. The waiter went to the tap, above the sink on the wall, he filled a glass jug with water, he took the jug to the American's, and as he put the jug on their table he laughed.

"Hong Kong no ice no snow!" The American's were now quiet.

On another evening they sat with another American couple, who had many young children with them. They were travelling the world, on a very limited budget, but were determined to show their children as much of the world as they could before they only had enough money to get back home.

Hong Kong was suffering water shortages and so each morning the water was turned off until the evening, which meant early starts to each day. Hong Kong was exciting, fast and crammed full of people. The smell, the noise, the lights. The millions of shops and manufacturing businesses, which seeped from dark cavern shop fronts and onto the streets. Vendors selling strange foods from hand pushed carts. Orange Julius. The trams and the red taxis and the thirty degrees Celsius, plus, heat and humidity. Such a contrast to the wet cold streets of drab old England.

There were huge skyscrapers built using bamboo scaffolding. In squares there were people doing Tai Chi and playing basketball. There were shops full of gold and dark alleyways where women sat picking the seeds off piles of bean shoots. With piles and piles of fresh vegetables. In a supermarket were live chickens for sale, which would be killed, there and then, for people to cook for their dinner. There was the Star Ferry, a few moments of, relative peace, between Hong Kong Island and Kowloon. There were huge, beautiful, shopping centres bedecked in marble and fountains.

Douglas was enchanted by the furniture; he wanted a Camphor Wood Chest. He loved the smell.

Douglas and Clare went to see the temple with ten thousand Buddha's. They travelled about the island to Stanley, and Repluse Bay, and saw the beautiful, colonial, Repluse Bay Hotel. You can no longer for it has been washed into the sands of time. Even Clare would have wanted you to experience that.

They took a trip into mainland China, and experienced the contrast between it and the excitement of Hong Kong. China, then full of drab streets, myriads of people, and even more bicycles, sometimes interrupted by an occasional pick up truck, horn tooting. There were people selling meat from open tables in the street. There was a shop from which tourists made purchases of souvenirs. Chinese men stood at the door gazing in but were not allowed to step in. One fellow dangled precariously over the middle of a street on bamboo canes as he mended something, what? Nobody could tell you, but that man should have had a job in the circus.

Their 'luxury bus', as the advertising put it, was a battered mini bus; Douglas's 'luxury seat' was the spare wheel. They travelled past abandoned building sites, to a reservoir and on to an artist's colony where there were many pictures of still life bananas, and apples, and bottles of wine. The tour provided lunch in a restaurant; it was a tasty meal, apart of which was some Sweet and Sour Pork. Clare thought it would be similar to that which she enjoyed when she went to the Chinese Restaurant in Leiden, in Holland, 'Rice Taffle'. As Clare bit she almost broke a tooth for instead of a piece of soft pork there was a bone. Douglas told her that many Chinese people think that the sweetest meat is that closest to the bone, so the idea was to nibble off the bone whatever meat could be found. Clare and Douglas enjoyed the meal. However, the toilet was second only to one Douglas had experienced in Kenya, a couple of years before. He told Clare that if she could hang on it might be for the best! The trip finished with a visit to a Chinese kindergarten. All very sweet little children, to remind the western visitors that we are all just humans really. They got back on the train and sped back to Hong Kong and had tea in the Peninsula Hotel. The Peninsula, which remained open through the Japanese occupation of the Second World War, with it's fleet of Roll Royce limousines.

The Honeymoon was good for the newly married couple and Douglas thought that Clare was trying to settle into their new life. He thought, maybe, the wedding night was just stress.

He appreciated the fun side of her nature and the jokes she made about getting into a Rick-Shaw and demanding a ride to the Peak '...and make it snappy'.

Douglas's performances in Hong Kong went well, In the morning paper it was written that Douglas gave the most splendid of performances, there was a nice photograph. Tony Banes interviewed Douglas on the afternoon RTHK Radio show. There was a piece for RTHK television and a small item on TVB Pearl.

Douglas had been a regular visitor to Hong Kong and Clare was thrilled to see the place in which she had spent some of her childhood. There was one, final radio show for the British Forces in Sek Kong, in the New Territories. They took the bus, with the chickens, and the pig and a load of Hong Kong Chinese people, and wound up the windy, windy road, through the tropical vegetation, and farms, and the terraced landscapes, and heat, and smell. They alighted at the Borneo Lines. Douglas said to Clare

"Every time I come here I remember Michael Bentine, 'It's a Square World' the television programme from the 1960's, I am sure he was the one who taught me about 'The Borneo Line's', it was written on the wall right by the bus stop. Douglas played '*Slow Boat to China*' on the radio show, Vaughan Savage, who presented the show, admired Douglas's ability as a jazz pianist, and rounded it of by saying

"Truly one of the best jazz pianists on planet earth, and the best one in this studio since he was here last year. The tune was dedicated to his brand new wife Clare, but it seems to me that he has already taken her on a Slow Boat to China." The jingle played and the news followed.

Douglas and Clare travelled a lot. The last tour was six months across Europe. They started in Belgium, went through France and Germany, They saw sights Neuschwanstein, in Bavaria, they were in Austria then Switzerland. Douglas was to play at the Montreux Jazz Festival. Bob James, Darryal Jones, Leonard Cohen and Miles Davis were all on the bill.

Then Douglas and Clare went on down to the very south of Spain visiting The Pardo art museum in Madrid on the way. They drove through fabulous mountains and forests and the seaside at Marbella.

During this trip Clare had frightened Douglas. In her angriest moments she had threatened to kill him and their child. So relatively speaking Douglas felt that it was better to be alone. She had wanted a child but when she got one the whole idea disagreed with her. She paid for a private doctor to sterilise her so that she could have no more.

Five years later, looking back upon their, failed, marriage. Douglas saw, with horror, that the days in Hong Kong were the best of it. Clare was never satisfied, and she left Douglas and their two-year-old child and went with a man, called Bruce, to Australia. The child or Douglas never heard from her again.

So Douglas became a single parent and the story of that is, again really another book. So here we skip forward almost a decade. During those ten years there were a few girl friends in Douglas's life. Good women, who would have made Douglas very happy for the rest of his life. Women who would have accepted his child as their own. Women he could have trusted. The problem was not with them but within him. Clare had wounded him so deeply that he was afraid to commit to another relationship. The echo of Arwyn was still a torment.

Then Yvette appeared, a beautiful woman from where? She seemed to arrive from the middle of a blizzard and completely foxed Douglas.

She bought with her a daughter of two years. Her motivation, Douglas later realised, was to make more children. Yvette was not really interested in Douglas, she wanted more children, Douglas did not mind having a family, he felt that it would be good, and he was turned on by this foreign woman, and soon they were married and soon there was Mummy, Daddy and four children, again this is for another book, but it is useful, here, to write that the life that Douglas and Yvette created was extraordinary. They owned a beautiful, and huge house, and the children had their own horses. There were new cars, all in all a beautiful life.

Once again Douglas could not believe what was happening, when one night he went to turn off Yvette's computer, something he did every night, and to his horror there was an email, upon the screen, open for the world to read, which alerted him to the fact that his wife, the mother of his children, was conducting an affair.

He thought to himself 'hang on, hold it maybe it is a passing thing.' He did not tell Yvette what he had seen. He did not want another broken marriage. He wanted his children to have a perfect family life, with loving parents. In this dream world, which they had made. He hung on and he hung on. Until he just could not hang on more.

Yvette ever more tetchy towards him until one day she turned to him and shouted. "I suppose you are having an affair. Are you?"

Douglas could not believe his ears, for never had he thought of it. He knew that Yvette was, and he knew that she was seeing more than just one man. He had found out by accident, the email, and overhearing Yvette talking to one of her friends. Now she accused him. That was the moment Douglas and Yvette's marriage ended. Douglas knew that there was no return. The fairy tale world that they had created, like some hot air balloon snagged by a stray arrow, sank to the ground. So neither Arwyn nor Douglas had had the lives that they had hoped for. Of course there were good times and bad times for them both.

CHAPTER 8
Raymond and Crystal

Raymond had never got personally involved with anybody at his work. Police Officers, suspects, witnesses never went in his mind when he left the police station to go off duty. He just never got involved in any way shape or form, that is until he came to deal with a prostitute who called herself Crystal. Crystal had managed to build herself a career without a pimp; by keeping herself to herself and being quiet. She had a good number of regular clients, who treated her well and paid her correctly. She ran herself like any good small business operator, she took pride in her business premises, she took pride in her appearance. She kept herself fit and had regular check ups with her doctor. She practiced self-defence. She was selective in where she placed her discreet advertisements. She filled in her tax returns and paid her taxes. Her home was several miles from flat which she owned, where she provided the services she offered. Her business had been lucrative for nearly ten years when an apartment, in the same building as her flat, became the subject of a police investigation.

Crystal did not know who owned the apartment, neither did she care, but whoever it was bought a whole posse of police personal traipsing right past Crystal's door, for about one week. During which time Raymond rang her door bell to ask if she had any knowledge of her neighbour. Not satisfied with Crystal's response of 'no', Raymond decided to look around and ask around about Crystal. It did not take him long to have worked out some suspicions of how she made a living, what her real name was, and where she actually lived.

Raymond put her under 'unofficial surveillance', that meant he did not ask his boss if he could, but if there was a problem, later, he would say that he had suspicions, and that he was just checking before he bothered to make it official. So he followed a man into the building, who had been let in by Crystal using the entry intercom system, Raymond nipped in as the door was closing, nobody noticed. Raymond stood in the shadow out of view of Crystal's door and waited half an hour for the man to leave. As Crystal was shutting the door Raymond quickly stepped forward and pushed he way in to the flat. Crystal was startled but she put up a fight as she tried to push Raymond back through the door. There was punching and scratching she tried to get enough space to swing her foot up between his legs, but Raymond managed to grip her arm and swing her around so that he was holding her firm from behind.

He said. "Calm down, I am a police officer. I already have plenty of charges I could bring against you from assault to running a disorderly house. I have photographs of many of your clients and witness statements. I could arrest you, or we could talk to see if there was some better way to resolve the current situation."

Crystal Said. "Show me your warrant card first, why should I believe you?"

Raymond pulled the card from his pocket and held it before Crystal's eyes so she could see it.

"I will not scream or fight, now let me go."

Crystal was, in Raymond's eyes, a very beautiful woman.

"Now how about we do a little deal? You continue your little business and in exchange for my not arresting you, you give me a couple of sessions a month and a small monthly stipend. Alternatively I can arrest you here and now and then drive over to your house to tell your husband all about your work. Oh but he surely knows what you get up to, or does he really believe that you sell insurance? Anyway it makes no difference he lives off your immoral earnings so I will arrest him too. Mr. Jameston, Mr. Philip Jameston, married to you Wendy, oh and your two beautiful children; private education, that must be great for them.

There were no fancy mobile phones, no miniature cameras, Crystal, had no way to record what Raymond had said, what good would that do anyway? He could arrest her if he really had proof, but what proof could he have? Even if he watched the apartment block, and took photos of everyone who went in or out; no one but her clients and her knew what went on inside, and payment was always in cash so was he bluffing, or could he really harm her? She was not sure.

"Well Raymond, I think you are full of shit, and I do not think you have anything that your bosses would let you arrest me for, in fact, I think I could easily make a complaint about you, you, after all, have broken into my apartment and assaulted me. I have never had a pimp, and I will pay protection money to a bent copper, So I will say this only once; get up off my chair and fuck off out of my apartment."

Raymond grabbed Crystals arm, handcuffed her, and arrested her.

"If you tell my husband I will, one day, find you and I will kill you." Said Crystal

Then Raymond did what he had told Crystal he would do. He drove to her house and told her husband, Philip Jameston, that his wife, Wendy, was a prostitute who called herself Crystal, and he, Philip, was, therefore, living off immoral earnings. Then Raymond arrested Philip, who had no idea what Raymond was talking about. The consequences of all of this were catastrophic for Philip, Wendy, their two children and their wider families. Raymond piled up the charges. The subsequent court case led to prison sentences. It was 2007. Crystal and her husband were due for release in the spring of 2016.

CHAPTER 9
The unexpected often happens

What bought Arwyn and Douglas to that café on that day? They were in Burton on the Water. No one will ever know. They had heard nothing of each other for more than thirty years.

The world had moved on, technology had sped into the Internet and Friends Re-United arrived, and got the social media thing off the ground. MySpace followed and then Facebook was on it's steep accent to dominate cyberspace. A space, which had never been thought of in 1973.

Many people found each other through these websites, not Arwyn and Douglas. One day, by chance, they found themselves in the same café. A cold, rain sodden day, chill wind and deep grey sky. Their mission to get out of the rain for a sit and a hot drink.

It was the year Bulgaria and Romania joined the European Union and Robert, Arwyn's father, was convinced, in his right-wing way, that at one minute past mid-night, on the first of January, England would be swamped by the entire populations of these countries arriving at Gatwick Airport, and Dover Harbour, to take a slice of the good life of his sacred England. Nasa's Messsenger spacecraft flew past the planet Venus and someone assassinated Benazir Bhutto, Prime Minister of Pakistan.

Arwyn had changed; she was heavier in the body, her face rounded, and now with crows' feet at the eyes, and a world-weary countenance, an halo about her. She still had her red hair but it was short now and curled. He could see she was in pain, not physical, but mental. The feelings that he had had for her all those years before were back in Douglas's mind in a nanosecond.

Arwyn looked at Douglas and said. "You haven't changed."

Of course he had, but the brain filters out what it does not want to see, and suddenly she was seventeen again, and here was the first man to kiss her properly, and deep inside she wanted him to kiss her right now, and she wanted Douglas to sweep her up onto his white steed and carry her of into a Barbara Cartland novella. Away from Gavin, debt, and a tumble down house.

It took sometime for Arwyn and Douglas to come together, Douglas wanted to be careful that his children were as secure and as safe as possible. He needed to do much. Something that Arwyn could not, and was not, able to understand. Douglas told her from the outset that whatever they did must in no way harm his children. He told her that it would take time to finish things properly so that they could begin a new life together.

Douglas found things heavy going for a long time. For years he had been in a loveless marriage he had had no sexual relationship for about five years. So when it did come to sexual contact between Douglas and Arwyn it was a shock to him. It was a shock to Arwyn too, for Douglas could not make love to her, he was impotent. He made her cum, sure enough, but it was not enough for her.

Douglas engaged in some therapy sessions. He told the therapist of his relationships and the devastation he had felt when he discovered his wife's infidelity. He found it impossible to commit the same crime. Finally the therapist recommended a visit to the doctor to ask for some Viagra and to relax and enjoy a new part of his life.

Arwyn became happier now and, as she had always done, enjoyed the sex. She did, however, hold high standards, in her mind, for this activity, and Douglas failed, to meet her expectations, on many an occasion. He made her cum but always from the outside, she wanted him to make her come from the inside. He could not, and the pressure she bought to bare made him feel raw sometimes.

On one occasion Arwyn bought a gift, nicely wrapped, with a ribbon. Douglas was surprised. "For me? Oh dear have I missed some anniversary? There was nothing in my dairy."

Arwyn chuckled. "You are always so nervous, why should I not just give you a present because I want too?"

Douglas apologised. "So many years of living on the edge of always getting everything wrong, I suppose. I am sorry."

Arwyn told him to open the gift. He pulled on the ribbon and removed the red wrapping paper. The looked puzzled. The gift was a medicine tablet container with the words 'Horny Goat Weed' printed on the label.

Douglas questioned. "What is it?"

Arwyn laughed. "It is the stuff that makes goats horny, I thought it might help the Viagra along. Here is a glass of water, try a couple."

Douglas swallowed.

Douglas was working hard at his career, the older he was the more he had to, for the fees were not what they had been in his younger days. He was holding two households together.

Arwyn's household was dyer, she lived in a ram shackled old house, which was unheated and falling down. It had not been painted since she and Gavin had moved in. There were holes in plasterboard, broken windows and the smell of neglect.

Douglas rented a room in a nearby house, and once Gavin had left, and solicitors had spent a lot of Douglas's money, Douglas became the owner of Arwyn's house. He had her name put on the title deeds, although it was his money that had paid off Gavin and some of the huge mortgage. They had to get another mortgage to cover the rest. It was Douglas's money that restored the property to a pleasant dwelling. Arwyn demanded as much as she could. Douglas paid off credit cards and invested thousands into new bathroom and kitchen. He rolled up his sleeves and did much of the work himself. He purchased for Arwyn new clothes and paid off her son's parking tickets. Douglas wanted to make Arwyn's life perfect. He wanted to wipe away the years of neglect they both felt and he thought, at every corner, it would soon be that he and Arwyn would settle down into a fairy tale happy story.

It is never possible to know what is in the mind of another person. What was in Arwyn's mind only she could know, but many thought that not even she knew. Douglas loved, and he gave, and he paid. Arwyn worked out how to get Douglas to pay; she did not find it difficult. She wanted to take her kid's on holiday.

"Probably the last holiday they would be able to have together." She told Douglas, and he kept on until Douglas went with her and she booked the holiday and Douglas paid Thomas Cook's a thousand and more pounds.

The trip Arwyn made with her kid's, on their 'last' holiday together. To Jamaica two weeks in the sun, in a beautiful hotel and all the food and drink they could cope with. The teenagers took Arwyn into the nightclub and to the Karaoke. She and they drank far more than would be normal, and they slept it off on the beech each day. Tracy bought some marijuana from a handsome black guy and she had sex with him.

There were trips away at weekends, there were trips away to Scotland, there were trips to Belgium and France. Then there was the problem of Arwyn's car and Douglas solved that problem with his money, but the car Arwyn chose did not suit her well as she thought it would, so he changed it for another.

Douglas could seem to an outsider as a bit of a chump. He was funding all of these things and doing his best to love and care for two families now. Torn between the two it was amazing to see how well he managed things.

He knew that for all he did Arwyn was still not happy inside herself.

One afternoon Arwyn and Douglas had settled down for a little quiet love making. It was the no pressure kind, the sort that Douglas found the most pleasing. Then Arwyn said. 'I know you try to please me but Gavin used to make me cum from inside, why can't you do that? Gavin did it every time.'

Douglas found this sort of competition very hard and he took it deeply into himself, he blamed himself.

In the meantime Arwyn had told him that despite the fact that the house in which she lived now belonged to Douglas it was not possible for him to move in. She had kept Douglas a secret from Darren, Justin and Tracy, her work and all but two of her friends.

Douglas remembered those long ago college days when as they entered on a Monday morning suddenly Arwyn knew him not, and she would tell no one of their relationship.

Each month Douglas was paying a hefty rent for a flat on the other side of Cheltenham. A solution came to him. The house in which Arwyn lived, his house, had a shed at the bottom of the garden. It faced away from the house and could be easily accessed from the gate in the back fence. The shed door was invisible from the house. The shed contained nothing but unwanted items and rubbish. It was actually a substantial building; it was made of brick and had a tiled roof. Over the course of several months Douglas cleared the shed and in it built himself a space in which he could live. Arwyn was at work most of the day, and her boys and daughter were out too. It was not that difficult. Within half a year he had constructed a bed sitting room complete with shower, toilet and office space in the shed. He dug a trench for a soil pipe; there was an electric supply and water already in the building. He insulated the walls and roof space, It was cosy. It had no windows and no planning permission. He lived in it for a month and nobody knew he was living there.

Arwyn had fallen into a pattern which Douglas remembered and again described as 'Push-Me-Pull-You', he had seen a film, when he was a child, about a doctor who could talk to animals. There had been a Lama type creature in that called a 'Push-Me-Pull-You'.

Sometimes Arwyn wanted Douglas and sometimes she did not. Sometimes she would fall into great depressions and sometimes she was fine. Douglas spent his time surfing the wave of the good times and drowning in the bad.

Douglas's life with Yvette had been often dyer but he had lived at a very high standard, and he had his children about him, even though the children were entering adulthood. Here, with Arwyn, he found himself increasingly jumpy for he found it was easy to upset her. He knew not, from day to day, if he would be in favour, or out of favour. He constantly quizzed Arwyn to find out what she thought would make her happy.

One day he asked her what would make her happy? She told him she had always wanted to go on a cruise. She went on at great length how her best friend, Barbara, had had such a great time and that she could only imagine herself feeling great if she had the same opportunity. So gullible, you might think, Douglas made the arrangements, they had to wait about six months but that was alright he thought, something magnificent to look forward too. So the tickets were purchased and Douglas really thought that this would be the panacea that would be the full and final cure.

The events you have read about so far happened over a period of several years. 'The-Push-Me-Pull-You' happened throughout. Douglas had given up so much for Arwyn; Arwyn had given up nothing, nor had given very much to Douglas. She knew she did not love him, but was perfectly happy for Douglas to think she did, especially whilst he was providing such a bounty. She knew that he was a better man than Gavin, but what she really wanted was something else, what, or, who that something else was she did not know.

So keeping Douglas about was the best she could do right then, at least until there was something better. After all Douglas would never let her down, and he would provide no matter how awful she was to him. This makes her sound cold and calculating, she was, but she did give Douglas, on occasion, just enough of what he wanted to keep him hanging on.

Deep in Douglas was the harm he carried from his first wife. The guilt he felt of the damage to his eldest, their, child. The pain he knew his precious boy had felt when his mother had left, he had been an infant then, but that kind of hurt runs very deep. Then the hurt inflected by society, and rules which plunged him into a boarding school, and finally the hurt that Douglas had caused on him when Douglas took up with a new woman, Yvette, and even married her. Douglas knew his precious boy had been harmed and that nothing he could do would repair it.

Douglas also knew that his other children had not escaped damage, a bit less in his daughter than his younger son. Definite scares were apparent and later his stepdaughter told him that her relationships with men had been affected by the relationship that Douglas had had with Yvette. Douglas and Yvette had one other child whom they had adopted, Monica. Douglas felt sure she had felt it to. That poor little mite had had a very rough entry into the world. Her real parents had been some of Douglas's best friends. Douglas was Monica's Godfather, so it was logical, as she had no other relatives that Douglas and Yvette would care for her, and they did.

So the stakes were high for Douglas. He had to do all he could to stop his relationship with Arwyn from disintegrating after all the damage inflicted already. The thought of yet more failure was more than he could bear. Douglas went to extraordinary lengths to keep the show on the road.

He did them with love, and kindness. Despite the pressure, and difficulty. He gave all he could to the cause of making a good life for Arwyn. He dreaming, constantly, that one day Arwyn would love him, as he loved her, and that harmony would be theirs to enjoy.

Sometime around and about this point Douglas had some concerts to perform in America. It was a thirty-day trip. The money and the publicity were welcome; it was getting more difficult to get that kind of good work these days. Once in a while Douglas thought he might end up playing for weddings; there was high demand for his financial assets and he had to keep the pennies clicking into his bank account.

The trip was quite satisfactory. Three radio stations were kind enough to give him live interviews. The DJ's played some of his older recordings and enthused over them. There was also a television performance, but it was only a small local station, which reached very few people. The trip finished in New Orleans. He was interested to see just what had happened to the city after hurricane Katrina had, all but, washed it away. He wrote a tune for a song, a guy he met, who had written about George. W. Bush's response to the disaster.

Douglas said to the man. "You know that is such an old story now; no one is going to buy that as a new song."

The feller smiled and replied. "Well I ain't going to sell it as a new song! I will say it is an old song, written at the time of the disaster, an experience like that ain't never goin' away. Who will know? Just me and you. Now just play that bit in the middle again. Are you really sure you are just giving me this tune, you want nothing for it, no payment, no royalties?"

Douglas pulled the manuscript towards him and wrote the sheet that the melody now belonged to his new friend.

"I can't believe you did that brother."

"Why?" Asked Douglas. "I can see, that even after all these years you are still struggling to get things straight. I do not see much evidence of wealth down your street. I hope you make some money from the tune. If you make a lot remember to share it, with some of the poorer folk around and about here."

Douglas returned to England. On Virgin Atlantic, did it really take twenty hours? There was some advertisement for this airline saying 'You'll be treated like a rock star!' Douglas said to himself. 'Shall I tell them I was once a big Jazz Star, and I have just been reprising my career in New Orleans.' In the end he decided not to.

Douglas thought it was time to let Arwyn in on the secret of his home in the shed. He told her to close her eyes and he led her by the hand.

"Mind the step," he told her.

When she saw the shed she could scarcely believe it for how it had been constructed without her knowledge? She could not understand. One part of her was mad and angry; another part was scared that her children might find out that she had a new relationship, with a man who was not their father. Another part of her was glad that the man who had sorted out the finances, made her house liveable, and the man who had paid for holidays, and who obviously loved her totally was now, almost, under the same roof as she. It was what she wanted, and what she did not want all at the same time.

*

The cruise around the Mediterranean was great fun. For weeks before Arwyn had been collecting new items of clothing to wear on board. She was excited and found it hard to not talk about it. When they finally boarded the ship she was in an ecstasy the like of which she had never been in before.

Arwyn thought the dressing up for dinner was great; Douglas in is Dinner Jacket and bow tie, she in yet another new dress. Arwyn videoed the ocean with her eyes, and sorted the pictures in a special place in her mind, so that she could never forget.

The food, on the cruise ship, was so beautifully presented, and there was so much variety, and there was so much quantity. The shows, and entertainment were superb. One cabaret, on board, was a comedian who's arms kept getting longer and longer. Douglas and Arwyn laughed, as did all the other cruisers, until tears dripped from their chins.

Douglas said to Arwyn. "Did you never see that old gag before? He did it so well. What was that joke again, the one about the Dachshund and the postman's trouser leg?"

Her breath was simply taken away when they ducked in and around the picturesque Greek Islands. The visits to different harbours and a concert of folk music, in beautiful concert hall; just down from where the ship was docked.

It was more than a fantastic experience. Arwyn had more than enjoyed it, every moment from sitting in the Jacuzzi to wondering what kind of shape the steward would make from the towels when they returned to their cabin that evening. She had felt like a Princess, the only thing, unbelievably, was that she had reservations about certain parts of her Prince.

Harriet and George

There were several locations, on board ship, where dinner could be taken. On one occasion the waiter lead them to a table with four seats around it. Arwyn was wearing a long evening gown, green with some embroidery of yellow flowers on the right at the front and over the shoulder. The left shoulder had a gap through which Arwyn's shoulder could be seen. The green shimmered in the light, it was most attractive. Douglas was wearing his dinner suit and bow tie, they sat down. The waiter bought them drinks and a few moments later they were joined by another couple. Douglas thought that they were very nice, Arwyn enjoyed speaking with Harriet and Douglas was getting along famously with George. They had a discussion about how the captain of this ship insisted that all passengers clean their hands with the hand cleanser, on their entry to any of the places where the passengers could eat or drink.

"Absolutely the correct thing to do." George informed the company. "I read of a cruise where many of the passengers suffered from gastroenteritis, an absolutely awful thing to get at any time, but on one's holiday, simply ghastly. On a ship where it is so easy to infect all the other passengers. No this Captain is a first class sort, and good for him."

Harriet asked Arwyn. "So where do you two live?"

Arwyn replied. "We were both bred and born in Cheltenham. What about you two?"

Harriet said. "Well you will not believe me when I tell you. We are both from Gloucester! Would you believe that? George is a Doctor but his surname is not Foster!" This was followed by some laughter.

The waiter bought salmon mousse with brown bread for a starter.

Douglas said. "I really like the butter they serve on this ship."

Each mousse had been prepared in a mould, which had the shape of a miniature salmon. There was discussion as to how hard the kitchen staff must work to make such wonderful food, which was always so wonderfully presented. The main course was steak au pouvoir, followed by a desert of lemon sorbet.

The two couples got along so well together that after they had eaten they made their way to the piano bar for a drink. The piano was played expertly by a woman who had long blonde hair and who wore a splendid, long, dinner dress. Both Arwyn and Harriet thought the dress magnificent. The music was popular classical music. The classical tunes people could hum to. It was a very nice evening and they agreed to meet up to repeat the evening together on the following day.

As Harriet slipped off her evening gown, and George undid his bow tie, Harriet was the first to speak.

"Is it not so desperately sad to see such a wonderful couple as Arwyn and Douglas so, so very far apart? He loves her with all his heart, but she really has not signed up for that."

George looked at his wife and felt totally bemused. He asked. "What the Dickens do you mean by that? Perfectly suited couple, first rate fellow that Douglas, a Jazz Pianist of the first water. I have three fine CD's which feature him. When I was in the Forces, stationed in Hong Kong, in the nineteen eighties, up at Sek Kong, I actually heard him play, live, on British Forces Radio, BFBS, he played *'On a Slow Boat to China'*, absolutely first class performance.

Harriet asked. "Did you talk about that to him?"

George coughed a half laugh. "Absolutely not, when I heard him, all those years ago, he had his 'new' wife with him. From our conversation with Arwyn and Douglas this evening, Arwyn is obviously not Douglas's first wife! I did not think it appropriate to bring that up over the steak au pouvoir! So what is it that you think is wrong Harriet? Women, you must always see things that are totally un-see-able by the rest of us."

Harriet said. "Look at Arwyn, listen to what she says and watch how she makes no attempt to make physical contact with Douglas. I am always reaching out to touch you darling, for you know I adore you. I am afraid that Arwyn has got herself into something and it is not quite meeting her expectations. You must see it, she wants to move on."

George was quite shocked. "You realise that he is paying for the entire trip."

Harriet said. "How on earth do you know that?"

George said. "Well we were speaking about how we had come to book this cruise, and we got to discussing the price of the tickets, and one thing led to another. Anyway I like them and I am looking forward to another interesting evening tomorrow. May be it will all turn out right for them."

Harriet already had the measure of it. "Not if someone pulled the plug out of the Mediterranean Sea and this cruise ship found it's self on dry sand is there any hope of that. You men are clueless!"

Even Barbara, Arwyn's best, and longest friend, found it hard to understand. Gavin and Arwyn had been together for twenty-five years, they had been in debt all of that time, money was always a nightmare; sometimes there were Bailiffs at the door. The house had been a mess from the start, and Gavin was not always an attentive Father, and was often, it was felt, uninterested in Arwyn's life at all. In one blazing row he had asked Arwyn if he really was the father of her children! By contrast Douglas was an absolutely super man, patient in the extreme, with a gentle nature, that was generous to a fault, in every direction. Barbara could not believe all that Douglas had done for Arwyn, nor why Arwyn was still not satisfied. Barbara could not understand why Douglas put up with all that he put up with. Other observers felt the same.

When Barbara and Arwyn met up for their monthly meeting, after the Cruise. Arwyn was full of it. She regaled Barbara with visions of food, food and more food. Sunny beaches, and Greek architecture. She enthused about the little white villages, which sparkled in the bright sunshine against a blue sky. She showed Barbara the photographs she had taken. Barbara listened intently and when the rush of Mediterranean glory had abated.

Barbara said. "I thought that you told me that Douglas went with you on this cruise. You did not mention him once in your stories, and you have not one photograph of him on this trip with you, you told me he paid!"

Arwyn looked a little shocked, then a little timid and then she felt herself flush with embarrassment.

Arwyn could not find it in herself to tell her boys about Douglas, now living in the shed for a good few months. Although they were now young adults, to Arwyn they were still her baby children, and had to be protected at all times, and in all ways, from all harms.

Then, one day, Arwyn's oldest boy, Darren, was walking the dog, down the road, at the back of the house as Douglas was coming out of the shed, the collie ran straight to Douglas, he knew Douglas very well. It was a shock for Darren. Later he quizzed Arwyn. Arwyn told him that she had rented the shed space to someone to use as a storeroom. Darren was not that stupid and the next day he knocked on the shed door. Douglas answered.

The anger that greeted him was unexpected. As soon as the door opened Darren's fist lunged out and caught Douglas on his left cheek. He staggered back and fell; his head hit the ground with a thump. For a moment the wind had left him and he found himself unable to move.

Darren found himself frozen to the spot. He seldom went into this old shed, the last time was, some years before, when he went to put a box of old childhood toys in it. The room was completely transformed; it was a proper place in which anybody could live. His brain was fixed on these thoughts; he paid no heed to Douglas, who was still full length on the floor. Then Darren saw the, large, framed photograph hanging on the wall. It was a picture of his mother and the man he had just punched. They were framed in a sunset and facing each other. Their eyes looking into each other and their lips were joined. It looked as if the photograph had been taken in Greece, there was a blue sky and white houses. In the bottom right hand corner was a small picture, about a postcard size, pushed into the frame. The photo was similar to the large one but the couple were touching chin to chin. Darren had never seen such a pose.

The rage in Darren was uncontrollable, his foot lashed out to kick at Douglas. What made Douglas move, when only seconds before he was paralysed, who can tell? Douglas rolled and Darren's as foot kicked and now Darren found himself falling back, he too was on the ground.

It took a while to calm Darren down. Darren got very angry at times, and was quite capable of swinging his fists. It could have been the shock of coming across a strange man in the shed, of what he considered to be his house, or may be it was the shock that his mother had been far from honest, and open with him, but the day Darren discovered Douglas in the shed was a day of real discovery in Darren's life, and a day that changed his perception of his mother for always after. Darren was full of hate and anger and murderous thoughts filled his mind.

When the dust had settled and Darren's brother, Justin and sister Tracy, had been let in on the secret, Douglas told them that he was not going to try to be their father, but if he could help them in any way, they should only ask, and he would help if he could. Indeed as the time went on there were many times they asked, a lift in the car here, a photocopy there, and sometimes more serious help like loans of money, which were never repaid, or problems with girls, Tracy never had problems with boys.

The boys nor Tracy never really knew the extent of help their mother had accepted from Douglas. They knew that she had accepted all willingly, and they had some appreciation because they were better off than they had been before. There was some jealousy, and there was some difficulty, in their minds, of the position of their real father. For in the intervening years he had found a new partner and had started a new family.

Gavin's new family played on Arwyn's mind, it made her feel inferior. What was wrong with her? She would speak to herself when she was alone at night. 'Why would he not marry me?', 'I could kill that bitch'. Then when Douglas asked her to marry him, for the second time in his life, and Arwyn crucified Douglas with her tongue.

"I am happy on my own for the time being" She had not even paused to give the idea a thought.

Douglas knew that that was untrue, and it made him unhappy, that for all he had done, and been through for her, she was not prepared to make the commitment. So 'The-Push-Me-Pull-You' continued through more hours and days and weeks.

Douglas knew not how to extract himself from all of this. He knew for sure that this bed was one he had made. It was like the 'Apple Pie Bed', that he had once experienced, when he was about ten years old, on a Boys Brigade weekend, where they had slept in dormitories in an old house. In those times people did not use duvets, instead they had sheets and blankets. If the top sheet is folded down the middle and then tucked in, no matter how anyone would try it was impossible to get into the bed. The fun in watching some poor fool trying. It would enviably produce much snorting, and amusement, for those who performed this dastardly deed.

Then Arwyn came across another crisis, which she had not the resources to cope with alone. So she dialled the 'emergency number', and like a fool, Douglas picked up the phone and went running to help her.

It was Arwyn's parents; they were no longer able to cope alone in their own home. Her mother was living with dementia and her father could no longer cope physically with his wife's demands.

Arwyn wanted her parents to move to live with Arwyn, Douglas and Arwyn's children. Douglas realised it was a huge commitment. Later he thought that Arwyn had completely misunderstood the level of commitment that would be required.

Douglas agreed, and within a short time Douglas had rearranged the house by splitting the living room in two parts with a structure cobbled from some timber and strawboard so that Arwyn's mother could have one half and her father have the other. Douglas converted the dining room into the sitting room and the kitchen, which was large, became a kitchen diner.

It would be wrong to say that Arwyn did nothing for her parents, once they had moved in, but anyone could see that it was Douglas who bore the burden. He behaved as if the elderly pair were his own parents. He took them to the doctor and the hospital, the social workers called Douglas if they needed to check up on Arwyn's Mother. So this continued for quite sometime.

During this time Arwyn continued to blow hot and cold in Douglas's direction. Indeed for several weeks Douglas made notes in his diary, as to Arwyn's attitude towards him, was she friend or enemy. Some days he found it all but unbearable. He slept alone, in his shed, and on occasion he would wake and find Arwyn lying beside him asleep in the bed. On occasion she would arrive before Douglas went to sleep. These occasions were when Arwyn felt in need of sex. Douglas was confused by all of this, and it was often not easy to cope with the demands Arwyn had. Douglas found it difficult to be in an unholy row with Arwyn only hours before, about really nothing, and then find her trying to cuddle up. The cuddle was nothing to do with 'I'm sorry'; it was purely for her own gratification. Once the sex had taken place she would leave, and go back to her own room, in the house, leaving Douglas feeling used, unloved and having absolutely no idea what was going on, or how to extract himself from the situation.

Douglas was truly stuck for he had burnt all his bridges to be with Arwyn, and he had committed all his funds. If they were to agree and sell the house there would not be enough money to do anything such as buy another house. For the cost of reparations to the building, making it liveable, had been huge, and it would take some time for that investment to seep into the possible sale price. Besides what now of Arwyn's parents and her sons and daughter, not to mention Arwyn. Douglas could not think of disenfranchising them. So he elected to sit it out, ever in hope that Arwyn would get to grips with her emotions, and understand just what Douglas had done for her, and was still doing for her, and that he was really worth looking out for and loving.

In the meantime Arwyn's career was speeding a head, deputy head teacher now, and then promotion to acting head teacher. For a term. She met Barbara in a Costa Coffee in the High Street one morning.

Barbara asked her straight out. "How was it all going?'

Arwyn told her that she was sick of her Father taking over the house.

"Somehow he seems to think he has his empire of grocery shops once more, he seems to think I work for him." Arwyn growled. "As for my mum she drowns in a sea of dirty tissues, and every time they are cleared away, within a couple of hours there were yet more to be cleared away. She has to have a commode because she cannot get to the toilet on her own steam, it is only by the front door, but it is too far. So that has to be emptied, and I hate it, I leave it to Douglas whenever I can! My Dad is my Dad, so I cannot not love him, but he is always dirty. Mum spends most of her time sleeping, and when she is awake she eats and goes to the toilet. As for Darren had made his girl friend pregnant and the 'stupid girl' wants to keep the baby. Barbara I know that girl, she will soon be making monetary demands on Darren, and he will not have the money to deal with that. So I will have to get Douglas to fund it. The problem with that is I am fed up with being with him, although it would be absolutely impossible to cope with Mum and Dad without him."

She paused then she mused. "I thought Douglas was what I wanted. He has been so good to me. He continues to be good, even though I treat him like dirt most of the time."

Barbara questioned her. "Wow that was a tirade. Oh and by the way, I am fine, thanks for asking. What is it that you want Arwyn?"

Arwyn replied. "I don't know, but not this."

Arwyn's depression mixed with her unkindness battered Douglas like typhoon and then she tripped out these words.

"Can we sell this house and move to another which has some separate space for my parents? Their own room, or an annex. My father is willing to put in some of his money to make it happen."

Douglas paused, he thought then he spoke. "I am not sure." He told her that he felt that she did not want him, and that she was using him as a care assistant for her parents. He pointed out that it was his money that had sorted out her life, and his money which was in the house.

He said. "What of the debt that was unpaid from Gavin? That money would have to be paid up just to make a move possible."

After some considerable time a suitable house was found and a suitable buyer was found. There were all the usual problems, of course, but through the solicitor, and with the agreement of Arwyn and her Father the house was purchased in equal shares between Arwyn and Douglas alone. No explicit agreement was made with respect of Arwyn's parents but Douglas would never have seen them in a difficult situation, for Douglas was not the sort of man, who could harm anyone.

The house was a bit out of Cheltenham. The other side of the racecourse. It was set alone in it's own acre plot. Surrounded by trees and a track drive down to the country road, which lead out to the main road.

It was quiet, idyllic and with a purpose built 'granny-annex' perfect for Arwyn's ancients. More of that later.

Douglas's financial situation was now over stretched. He still had to fund his children; Arwyn had soaked up his remaining capital, which was now all in the new property. So Douglas was, more or less, hand to mouth now. He needed gigs for the royalties on old recordings were in short supply and at this time there were no record companies willing to take a chance on a new album from this 'Douglas Has Been'.

CHAPTER 10
A Day at the Races

You placed a two hundred pound bet on Lord Windermere! Where did you get two hundred pounds from?" Asked Tracy.

"I 'borrowed it' from Douglas." Chuckled Darren.

"You borrowed it?" Questioned Justin. "Did you ask him?"

"It will be fine, Lord Windermere will win, we are going to make a fortune, I will put the money back before Douglas even knows it is missing."

Justin's voice had a rising inflection. "Darren, Lord Windermere is twenty to one, he is the outsider. Why Lord Windermere?"

Tracy put her finger to her lips. "Shush Dad's coming back."

Gavin, their father, always took them to the Cheltenham Races on Gold Cup Day.

"I know it is going to be my lucky day, it is Friday the fourteenth! I have just placed a bet on a great little Irish Horse." Snorted Gavin.

Darren asked. "'Lord Windermere'?"

Gavin said. "No, of course not, that old nag? No chance. No the winner of the Gold Cup 2014 will be, now mark my words my children, the winner will be 'On His Own'."

Tracy said. "Well it won't be much of a race then Dad! One thing is for sure; if he is on his own he will definitely win! How much did you bet?"

Gavin looked proud. "I put down, what boys from the smoke used to call, a monkey!"

Justin said. "Well Dad we are not 'from the smoke' so how much is that exactly?"

Darren said. "Five hundred my son, and when we win we are going to celebrate, we are going to celebrate big time."

Tracy made a statement. "Well if it were my money I'd have put it on 'Bobs Worth', the winner from last year, and the favourite today."

The huge crowd roared, binoculars at the ready, betting slips clutched in hands. Three thirty five and they were off. Up to the first jump, easier for the horses than a down hill jump with 'Knockara Beau' in the lead, followed by 'On His Own'. 'Last Instalment' moved into the lead, but then dropped back and then he fell. At the last jump 'Silviniaco' and 'Bobs Worth' were in command but 'Lord Windermere' beat 'On his Own' by a head.

Tracy looked at her Dad and exclaimed. "A monkey Dad? Five hundred quid! What would Mum say?"

Gavin said. "She need not know. Hold on there is a Stewart's enquiry."

Justin asked. "Why what has happened?"

Tracy made a short, sharp screech. "I think I just saw Lily Allen."

Gavin questioned. "Who? What one of your friends?"

Tracy answered. "No Dad the singer, she writes songs, she sings, I have a CD '*Alright, Still*'."

The wait of twenty or so minutes for the result of the Stewards Enquiry was torture for Gavin and for Darren. Darren had picked the winner so, he breathed a sigh of relief, for he had not been sure how he would replace the two hundred he had stolen from Douglas. Gavin grovelled.

"Now there is no need for your mum to know about all of this." Darren said.

"Why is that Dad, because you haven't given Mum any money towards your children's keep for a while? You know she always tells us if you have not paid up."

They had a take-a-way kebab, which Darren paid for.

When they got home Arwyn asked them if they had seen the horse that had crashed into the rail, right into a cameraman. Arwyn said. "The horse and rider were badly hurt."

CHAPTER 11
The days roll on

They say that opposites attract, and it is perfectly true. In the case of Douglas and Arwyn. Douglas was ever the optimist whilst Arwyn could always point out the downside of whatever it was. Douglas would have some terrible news and be taken a back for a little but would then say.

"How do we deal with this?"

Arwyn would curl up in a ball inside herself at any moment of stress and would be irritable and sullen, and then would fall into a depression.

These deep bouts of depression and unhappiness would come in great waves over Arwyn, then Douglas would do whatever he could to relive the situation, sometimes he could, other times he could not. Sometimes Arwyn would sulk and be quiet sometimes she would wind Douglas up and up until there was a row. For then she could employ a technique she learned on an 'in service training day' at school, 'pick on something and keep bringing your 'opponent' back to it with a question that is nothing to do with whatever the argument is about'. For example there is a, stupid, argument about washing up.

He says to her. 'It was my turn yesterday.'

She says to him. "Why do you get so worked up?"

So the argument shifts from the washing up to him getting worked up. No matter how hard he tries he never returns to the washing up. At the training day Arwyn had learned to use this technique to defuse awkward situations but with Douglas she learned, very quickly, that she could wind him up, and up, and she knew that he would never be violent, that was not him. It became her way of defusing the hurt, and harm, and hate which she felt deep, so deep, within.

Once, long ago, she had overheard, her mother in conversation with one of her mother's friends. In this conversation her mother told the friend.

"My daughters you ask? Well it is Susan who is the one with brains; as for Arwyn well she won't amount to much. It is ok with that red hair of hers, and that pretty face, she'll find a man to pay her bills. Ah but Susan yes she is the intelligent one, not Arwyn. You know surely that Gwyn, 'blessed', 'holy' Gywn will be a millionaire one of these days, dear, dear Gwyn."

Of course Dorothy had not intended that either Arwyn, or Susan, or Gwyn would hear that conversation, she knew that such talk would be hurtful to anyone. In this case it was devastating. It dislodged Arwyn's foundation stone. For the life of her there was no way she could shift it back into position. She carried that criticism with her for every moment of her life thereafter, and it festered within her, and her life became an endless ribbon of trying to prove to herself, and to her mother, that her mother's statement was wrong.

One could easily say that Arwyn's mother shaped and pruned Arwyn's self-image on a regular basis. In away she was not to blame. For she was, in her mind, trying to do her best. Arwyn's mother believed in 'reality', and 'facing up to things'. She was never one to hold back on her view of the world, and all that was in it, even though her experience of the world was limited, and from one perspective, hers.

Douglas had never been criticised by his parents, whenever there were 'battles' with other pupils at his school, when he was a boy, both his mother and father had supported him and helped him to understand that often those who criticise are those who have been criticised. So Douglas grow into an adult who could see that often people are damaged, and this is where things got difficult for him, he felt he should do what he could, when he could, to help people repair the damage. He did that by being open, giving, and by being sympatric, and if possible empathetic.

With Arwyn there were times when she could frustrate the socks off Douglas. One day, quiet a while back, in the time line of the story, she started going on a about money and happiness. Douglas listened to her rant for quite a while and then he butted into her rage.

"In these past months I have paid up your debts, repaired and made your house liveable, bought you presents, paid your sons parking fines. We have been on holiday and you have had not one, but two new cars. That was a lot of money, did that make you feel any happier?"

Arwyn said. "No."

Douglas said. "So it is not money that makes you happy then!"

Ever the optimist Douglas woke every morning wondering what good the day would bring and what good he could bring to the day.

In the mist of one row with Arwyn he asked. "Do you know what? I have never woken up in the morning thinking who can I upset today!"

What Douglas had not yet learned was that Arwyn had developed this technique because she realised, long ago, that it was a way to manipulate others to obtain what she wanted. She had done it to Gavin many, many times, and Douglas was just as stupid, and he had some money.

It was really what Arwyn asked for Arwyn got and Douglas paid. Sometimes Arwyn rewarded him with a smile, sometimes she would be concerned, and on the odd occasion she would provide a gift. Sometimes she wanted sex and sometimes she wanted love. Douglas went around in ever decreasing circles trying his hardest to provide all that she wanted and required.

There were days when things were nothing but nice between them. Arwyn had no bad words and no excessive demands.

One sunny day she said. "Lets go to the seaside, like we used to do."

It was a warm summers day so they threw some towels, some swim suits, and some sun cream, into a bag, got in the car and off they went. Weston-Super-Mare was only an hour or so, but then the sea is never much further than fifty miles from you anywhere in England. They took a turn round the Grand Pier; it had not long reopened after the fire all but destroyed it in 2008. They went down on the sands soaked up the sun, and splashed in the Bristol Channel, and then had a fish and chip supper from 'The Water Front'. It was the kind of heavenly day that Douglas would have been happy having every day. Arwyn wished it too. Douglas pretended to be Marlon Brando, well '*On The Water Front*' was the film, and Douglas, with a cheeky glint in is eye, reminded Arwyn of '*The Last Tango in Paris*' She looked at him across the table of the Fish and Chip Shop.

She laughed, then spoke to him. "I may not always say things that make you feel good Douglas, I do know that I can be an absolute cow sometimes. Actually sometimes I have thought 'why does he not murder me?' I am grateful for what you have done to get the new house and for the things you have done for Dorothy and Robert, the truth is that without you it would not be possible."

Douglas was shocked by this outburst. It was not on his list of expectations for that day, so of course he pushed a little too hard for more compliments.

"So do love me then?" He found himself in an awkward silence.

The Russians had the winter Olympic Games in Sochi, in the early part of the year. At the end of the summer many Scottish people felt betrayed as Scotland failed to break free of England, the Independence Referendum so close a result. Douglas noticed another headline. One might think, that it was appropriate; apparently it was the 'International Year of the Family'. Douglas arranged and executed the move to the new house.

He asked himself. "So are we a family now?" but no one replied.

The new house was not a new house it was over one hundred years old. Originally it was built for the son of a farmer, as a wedding present from his father. What a fine house it was too. Standing alone and proud at the end of a leafy drive. Quiet and tranquil, a spot away from the crowd. Disturbed only by butterflies and the odd mooing of a cow amongst the buttercups.

Then came the day to move to the new house. Lock, stock and Arwyn's ancient parent's, the collie, and Arwyn's two sons, and her daughter. A removal company sent their truck, and a gang of husky men, and the furniture was loaded transported and decanted into the new property in, an impressive, short space of time.

What was in this for Douglas? Well he hoped that it was a reaffirmation that Arwyn and he had a relationship that was one to one, intimate, exclusive and happy. He felt that with this, things would have to be better, and that surely Arwyn would have to love him properly. After everything else he had also become nursemaid to her Neolithic parents. It was he who took them to appointments and the doctors or hospital. It was Douglas who pushed Arwyn's father, in his wheel chair, up the slope to the bank. It was Douglas who cleaned and tidied and made sure things were comfortable and secure.

So let us ask the question again 'What did Douglas get out of all this?' The answer? Not that much.

The configuration of the new house gave rooms, nooks and crannies for all to have their own decent sized space. The old folks in the 'granny annex', which was perfectly perfect, with a lot of space, hand rails, a wet room, easy to navigate and light and airy. Up the stair, the main house, was a room each for Darren, Justin and Tracy. There two other rooms for Douglas's children, ready if they wanted to come to stay. There was another, spare room, for guests. Douglas and Arwyn had the 'bridle suite' with their own, en suite bathroom; it was complete with Bidet and Jacuzzi. Douglas had a study on the ground floor. There was a large, bright and airy sitting room, with patio doors to the barbeque area, and the garden beyond.

The whole place had the air that all the works had been done professionally. Douglas marvelled.

*

"This is where I, Craig, came into the story. You had not forgotten that I was the one telling you this story. You have been eves dropping whilst Davy and Norman sat in the Rose and Crown, You do remember. That's Ok then. I promise I did not make the next little bit up!"

*

"Look at the grouting on this wall in the downstairs lavatory, absolutely wonderful, a truly professional job. The person who did this must have done a great apprenticeship, the rigorous kind, like my grandfather did, the kind people do all over Europe, the kind every work person here should do." Douglas said.

Arwyn replied. "Why to you say Lavatory?" She mimicked a 'posh' voice. "It's a toilet!"

In this Douglas was reminded that there was a chasm between them. He did not want to see it, but he could see, that education, and aspiration, were important elements in any relationship.

Arwyn, and her parents, and Darren, and Justin and Tracy stayed in an hotel for about a week whilst Douglas organised and arranged furniture to make the new dwelling habitable.

Arwyn came over to help on the first evening after the move. There were boxes, and bags, chairs and tables, clothes and kitchen equipment piled on just about every space. Arwyn panicked when she saw. She burst into tears and accepted Douglas's comfort. He told her not to worry it would all be fine. Douglas moved some boxes and arranged a mattress on the floor and he and she laid down on it. They made love that night as tenderly as they had done thirty-nine years before; in that caravan on the first time they had sex. Douglas screamed for joy inside his head for he thought he had made it. This is what he wanted, her love, her affection, and she felt secure as she had done all those years ago, when she would sit on Douglas's lap in the arm chair in his bedroom telling him all about her school days, changing her voice to mimic her old school teachers that she was telling him about.

 Douglas soon brought order to the house he pieced together new beds, wardrobes and cupboards. He did not notice anyone helping him, because no one was, it did not matter he was a skilful handyman and often found it easier to get along with jobs on his own. In the annex he made the space for Arwyn's mother, Dorothy, and another for her father Robert. Douglas installed the Robert's television, a vital necessity for him. He installed another television for Dorothy, but it was not much used as she spent most of the day and the night sleeping. Dementia was claiming her more, and more, each day, and there was no return on that journey. Arwyn's father was increasingly less able to cope with his wife's loss of short-term memory, and his frustration was often apparent. One great thing about the move was that there was a bathroom, right by Dorothy's bed, and she could actually do the journey, more often than not, on her own.

Douglas and Arwyn slept together every night for nine months. Douglas had purchased a brand new bed with the most comfortable of mattresses.

During this time their relationship was good, and even a stranger could see that there was love between them. They sent each other text messages, and of all the times they had been together, Douglas considered this time to be the happiest.

A short musical interlude

Robert called Douglas over to the annex, one morning when Douglas made them both a cup of coffee.

Robert said. "You know me Douglas, I am not one to make great song and dance about anything."

Douglas retorted, jokingly. "Except tennis and your time on the ocean wave!"

They both chucked.

"Well I just wanted to tell you how grateful Dorothy and I are for all that you have done to set us up in the wonderful new place. Honestly I never dreamed we could stay in such a mansion. Just as a small thank you I have bought a gift for you. Arwyn told me it is something you will enjoy."

Douglas removed the wrapping paper and let out a whoop.

"Jolly, yes, wow that is something. Thank you very much The Complete Miles Davis at Montreux. You know that I played there in 1985, Miles was there. I met him, only for a moment or two, sharp dresser not a man to suffer fools. I think he was only sixty-five when he died. What lips that man had."

Robert said. "What do you think Chet Baker or Miles Davis who was the greater trumpet player?"

Douglas said. "How could you ask such a question? I will tell you a story of a friend, David Bedford, great musician; He did arrangements for Elvis Costello. Have you ever heard 'Shipbuilding'? Chet Baker is on that."

Robert said that he had and then asked. "What did Miles play when you saw him?"

Douglas replied. "Oh I don't know how many tunes he played. I can tell you one that I remember that you would surely have heard. *'Time after Time'*".

Robert started to sing the Cyndi Lauper song, then he said. "You know all that Jazz stuff is actually rubbish. You need to listen to some good music. Rodgers & Hammerstein, now that is real music, *Oklahoma where the wind comes sweeping down the plane and the waving wheat can sure smell sweet when the wind comes right be hind the rain.*" Robert laughed.

"Yes, I am sure you are right! Joked Douglas. "Thanks for this."

Douglas went off about his business. He had to go off to a gig. Douglas still performing with his band, he knew nothing else. Jazz festivals had become the bread and butter and there were still royalties from old recordings and the odd club to keep the wolf from the door. He had no reserves in the bank now, he had to earn.

CHAPTER 12
Back to the other things in life

Darren's girlfriend had their baby and Arwyn delighted at becoming a grandmother. Many were the days she was babysitter. Arwyn was still teaching.

They had meals in restaurants; there were family gatherings, visits to the cinema and theatre. Friends came and went.

Arwyn got together with a Barbara to discuss the decoration for the living room. Barbara all but drooled.

"I have found this guy who is a decorator, by god, he is fit! So what wallpaper is it going to be? This or this. I am going to sit on that chair, outside on the patio, and watch him strip your walls Arwyn!"

The young decorator was everything as buff as Barbara predicted. Arwyn looked at his biceps and had a hot flush. Both women sipped on their white wine and ogled. It was a hot summer.

Douglas got to work in the garden and started to make it look nice. Sometimes Arwyn and he ate together, sometimes alone, sometimes Arwyn would cook sometimes Douglas would cook. Sometimes the sun would shine but Douglas thought there is not much rain these days, thank heavens.

July 10 came, it was a very special day, and it was Arwyn's birthday. How he had got tickets, Douglas was not prepared to say, but someone who he had played for, late last year, had had a hand in it. So there they were at Wimbledon, the one hundred and thirtieth tournament. Andy Murray, of Scotland, was to play Milos Raonic, of Canada, in the men's singles final. Arwyn and Douglas could easily see the Duke and Duchess of Cambridge, from where they sat. They saw David Cameron, and Alex Salmond. Cliff Richard was wearing a Tartan Suit, which Arwyn thought was well over the top. They saw Andy Murray go apoplectic, they thought at his coach, Ivan Lendl. In the end it was six, four, seven, three, seven, two. So Murray won three sets to love. Douglas had given Arwyn an experience of her life. She had wanted to do this since her father, Robert, had told her of his visit in 1969, when he had watched Arthur Ashe beat Pancho Gonzales in the forth round. Robert was full of it too, and very jealous that no ticket had been produced for him to go with Arwyn and Douglas. He made it quite clear that he was not happy to be left at home to watch it on the television.

Arwyn made love to Douglas that evening and slept close to him.

About three months later, at first, Douglas did not notice the return of the 'Push-Me-Pull-You', Douglas was in such euphoria he had not noticed Arwyn's little mumbles and grumbles. The tetchy way she was dealing with her father and the lack of patience she had with her ever-dependent mother.

Then she started with niggles about her youngest son. Then, in the middle of one Saturday-night—Sunday-morning there was a banging on the front door Arwyn and Douglas awoke and found a policeman and Tracy at the front door. The policeman explained that Tracy had been at a party, which the police had raided, drugs had been found, and the policeman believed that Tracy had been smoking Cannabis. She had none on her when she was searched so the policeman was giving her one chance; he spoke in a 'Cop-pery' way.

"Be sure you understand, I will make a note of this and my colleagues will be made aware, if, Tracy, you are found in such circumstances, ever, in the future, action will be taken. Drug offences are serious matters. You do not need to be messing with any drugs, nor, in my opinion, should you be messing with the kinds of people who were at that party. A nice young woman like you, living in a beautiful house like this. Mind you hear me now."

"You Copper's…' Tracy was about to say more but Arwyn squeezed her arm by way of telling her to keep quiet.

The policeman put on his hat and vanished into the darkness of the garden.

It was all quite a shock for Arwyn.

May be it was that that accelerated the growing of the rot again. The rot in the relationship between she and Douglas. May be Arwyn had thought that all those things were behind her, only to be confronted by such things again. It churned up her emotions and she began to have feelings that life had not been perfect, it was not perfect, and she wanted it to be perfect. She started to question things again. What was she doing with this life of hers, living in a house with her parents, and a man who was Ok, but actually, she asked herself.

"Is Douglas really that good? Was she in charge of her own life?" She asked herself? She replied "No."

She started to reach into her memories looking for her desires, and passions, and she came unto a locked door. She hunted for the key and found it under a flowerpot, and she opened it and pulled the door open, and she found, in the darkness, what she had been looking for, her sexual desire. It came upon her like a daemon. She craved for something more than she had with Douglas. The voice inside her head kept saying.

"Yes Douglas is Ok, he is a good man, he loves me, and I like him enough, but I want something that is raw, and that excites, and sets me on fire. I want a man to take me and make me cum, from the inside, until I scream for him to stop." She was running on to sixty years of age now. Time had taken it's toll on her body, lines had come to her face, weight had grown around her hips and tummy, but in her mind she was still the beautiful young thing that Douglas had fallen for forty years before.

So these few months of what Douglas had craved for was decaying at rapid speed. He was not really aware that it had, for he was still locked up in the euphoria of the new house and how well he thought things were going. He was still not interested in other women, just Arwyn, and he treated her like a Goddess, whilst she was craving to be treated like, she thought, some men might treat a Whore.

When Arwyn looked back at Gavin, even back to Colin the scaffold builder, all the men she had slept with, only Douglas treated her with total respect. All the others had, in one way or another, treated her with disdain. It suited her low self-image, which Douglas spent most of his time trying to improve, but improvements like that can only be achieved by the willing, and only under their own terms, from within. No one else can do it for them. Anyone can pretend to themselves, and to the world, that they have made improvements, but like the alcoholic it takes but one drink to stumble, and fall back, on the old, and comfortable, comfort zones of the past.

Arwyn was beginning to realise that this was about something more. Her Mother, now faded and unable to lay down the law. Arwyn had oft times been so self deprecating so laid back, but that was not really her she wanted to be in charge, like her mother, like her sister Susan. My god she thought to herself, 'I am nearly sixty years of age and I have only just realised that I lived in fear of my Mother all these years'. I should have been like my sister and fought back. When all these years I have tried to be like my brother, holding back, not rocking the boat. Just like my father always did. No more; I am in charge, this is the rest of my life.

CHAPTER 13
Kicked Out of Bed for Snoring

Douglas knew that he was not the world's greatest lover he tried hard, but the truth is that it was love, and not sex, which turned him on. Back in the previous house, when he realised that he was failing with Arwyn's sexual appetite, he went to a shop that sold women's sexy under-ware, Anne Summers. Although he did not think it was sexy. He, with embarrassment, seeping from every pore, asked the young woman shop assistant which vibrator would be the best? The young woman, with not hint of embarrassment spoke in clear tones.

"Well this is the one I like best."

Heavens he thought, she uses one. So he bought it along with some special gel, which was supposed to intensify orgasms.

Arwyn quite enjoyed these things. Douglas thought he had managed to improve things, but like wall paper over cracks in the plaster the ill was uncured.

Justin and Tracy

"What do you actually think about Mum and Douglas?" Asked Tracy of Justin.

"Not much really. Douglas is Ok, he is good to us, but he is not like Dad. You would think he'd do drugs and drink, that is what Jazz people do, but he doesn't" Said Justin.

"Well you are right about that. Douglas is, well, sophisticated. You could never say that about Dad." Said Tracy. "The problem is that Mum is not happy."

"How do you work that out? She seems Ok to me." stated Justin.

"That's the trouble with men." Admonished Tracy you miss all the important signs. Men the emotionally illiterate."

CHAPTER 14
Black Out of the Blue

Now the most awful time of Douglas's life was about to begin, he did not know it. He thought that his investment of love, time, care for Arwyn and her family, all the work he had done to move the whole caboodle to a new residence and the very many piles of money he had invested had got him the love of the woman he loved. Please understand that he was not trying to 'buy' love and affection, not a bit of it. He thought that Arwyn was his girl and he thought that he should do his best for his girl. Blow, you may take that the wrong way too. He did not think of Arwyn as 'his property' but he did think that they were exclusive to one another and that they were now set up to enjoy the rest of their lives together. Douglas loved Arwyn and he had worked so hard to leave his previous marriage, without too much harm to his children, he had given up more than Arwyn could know. Of course before that he had coped as a single parent. So having been let down by two women he, for a few happy months, had been living under the illusion that all was well in the state of his little world, and his ship was cruising in the sunny climes of the Caribbean. He would have believed no one if they had told him that his internal vision was totally false.

Arwyn may have started out with the idea that she wanted to murder Douglas, or at least to destroy Douglas's mental health, but probably not, people do things because they want to get things for themselves, if destroying people is what it takes, then they destroy people. Anyway the effect upon Douglas was about the same as an earthquake of huge magnitude.

His first marriage had been smashed by the infidelity of his wife and Douglas had been left as a single parent, with no support. He gave his second wife the children she wanted, and a life extraordinary, and was then brushed aside.

Now Arwyn, the woman he had done the most for, who was living in the most disgusting state when he had showed up, was about to crucify him, leave him for the vultures, and totally disembowel him. Oh Arwyn did not do this alone, she could not have done, for in common with Douglas's two previous wives Arwyn did not possess the ingenuity, the knowledge, or the heartlessness that were required. Oh sure Arwyn knew exactly what she was doing all the time. What she was about to do was deeper and darker than anything she could have dreamed up on her own.

Douglas was putting up with the Push-Me-Pull-You. There were tell, tell, signs that things were not as they should have been. Arwyn's friends would show up and Arwyn had not mentioned they were coming, she excluded Douglas, well why should she tell him? Maybe because that is what people do. She would go out in the evening and would not want to say where she was going. She stopped asking Douglas how he was and paid little attention to him. Then one night whilst Douglas was deep in sleep he was awoken by a sintering pain in his chest. He realised that Arwyn had just smashed him in his chest with her fist. She was screaming at him, she was shouting at him to get out of the bed and sleep elsewhere. She shouted she could no longer stand him lying next to her snoring like an over grown pig. Douglas got up and left the room. It was the last time that he slept with Arwyn.

A cold, cold war began. Douglas retreated to his study, coming out only to honour his commitment to Arwyn's parents, and to take care of things he needed to around the house. Arwyn did not bother to knock on Douglas's door, unless there was something she wanted. One evening she opened his door without knocking, without any sign of a smile she barked.

"I need the cupboard to be mended."

Douglas said to her. "I find things so difficult, you never smile, and you never asked how I am. Those things were the oil that keep things smooth between people."

So the Push-Me-Pull-You continued.

Sometimes Arwyn would have a cup of tea with Douglas and he would be all-hopeful that things were getting better.

Then, one cold grey day, before the spring, he inquired of her. "Have you found someone else?"

She gave a half laugh and denied. "Of course not."

Douglas was relived by this lie, and he did not want to see through it, so he did not. Life remained in this unhealthy state. It got no better for a couple of months. It was then he noticed that Arwyn was loosing weight; he asked her if she was ill. This made her angry; she told him she was trying to lose weight. Then she bought some new clothes, she started going out more and then one night she did not come home. Douglas returned to the question he had asked her before.

"Have you found someone new?" Again she replied that she had not.

He asked her what she did when she went out she said she had been with Barbara who had joined a walking club, and they did a lot of social events. She told him that she was off to a Thai Night. One of the others in the group was from Thailand and they were meeting at the woman's house. Douglas asked if he could come. Arwyn said it was members only but she declined to let Douglas know how to join.

He asked her about the group was it all women? What other things did they do, what kinds of people belonged to the group? She replied that there were many people, then she added a caveat, which Douglas found strange. He should have really taken on board fully what Arwyn said, but he failed to grasp the importance.

Arwyn spoke in a strange way. "There are quite a few policemen, high up policemen, so you had better watch out."

As this story further unfolds you will begin to understand that this was actually a threat. That this threat was already in the process of being carried out, but Douglas was churned up in side and was desperately trying to get a grip and an understanding. He felt that things were not good and for the first time he came upon the idea that whatever he did now would not return things to how he had wanted them to be. His optimism, however, kept him blind to what was really going on, he even believed Arwyn about the Thai Night, and the Walking Club. He just could not believe that Arwyn would harm him after all that he had done to be with her, and all he had done for her and her family. After all only a little while ago they had signed up for this house together, for most people buying a house is the biggest thing they get to do, and is a serious business. So surely she must have been serious about him too?

*

A few years after all of this Douglas's best friend interrogated him.

"Can you not see the signs? Your trouble is that you think people are nice, some of them are not. Do you just fail to read the messages people send to you?"

*

Douglas did pick up on this next signal, for it was so loud and so clear it was as if his shirt had been ripped from his back and Ice Cold Winter himself had laid his hand full square on the middle of the naked flesh of his stripped, white and pasty, torso.

For all the preceding weeks, although Douglas had suspicions, he could still feel the glimmer of love, or at least affection from Arwyn, just enough to keep their relationship alive. Like raking through last night's barbeque, the white dust, a couple of black charcoals and there an ember, still warm, and glowing red as it catches the exhale of your breath.

It was a bright spring morning and Arwyn was in a new frock, heading out to walk with the collie. It was warm but as she passed by Douglas he felt that winter, and it stopped him in his tracks, and before he had realised Arwyn was way down the path and she was gone, Douglas was not sure which way she had gone. What could he do? He knew instantly that she was gone, not just on the walk with the dog, but completely gone from him. She had not said a word but he knew it was all over. Those scenes that can be seen on television shows about the environment where the cameras, on a bright sunshine day, capture a huge iceberg breaking free from an ice shelf in an avalanche of snow. All he could do was to wait for her return. His brain was on fire and his body was freezing. Why had she left him? Who had she left him for? Never before had he felt 'unstable' but it was in these moments he began to be aware of how mental illness could strike just as a flu can strike and he realised that both are as deadly.

He climbed the stairs to the bedroom that they had shared, the unmade bed that he had bought for her. The room was in a huge mess, clothes here there and everywhere. Papers, discarded envelopes and magazines. Then he saw a mouse emerge from the clutter and scamper away. He had not been in this place for several months, since he had been banished for snoring, and so he had not been able to tidy and keep things clean. Wondering if there were more rodents he pushed a pile of debris with his toe and his eye caught sight of a paper. He recognised it, it was a ticket to a Dinner Dance, which Arwyn had said she and Douglas would go to. Douglas could clearly see, stamped by an old fashioned rubber stamp the word redeemed. Attached to the paper a photograph of Arwyn sitting close to a smiling man, who had his arm about her and a look across his face, it is a cliché but, like the cat who had fallen into the vat of cream.

Douglas bent down to pick up the paper and the photograph. Time stood still, his mouth went completely dry, he could smell is own halitosis pervading the room, it was ever like this if his mouth became this dry. Beads of sweat streamed to his forehead, his breath was in short pants, and for moments he was paralysed.

Douglas's world was imploding, slow motion visions of avalanches of ice bergs smashing into the arctic ocean and Samuel Taylor Coleridge's *Ancient Mariner* came into Douglas's head *'ice mast high came floating by as green as emerald'*. Had Douglas shot the Albatross, no that was Arwyn, but green is the colour for jealousy, and a spark hit from the coal in that barbeque, and a cold north wind ripped through the pleasant spring day. Every pain Douglas had dealt with until that moment in his life came together and stung him again, and again, with an intense ferocity which wiped any notion of any type of pain he had previously felt, in all the fifty and more years he had struggled for his existence.

The paper dropped to the floor and lay amongst the mess of the bedroom, which Arwyn had made her home. Douglas moved his feet and stumbled down the stairs and out into the sun and it's warmth. He sat on the garden bench with his hands on the table. He had never felt so sick, he had never felt so foolish, he had never felt so duped and he had never felt so alone.

Douglas came from a strong family, they were of good self-image, and they were a family who did whatever good they could. They were Methodists; he was a Boy from the Brigade, 'Sure and Steadfast'. His people were optimists, who saw a blocked road and took it as an opportunity to take another route, and enjoy some different scenery. So Douglas soaked in the sunshine, and the optimist inside him started, madly, redrawing the map, what must he do to get her back? Was the question pounding with his heart and through his arteries.

Many might have asked what kind of fool was this Douglas? Why on earth would he not just accept that it was over and get over it. Douglas would have replied.

"So you have never really been in love then?"

Of course there was more, as the story has previously stated Douglas gave up all for Arwyn and he had given her everything he had. All his money was now in the house and her ancient and modern relatives were dependent upon this accommodation and the circumstances, which had been created. Apart from that Douglas had survived two terrible previous relationships and he wondered if it was all down to him, was he all to blame? As he sat there chastising himself. He thought 'it is sex, I am just no good at it.' Arwyn's dog appeared begging for some attention. Then Arwyn appeared. Some bits of sunlight escaped through the gaps in the leaves of the trees and caught in her red hair. Douglas realise that she had slimmed down, he saw the beautiful dress she was wearing, and the make up and he knew that she had not been 'improving' herself for his benefit. For Douglas had not asked her to change he accepted her as she was, a bit over weight and older than she had been. He remembered her at seventeen and that was enough. The lies were now becoming apparent to him, though he had seen a tube of teeth whitening toothpaste in the junk her the bedroom floor, and some stuff to colour her hair, he had not realised she had been hiding the grey ever since they had got back together, naivety had told him that her hair was, amazingly, still the same colour as it had been forty years before. Douglas realised that it was all lies. It had not been good with Yvette but he had had a good business with his music, and his children were near. Now what was he to do? Arwyn was there in front of him gleaming, and beautiful, and his heart would not let his brain let go.

He looked up and asserted. "I don't want you to go off with someone else."

She looked at him and said. "What are you on about? I am not going off anywhere."

Douglas retorted. "I felt it, when you passed me earlier, I know, you have someone else, I can feel it about you."

She looked at him and her internal calculator began calculating, actually she needed to move quickly on this for she did realise that her current living accommodation, for her and her relatives, were on a fulcrum, and she knew that the whole edifice could crumble. She had been playing the game of 'having a bit on the side', this is how her best friend Barbara and she giggled about it, for a good few months now and she was well pleased with the way she had got away with it.

Hang on though this was now going to be difficult and that difficulty was something she really had not calculated, for she did not think she would have to. Pushing Douglas away and then pulling him back had worked for so long, she never thought he would work it out. It is amazing how much stuff a human brain can process in a nanosecond, all that and more. What had Douglas said? He felt it and then Arwyn realised that it was on this morning she had felt it too. Up until then it was 'just a bit of fun on the side' but after her, secret, telephone conversation with her lover that morning, yes she had fallen in love, yes that very morning.

She kept her phone on vibrate, and she had been snug and cosy, and still much asleep when he called her. As his rich voice poured into her ears and he said some sexy things to her, she felt her own hand between her legs and she imagined that his tongue was there and in a moment she was squeezing her own hand between her thighs and arching back her body in orgasm.

Even as all these things passed through her head she knew that keeping Douglas on side, at least for now, was a major priority. Ok he had rumbled her, but no need to own up just yet, keep this show on the road for the sake of keeping roof overhead, kids off the street and parents out of a nursing home.

So without batting an eyelid Arwyn simply denied that there was any one else and then she said.

"Why do you get so worked up? It has been you who have been strange all these weeks."

Douglas reminded her of the punch that night she had thrown him out for snoring and she said.

"What punch? What are you on about? Stop being so ridiculous there is no one else. Now I have things to do. Pull yourself together."

That evening Arwyn took an overnight bag and she was gone for four days. She did not tell Douglas she was going away. She just went.

Douglas tried phoning her but there was no reply. He went to the bedroom and dialled once more. He heard the vibrations of her phone and found it beneath her pillow. He looked at it, he scrolled through the contacts and the texts he found the picture of the man he had seen in the other photo, and the texts from the man to Arwyn were explicit and enraged Douglas. The man called Arwyn 'little miss get your knickers down', he spoke of 'fucking her against a wall like the whore she was', he called her 'a slut that was good for only one thing banging until she screamed'. Arwyn's responses were to encourage more. She had written 'I can't wait to suck your dick', 'I want you to ram it in me', 'remember the last night, drunk, naked and fucking on the stairs'.

Douglas should have left her by this time but the brain takes time to adjust to the new situation. He knew nothing of this side of Arwyn, he could not believe she wanted that kind of sex, he did not know how he could give her that kind of sex. He could never have called her the things that he had read.

Yes he was concerned that she had not come home, but he realised that it was a Bank Holiday weekend, and yes he thought maybe he should phone the police, but he just knew that she was with him, whoever he was, and that they were probably in some hotel, by the seaside, fucking.

Douglas tidied Arwyn's bedroom, he trapped the mouse and washed her clothes, he ironed them and put them neatly away, and did some jobs around the house. When Arwyn at last returned he said

"I hope you have had a nice time, your parents are good, although Dorothy nearly took a fall, fortunately I just happened to be there and caught her. and your boys are at parties tonight. Tracy has a new boyfriend, I am not sure what you will make of him, oh and she now has a tattoo, nothing too bad, just on her ankle."

Douglas wanted to recapture the time before all of these awful new events, but could not focus; in fact he was at the beginning of a nervous break down. Over the next days Douglas set to all the jobs that Arwyn had mentioned recently. Cupboards were repaired, a new toilet installed and the plaster on the wall, behind Arwyn's bed, was smoothed out and made flat and painted, Arwyn had made a mess of hanging a picture.

He wrote a letter to her telling her that although she said she had not, he believed that she had fallen in love with someone new. He said that he realised that it was her right to do so, but asked her not to leave him behind. He said that, although he would rather not, he would even settle for a share of her affection, sooner than lose it all. He said there are places in the world where women take on two husbands, and if that is what it would take to be with her he would. Of course he realised that this was fanciful, and as the words left his pen he realised the nonsense that was flowing. He just had not understood, before, how anyone could be come so desperate in such a short time. His life felt as if it had been kicked into lower earth orbit and that somehow the whole world was now being viewed, by his mind, through a different lens, and from a different perspective. He put the letter on the passenger seat of her car with a single red rose.

He stopped eating; eventually he had to go to the chemist to buy something to help him to sleep. His world in turmoil he grabbed at anything he could for stability.

Douglas fought huge battles in his mind with ideas of his own death, and the deaths of Arwyn and her lover. Murderous thoughts had never entered his had before. He had to control them.

In her attempt to 'keep the show on the road' Arwyn took to knocking on Douglas's study door to take tea with him. Douglas forgot that 'Push-Me-Pull-You' thing every time, thinking each time that everything would turn out right, if he was just kept cool and would ride out the storm. Arwyn stopped out night after night, and then one morning she returned with her car smashed, she had had an accident and she came directly to Douglas and asked him to hold her. The fool in Douglas's head said see she has come back to you."

On another evening, whilst Arwyn was out, Douglas collected the washing and to his shock came across a pair of Arwyn's knickers decorated with a slogan 'little miss get your knickers down'. He remembered the text message he, may be should not have read, 'little miss get your knickers down'. For any one observing this tragedy, as it has been unfolding would see that it was at this point Douglas's mental health detached from reality, and now found itself not in low earth orbit but in space in real orbit. He could not now see a future on earth. For he had given more to Arwyn than anyone, and he had given her space whenever she needed, he had kept at bay his own desires and needs. He knew that she had another man but that she had not the guts to tell him straight. She had not the guts and he could not understand why. Surely she knew that Douglas could not hurt her in any physical way, he was simply unable to do such a thing. Or may be she had detected the ominous battles he was having deep in his psyche, may she had felt the murderous thoughts he had had.

Douglas sat down at his computer and used it to construct a time line of the past weeks. He collected the information from the telephone bills and understood when Arwyn had taken up with this other man. He was shocked that it was not long after she had thrown Douglas out for snoring and he was amazed that he had not recognised it all sooner. Then he saw, with a sick making clarity, that he only noticed on the day that Arwyn switched her allegiance from him to the other man. So he had had his eye on the ball, and he had recognised the very moment that Arwyn had stopped loving him. As the flood of text messages from Arwyn to her lover were listed on the itemised bill; of the phone he had given her, and which he had paid the bill of, from the time he had been in the shared house, before he made a home in the shed.

Douglas knew why he wanted Arwyn to come back to him. It was because when she did love him the world was the best place he could be in, and he felt as an eagle high on a thermal looking down on a glorious sun drenched landscape, great open plains and meadows, snow-capped mountains to the north, long sandy beaches to the west. Douglas knew why, and now his brain, mentally deranged at this point, had to work out how to get Arwyn to come back to him.

He made lists of other works he knew Arwyn wanted to be done. There were places in the world she wanted to go. He constructed a booklet of pictures of the good times they had had together. Pictures from the first part of their relationship and pictures from all the things they had done together in the more recent part. He printed one copy on his printer. His mind kept saying you have to get her back.

Arwyn came to him one morning and said that she was going to visit her Niece in Paris over the weekend; she was going to fly to Paris-Charles de Gaulle where her Niece had agreed to collect her. Arwyn had a challenge that she needed to get to the airport this end to catch the flight. She asked Douglas if he would drive her. Arwyn made a fuss of Douglas that morning. They went shopping together, Arwyn liked a vase, and Douglas bought it for her. They went back to the house and Arwyn went up to change, Douglas followed. He had in mind the text messages he had read; he wondered if Arwyn had wanted him to call her 'Sexy', it was not what he would have done normally. Douglas stood in the bedroom doorway. The bedroom in which they had shared the same bed, and as she wanted to step out on to the corridor, for the first time since she had thrown him out of bed.

Douglas reach out and touched Arwyn, he said. "You look so sexy."

Arwyn stopped and looked at him. In her eyes he saw a glint of the Arwyn that had loved him, he saw the faint beam of the woman who had lured him away from his previous life. He touched her on the hip. She then said. "You know that what you have just done amounts to sexual harassment."

Douglas said. "What? What do you mean?"

She said. "I did not give you consent to touch me."

Douglas said. "I am sorry, but I thought that you were my *Partner* you never complained of my touches before, we made love in this bed, not so long ago. You told me that there is no one else when I asked you."

Arwyn was shrouded in a cold atmosphere she said. "Well I am letting you know now, you need to ask before you touch."

At first Douglas thought she has just told me is 'she has someone else', but then he thought no she told me I had to ask before I touch her.

Douglas knew that this was not the Arwyn he had known, but a Arwyn who had been tutored.

It was raining when they arrived at the dropping off point, at the airport. Douglas said.

"I love you Arwyn, please do not leave me. If you have found someone who lifts you up and provides things, which I cannot, please let us all get together and be friends and find a way to make it work for all of us. There is no need for any of us to suffer."

The airport traffic warden tapped on the window, and then tapped his watch.

Arwyn looked at Douglas and said. "How would that work for anyone?"

That was as close as Arwyn came to telling Douglas that she had fallen for another man. She got out of the car, slammed the door and splashed away into the terminal. She looked back over her shoulder at him as she went to the terminal door. Her glance was as the Snow Queen and Douglas froze as Kai had done in Hans Christian Anderson.

Whilst Arwyn was close Douglas's fragile mental health was spinning all over the place. Now she was gone he plunged into a swirling whirlpool of haunting agony. He could not understand just how this woman, his Arwyn, to whom he had given all, with only hope that he would receive in return, could have left him for another man. No matter how he tried he just could not make it compute. Nothing in his life thus far could give him a key on which to grip. He could not understand, he could not cope.

*

Serena Williams won the Wimbledon Tennis for the sixth time 6—4, 6—4, against Garbiñe Muguruza. This pleased Arwyn. She wondered why she had not pursued tennis as a career; of course her mother would never have allowed it. It was midsummer.

CHAPTER 15
All Cops are not Good Cops

Raymond had been in the Police Force for nearly thirty years, he would soon retire. He was younger than Arwyn. His career had not been exceptional but, from 'Bobby on the Beat' until Detective Sergeant, was good enough for him. It came at cost of course, failed marriage, and various other relationships, which had never really worked. He had one daughter whom he had not seen since, well when was it? Raymond would have been hard pressed to tell you, it was such a time. He still had a long way to go on his mortgage payments, so he was far from debt free, he liked to drink and to have a bit of fun. He would back a horse or two; well it was a horse race town that he lived in. Of course smoking was expensive. He had climbed the police career ladder, slowly, and by making arrests which, on occasion, he helped along by planting a little heroin, or threatening some poor soul with a much worse crime unless they confessed to a less significant one. Well it was all about targets, and Raymond found he could meet the quotas, if he just managed to cheat a little bit. Besides the people he chose to frame would have gone down for something if they had not gone down for what he had charged them with, so Raymond had no conscience about it. He had learned to lie quiet early in his life, for as long as he gave his father the answer his father wanted his father would keep drinking, fall asleep and forget whatever it was by the morning.

Raymond had no real idea why he became a policeman, he needed a job, he saw a recruiting poster and he applied and the police were desperate enough to employ him, so he had a job. The job made him neither happy nor sad. It was just a job. When he was finished working in the evening he just did not think about it until he arrived at the police station for work the next morning. Raymond had never been abroad, he voted for the Tories whenever there was a general election, although he often felt more right wing, and had thought, that sometime, in the future, he would vote for a party more to the right, if a candidate was available to be voted for. In his small back yard, various pots of flowers and plants were unattended but every morning he would raise the St. George's Flag and each evening he lowered it, he loved his Queen and his Country, where a few less foreigners would make things happier all round.

There was one thing in his life that he really liked, he owned a TR7 sports car, and it was getting more and more expensive to keep on the road these days. Spare parts less easy to find with each year that past. It was yellow, you would not miss that car anywhere near his home, or work, for it was the only one about those parts.

Raymond was not a great reader, but he would read the newspapers that supported the Tory party if he found an abandoned copy in the police station canteen. He could not cook, his house was not untidy, but it was not smart, and did not look cared for.

Most evenings he spent trawling dating web sites looking for women to have sex with. Somewhere in his head there was a flashing light above a sign, which said look out for women to share your life and brighten your later years, but that light was usually shielded from view. He was not that fussy about a woman's looks or her personality he would have sex with just about anyone who was willing.

That is how he came across Arwyn. He wanked off at her picture, he fancied her straight away. He did not know that Douglas had taken that photograph. Raymond was not always successful arranging dates from web sites but in this case Arwyn responded almost immediately.

They met in a bar in town, they had a drink and chatted for a while and the Arwyn got cold feet and started to back off. Raymond wrote down his mobile number and gave it to her. He told her to call him. A week later she did.

Douglas knew nothing of Arwyn's profile on that web-dating site. Douglas did not know that such sites existed at that time.

Arwyn thought that Raymond was good looking and she found him sexy. Raymond was over one hundred and eighty centimetres tall, he was quiet thin. His hair was a fairly light brown with flecks of grey, thinning on top. The shape of his face was oval rather than round. He had thick eyebrows and deep eye sockets which contained green eyes behind hardly any eyelashes. Most of his clothes were purchased at his local super market. Some of his shirts were garish, some would say a bit 'loud'. His ears were larger than his face really should have supported.

Arwyn's calls to Raymond became a regular event daily, and then twice daily, and then several times a day interspersed with many text messages.

Then a flood of text messages. It was not too long before they got together at his house, and she was not inside his house more than a couple of minutes before she let him fuck her on his living room floor.

There was no love in it, she looked at him, she dropped her clothes he unzipped his trousers pulled out his cock and pulled her on to it, a couple of minutes later they both had an orgasm. Arwyn came from the inside. Then they drank two bottles of wine and fucked again.

It made neither of them happy, it made neither of them sad but it cleared the sexual tension both of them had had. So when she could now she would turn up at his place and they would repeat the above paragraph.

As the sessions progressed they started to unfold their life stories to one another and at some point Raymond said that he wanted to see Arwyn's house and he wanted to have sex with her in her bed. She knew that Douglas had to work away over the weekend, she knew that she could sneak Raymond up to her room without her parents knowing, and her boys and Tracy would be out, so that is what happened. Arwyn got an extra thrill out of it for it was behind Douglas's back and there was a small chance they she would be caught out and discovered mid orgasm.

For Raymond it was just the nosey side of his nature. He wanted to see what Arwyn's place was like. He wondered if she would be a companion for his later years. She was good looking enough, and she banged like a 'good'n'. He was made up. By this time Arwyn had divulged that she owned half the property and the Douglas owned the other half. Raymond had taken that in because he did have a thought that maybe this was a way to clear his mortgage. He could get a good looking, sexy, woman, sell his place, get money to pay up the mortgage, and move in with Arwyn. The only problem he could see was Arwyn's parents. Raymond was not interested in them, not in the least. Anyway there were nursing homes, and if they were destitute the Social Services would have to find them somewhere, even if they had to split the couple up, and put them in two different homes, nothing wrong in that and he fucked Arwyn again.

*

Arwyn, away in Paris, and Douglas in a state such that he had never before experienced, after some deliberation with himself, he decided to take the bull by the horns. He got into his car and drove to the address he had noted from Arwyn's phone. He parked up and was trembling. He got out of the car and walked around the block three times. Then he went up to the door of Raymond's house and rang the bell. He waited a moment and then Raymond was standing in front of him.

Douglas said. "I am Douglas, I think you know that already, would you have a few moments to talk?"

Raymond stepped back, Douglas went in and Raymond told him to take a seat. Some might think this a dangerous and reckless act. Douglas was in freefall in his mind and this registered not as dangerous, but something beyond. It was like a movie he had seen where an astronaut flew to an asteroid to blow it up, and stopped it colliding with the earth. His life did not matter, he was going to die anyway. In Douglas's head he was already dead, there was no place in his brain that could tell him different.

Douglas said. "Arwyn has not told me about you, but I know that you and she have been seeing one another. Of course I cannot stop that but I was wondering just how much you know of the history I have with Arwyn. The commitments that she and I have together, and I would like to find out if you think your relationship with Arwyn is something that is serious, and do you want it to be a long term thing?"

The words came from Douglas as if he were interviewing a candidate for a job but Douglas was quaking inside. He wondered if this man, this Raymond, could be violent, he actually wondered if Raymond could kill him. He sat for a moment and waited for a response.

Raymond spoke with a chuckle in his voice. "You have pluck, I'll give you that. You know that I am a police officer, I could easily find something to arrest you for, whisk you off down the nick." He paused. "Yes I am serious about Arwyn, yes I am, and we're going to be together."

Douglas wanted to say something that might change Raymond's mind and something came to him, he said. "You do not know her like I do, she has great depressions, and she is very moody, and look she has cheated on me, down the line she will cheat on you, you know it."

Raymond replied. "I don't really care if she does, for now the sex is great and we are having a good time. What you need to do is to forget her, go find yourself someone new, there are loads of women out there."

Douglas grasped at the seat beneath him. The protector of Arwyn within him wanted to punch this policeman hard, but he managed to control that emotion and then he said.

"Have you been to my house? Have you seen Arwyn's parents?"

"Oh I have been to your house." Said Raymond. "But only into the bedroom, Arwyn told me that you once shared with her, and I fucked her, on the bed she told me that you bought for her."

Raymond was hoping to provoke Douglas enough to produce an assault, something in Douglas told him that that was what Raymond wanted him to do. Douglas pushed his hands under his thighs and tears came to his eyes.

Then Raymond said, "If you had had some proper security in and around that house of yours, you need some cameras, you never know who will come and rob you. I have a mate who could let you know all about that sort of thing. These days you can get cameras that are disguised, nobody takes any notice of them, put a few in the house living room, bedroom, they are so cheap, if you had had some up you would have a nice sexy video of me screwing the women you thought were yours."

Douglas's eyes were wet, his mouth was dry, he felt sweat in his armpits.

He said. "Look I realise that she wants you now, although she has not told me that you even exist, but she needs what I give her too, look I do not want to share her but I would share her if it means I do not totally lose her. We could sell your house, sell my house and buy a big house where we could all be together."

Raymond laughed a great cackling laugh.

"What are you on? You are pathetic, I tell you that I fucked your woman, in your house, on your bed, whilst her father and mother were in the annex next door, and you want us to buy a house together and be one great big happy family! If you had said those things to me you would need immediate medical assistance, and an ambulance right now, so you did not bleed to death. Get your sorry asshole out of my house and whimper away. Oh watch out sunshine, for if you do not stop harassing Arwyn, you will end up in prison, and believe me when I say I know all the right people to make that happen.'

Douglas was stunned and Raymond said. "Now fuck off you stupid, pathetic, little cunt."

Douglas started his car was quaking inside and shaking outside. He was blind with tears and he knew that he needed to protect Arwyn from this evil man.

His brain started searching for some ideas to stop this evil man, stop him forever.

*

Raymond collected Arwyn from the airport.

"Douglas came to see me."

Arwyn said. "What? How did he know? I did not tell him."

Raymond said. "He is probably stalking you, following you. He suggested we all live together, one big happy family, he is mad. It is ok though I have a plan. I'll get him arrested, you never know he might even go to prison."

Arwyn said. "No I don't want that to happen. What have you done?"

Raymond replied. "Nothing much, I just told him he should get some security cameras fitted. I gave him a card of a man who installs that kind of thing. I told him we had had sex on your bed."

Arwyn looked at Raymond in disbelief. "You what?" she said.

Raymond laughed. "He is a pathetic waste of space. He just sat there on his hands crying. Look we need to get rid of him there is no point in screwing around. Talking of screwing let's go to mine."

*

By the time Arwyn got back to her house it was getting dark, it had rained the whole day and Arwyn's Father called out to her, he was standing at the door of the annex, as he heard her. Douglas's car was on the drive but the lights in his study were off, at least there was no light from the crack at the bottom of the door. Arwyn wondered where Douglas was.

Robert was in distress, Douglas had told him that Arwyn was in a relationship with another man, and Robert had immediately panicked for he knew that the situation of him and his wife was dependent upon the relationship his daughter had with Douglas. Before a few moments had past Arwyn was in a blazing row with her Father. Douglas had come out from the study, where he had been in the dark, crying. He could hear the shouting and walked out in to the garden. He stood still listening. He heard an argument between Robert and Arwyn.

He heard Arwyn say. "Douglas is nothing to do with me, he is not apart of this family he is nothing, do I make my self clear, he is nothing. He lives here because we let him."

Robert said. "When I loaned you the money to put into this house, you assured me that your relationship with Douglas was solid. Now you are sleeping with some other man and Douglas is having a nervous breakdown. What will your mother and I do if this house of cards falls? For Douglas will surely want to pull out of this agreement."

Arwyn said. "Shut up about our agreement, you loaned me that money, not him, he knows nothing about the agreement we made."

Robert bit back. "Douglas does, I gave him a copy of our contract, the one you signed at my solicitors. You cannot go around buying houses unless the solicitor knows where the money comes from. Money laundering laws, Arwyn. I really never expected this. I do not want to deal with this kind of thing Arwyn. I thought Dorothy and I would be safe, and secure, here for the rest of our days. You cannot imagine how I feel, whoever this man is, who has turned your head, I have feelings I have not experienced since the war. I killed people Arwyn, I know what it is like. I will tell you this I am so riled that I could murder whoever this man is, if your actions do not see me off first. I cannot believe this Arwyn, I am devastated, totally devastated, thank goodness your mother knows nothing about this, I never thought there could be anything good about dementia, but may be, at least she knows nothing of what you have done. "

Arwyn said. "Shut up Dad. Just shut up."

Douglas turned silently around and went back into his study. He sat down in the dark and started to think of things that he could do to stop the relationship between Raymond and Arwyn, and how he could win her back. Douglas was now in the free fall of a nervous breakdown. His brain was on fire his life was imploding within his cranium, he was trapped in a murky pungent viscous liquid, his life was grey ashes, and all he could think was how could he get Raymond out of Arwyn's life.

He did not have it in him to be violent; or did he? He would harm no one, could he? He could not stop Arwyn from leaving the house. He wondered what Raymond could become, would he be violent towards Arwyn. Suppose he took her prisoner. There was no evidence that Raymond would do such a thing, but just now Douglas was brainstorming with himself, and many possibilities were flashing through his dendrites. He could not stop Arwyn, he could not stop Raymond but maybe he could just know where she was, then if she did not return, at least he would know where to start looking. He could protect the house like Raymond had suggested, some cameras. He reached into his pocket and found the card Raymond had slipped in.

It was not difficult to fit a tracker to the car, which he owned, and Arwyn used. He would not follow her but if she did not come home at night he could switch on his computer and at least he could know where her car was. If she called he would be there to rescue her, it wouldn't take long. He loved her and he would protect her.

In the meantime Raymond had filled Arwyn's head full of the idea of getting rid of Douglas. He told her once Douglas was in prison she would have the house to herself and that if that happened Douglas would never be allowed back. Raymond told her that she would never be kicked out of the house for her parents were old and where would they go? No judge would do that to such old people. Raymond did not know if that were true, but he said it anyway. He told Arwyn to note down Douglas's behaviour. He said that all she had to do was to wait and Douglas would do something that crossed the line, or there could be an accumulation of minor things that could be used together to make a case against Douglas. Raymond said that he had seen things happen time and time again, in his work, and she should surely know that what he said was absolutely true.

Arwyn did question herself and Raymond. She admitted that Douglas had been very good to her and to Darren, Justin, Tracy, Robert and Dorothy, Susan and Gwyn. She told Raymond that although Douglas had become 'clingy' since he found out about her relationship with Raymond she had not admitted the relationship, in fact she had denied it. What had Douglas actually done? Put a letter and a flower a car. Repeated time and time again that he loved her and begged her not to leave him. He even offered to tolerate the 'affaire' with Raymond. He was never violent or threatening and the new kitchen was splendid because of his handicraft.

Raymond, in response, said.

"Who is it you want to sleep with him or me? In this country just the idea that he 'might' be arrested would be enough to ruin him, the neighbours, his friends, and family, would all question if the stories were true, and they would all be left with a nagging doubt. So," he told Arwyn "we probably don't even need to get him arrested, if your neighbours see a police car outside your house it will probably be enough. You see when a country has a police force it 'trusts' they tend to believe it. Many people here love these kinds of stories; they crave a bit of revenge. A whisper of sex in a crime and Douglas will be a monster for the rest of his days."

Two weeks later Arwyn phoned Raymond,

"He has installed some cameras, I did not see them at first, they are tiny there is one just outside my bedroom."

Raymond said to her. "It would be better if it were in the bedroom, but never mind you can easily say it was planted in the bedroom, with any luck we can get him done for voyeurism. He'll be away for a long time, they will put him on the sex offenders register, and that will be the end of him."

Arwyn was a bit shocked by this she said. "Douglas a sex offender, no he is just not that kind of person, he is just not."

Arwyn was being sucked into something now, the problem for Arwyn was that she had never really stood up for anything and now she was falling for this because there was nothing to stand up for. The idea of being in charge of her own life, where had that gone? Her Mother's constant control had faded into dementia and to take it's place Raymond's sun had risen in the east and blinded her.

Raymond said. "That really won't matter. What to do is this. Take the camera down and make a fuss about it with your son, not Darren, use Justin, tell him it was in your room. Drive over to me with it and I will call one of my pals at the station. You will have to make a formal complaint, and make a statement, and say that you want to have Douglas arrested. Later I will tell you what to say when they ask you for a victim impact statement. We can lay it on thick, with all these sex scandals in the news just recently, celebrities, any judge or magistrate will want to use Douglas as an example to others, they will throw the book at him and good riddance."

Arwyn was now totally controlled by Raymond. Douglas had never sort to, and never did control her. Somehow she was kind of happy that Raymond took control. She was quite prepared to listen and believe all that he said to her. Deep inside she knew that Raymond had a self-image, which was pitched much lower than her own, so that gave her the feeling that she was on top, that she was in control. It was the same feeling she had had with Gavin, but that she had never felt with Douglas. Douglas was always trying to get her to feel better about herself, but that was all too much effort, easier to stay as she was than move up to something better. Raymond was, therefore, 'better' she thought, yes she thought it is time to get rid of Douglas, I get a new man, who makes me cum from the inside, I get to keep the house and Douglas is no longer in it, sounds fine to me. She thought it over and over trying to convince herself.

It was Friday; Douglas was in deep despair he could see only black as he looked into his future. He knew he could not go back and undo what he had done. On the sea of what looked like black crude oil in the picture in his mind flashed the face of his children and the life he had left behind to be with this Arwyn. The faces of his dead parents, kept flashing in his mind, what would they have thought to see him in this way? His family were in his head too, and friends and he could not believe that he was now feeling like this. The black sea was endless and no matter how he tried he could not see the future, hope for the future had melted into the black sea and he realised that he was contemplating suicide. He checked himself, that would mean he was looking in to the future working out how to end it, therefore, that would be hope. Or would it? The black was about him again swallowing him. He knew that he needed help and he called the doctor, no appointments, call back at one o'clock we will fit you in if there is a cancellation. There was a cancellation, the last appointment of the day. He sat alone in the waiting room and waited and waited. He assumed that the doctor was busy, half an hour went by and the black was still all over him. He heard the door and looked up, the doctor was surprised she said.

"Oh what are you doing here?"

"I have been waiting to see you. They gave me an appointment." Said Douglas.

"I do apologise." Said the doctor. "Please come in."

Douglas melted into a soup of tears and story and the doctor listened, although she had an appointment herself, she listened. Then she said.

"Yes I am sure you need some help, so on Monday morning call this number and tell them I have sent you."

The doctor knew that Douglas needed urgent help with his mental health, but she also knew that what he needed was not available over the weekend. She thought Monday, that is millennia away, and will they even have time for him then. What else could she do, nothing.

Monday thought Douglas that is a millennia away. How can I survive until then?

The answer awaited him back at the house. He pulled his car into the drive and saw a police car parked. He got out of his car and two policemen got out of the police car.

"Douglas Tellam?" Said one of the policemen.

"Yes," said Douglas "can I help you?"

The policeman said. "Douglas Tellam I am arresting you for voyeurism, and stalking, and harassment."

Douglas was in instant shock he had just fallen into the Arctic ocean, he could not breathe, he was in absolute panic.

"You were not obliged to say anything but anything you do say will be taken down and may be used."

Or something like that said Douglas later to himself. He was not really sure of what the policeman had actually said. It was a mixture of reality and television and the great ocean of blackness which filled his head and he said to himself. "I wish I was dead."

Now he was cold with shock and they pushed his head down as he got into the police car, was this a nightmare? Was it real? What had the policeman said he had done? He was in the back of the car and a policeman was beside him and Douglas said through delirium.

"I did not put a camera in her room. It was outside her room."

The policeman said. "That makes little difference. Please do not speak Douglas, everything you say I must write down, wait do it properly with your solicitor."

If black could get blacker, it did.

The policeman drove the car very fast, Douglas mentioned it and then wished he had not. The police radio was on and various conversations could be overheard. The policeman, who was driving, joined in the conversation giving directions to a small ally way in the heart of the town then he a gave a warning saying that it was a dark an dangerous spot because of some of the people who lived there.

"They might be armed." said the policeman.

Douglas said out loud. "In Cheltenham? Things like that do not happen in Cheltenham." Then he was quiet for he had not thought things like this happened in Cheltenham, sitting in the back of a police car, under arrest. No, no, no...

Douglas felt cold for he knew that the love of Arwyn, to whom he had done no violence, was now being mingled with crimes, real crimes that hurt people. He knew instantly that murder and putting flowers into a car were equal in the eyes of the law and that he was surely to be punished; he knew that there was absolutely no escape.

Douglas also knew that the fifty and more years he had spent being nice to everyone, paying his taxes, driving without speeding, never drinking, caring for those less well off.

Douglas knew that although he had never taken drugs or smoked cigarettes. He had given what he could to charities…

He saw a busker in the town centre one day and noticed that his guitar was battered, and that it had a hole in its soundboard. Douglas drove home and collected a guitar, in a good hard case, which he had not used for some time, it was not a cheap guitar, Douglas drove back to town with the guitar but the busker was gone. So Douglas left the guitar in his car and one day the busker was there and Douglas took the guitar to the busker and said.

"You have a great voice and you play really well, I wondered if you could use this, I no longer need it and I think you would make good use of it."

The Busker, who had been living on the street, with his dog, for several years could not believe his luck. A few weeks later Douglas saw the Busker again, this time from a distance, he saw that the Busker was using the guitar and playing well, the hard case was not there the Busker had a flimsy canvas case. Douglas thought may be he sold the case and went on his way…

Douglas knew that all the good he had done in his life was as nothing in the society of twenty first century England, because he had already worked out that when the English want 'Justice' what they actually seek is 'Revenge'. He knew that if capital punishment was still an option many folk would be happy to turn up and watch. After all they still used to 'hang-draw-and-quarter' people in Victorian times. Douglas had known his great grand parents and they were Victorian's, so it was not so long ago. Indeed it was still possible to hang people for treason until 1998. Thank god I am not in America, or Saudi Arabia, or some other god-forsaken place came to Douglas's jumbled thoughts.

He asked himself. "Is this life over anyway?"

The heavy steel gates, with their barbed wire crown, opened from the middle and slid aside on their rails. The police car past through the gap and the gates crashed shut behind it as another wave of terror washed adrenalin through Douglas's brain.

All the training he had had, all the books that he had read on self-motivation, and self-improvement, fell out of his mind. He knew that he knew, he knew that he had learned how to cope with everything in life, but this was not included in the education he had had. The books of fiction, and films, and television cops and robbers shows never conveyed the feelings which engulfed Douglas.

He wanted to shout out. "Ok for whatever I did, and more, I am sorry and I will accept whatever punishment but just let me be free to leave. Please I cannot endure this."

Thoughts of prisoners, hostages, and kidnapped victims came to him. He had been in custody but a few moments, however, do people cope with years of this stuff? He felt that oxygen was being deprived, it was not, but he was unsure of how to breathe, he was not in control of his life now and he realised that he was now on a conveyor belt in the factory of justice.

The police car stopped and the driver turned. He said.

"Just so you know, Arwyn did not want me to arrest you, but this is a good arrest for me. Targets, you know. Raymond is a great bloke so you need not worry he will look after her. Oh and just in case you feel like mentioning this little conversation, remember we are all friends in this nick, and there are many things we can charge you with. Behave well and who knows this might be easier for you. So keep your trap shut and life may be a little easier."

The other policemen said nothing they climbed out of the car and Douglas was led into the custody suite.

'Suite', the sort of name people might associate with a grand hotel, or a large house, in a nice neighbourhood. Beyond the door they had come through was a relatively small space there as a 'bar' type of arrangement, not a bar conducive to a stool and drink, and some pleasant conversation, and background music. This bar was too high to lean on but a good height for the custody sergeant to lean over, and he did, and he asked the arresting officer some questions and then he spoke to Douglas. Douglas heard what the sergeant said but could not remember what he said a few seconds later. Douglas looked around the dingy space in which he stood, grey, dirty concrete walls, dim lights, and his eye fixed upon a blackboard, which was on the wall in a room behind the custody sergeant's shoulder, the board was set high enough for it to be visible even from the angle at which Douglas held his head back. He watched and he saw a hand chalk is name in a box entitled 'Cell 1'…. and the word 'VOYERISUM'. In capitals beneath it.

From then on indignity upon indignity were heaped upon Douglas. He found himself putting ink on his fingers and thumbs and each was pressed on to a paper, or was that he put his fingers on a glass and a photograph was taken? You might think this silly but he could not remember. When he thought back on this he tried, and tried, but could not remember. He could not remember if it was a woman or a man who had photographed him. For television shows and life wondered about his brain cells and intermingled in this very unstable environment. He could not remember many things, but he did remember her saying.

"I am going to take a sample of your DNA, I will put this stick into your mouth and roll it on the inside of your cheek. This DNA sample will be compared with all the open crimes known to the police, and should that sample be matched you will be charged with further offences. I will give you this one opportunity to let me know if you have been involved in any other crimes."

Goose pimples arose across Douglas's body. Never had he committed any crime, why does she not know this? I am a good man, he said to himself but he found it difficult to hold onto that thought. He asked how long the police would keep the samples and he thought he heard her say 'always'. Later he could not really remember, he said to himself.

'They must have standard phrases they use so that they are not caught out, but what did they say?"

At some point he was given a sheet of A4 paper on which were written his rights. 'What does that mean?' He wondered.

They took everything from him, as it happened not that much, just a few coins really. He had to remove his belt, and take off his shoes; he was then locked into a prison cell. He thought there was nowhere deeper, but he was wrong. Rights, what rights? He could not comprehend.

On the wall, high above him, was a video camera; the walls matched those of the custody suite. There was a bench seat with a blue plastic covered mattress upon which he could sit or lie down. I wonder when they cleaned that, maybe they never did. The door was thick and had a hatch in it, which could be opened from the outside. Then there was a toilet. In the eye line of the hatch in the door and in direct vision of the video camera. It had no proper toilet seat. It did have a tap which allowed cold water for hand washing, but it was a part of the toilet. There was no soap, there was no towel. There was a small amount of toilet paper.

Douglas never found it easy to use a public toilet, like many men, he preferred use a cubical, he was not sure why. The thought of sitting on a toilet in full view of whoever was at the other side of the video camera as abhorrent to him.

So many punishments and he had not yet been into a court room. Fortunately Douglas had not eaten much over the past few weeks, he thought that his weight loss was the best part of this horrid story thus far. So thankfully he had not reason to sit on the toilet. He had not drunk much, his mouth was dry but eventually he did have to urinate, how he was not sure, it was simply a relief in the end. The idea of washing his hands in the toilet, well not in the toilet but close enough.

He tried to lay down to sleep a bit, he did not know what the time was, but his brain was on fire and the horrors of the moment would not allow rest. Eventually the hatch on the door opened, for a tortured second Douglas thought it was the door opening for him to be set free. No the custody women handed him a phone and said the duty solicitor for you.

It was late in the night now, Douglas poured out the whole story and the duty solicitor said, that he would come in the morning and he told Douglas to relax and try and sleep. Douglas switched off the phone and realised that he had trusted the custody person, but was that really a solicitor he had just spoken to? He did not know, but he had had to assemble his thoughts, and get them into a coherent order to pass his story on. Douglas pressed a button marked 'Call', which was near the cell door. Some time later a voice asked him what he wanted.

"It says on the paper I was given that I can ask for paper and pencil. Please can I have some paper and pencil?"

About an hour later Douglas was provided with paper and pencil. He made a list of all the things that he thought would possibly be thought of as wrong by the police, in what he had done over the past couple of weeks with regard Arwyn. One of Douglas's problems was that he never knew how to lie; he had always to be totally open and honest.

So he wrote that he had found out about Arwyn's lover by looking at her telephone. He wrote that he took her phone and exchanged it for a phone which looked identical and in doing so was able to intercept calls and messages and using the forwarding service so that Arwyn and Raymond were unaware of Douglas's interference. He wrote that after the first text messages, Raymond to Arwyn and her reply, Douglas decided not to continue with this for the text messages were sexual and explicit. So at the first opportunity he swapped the phones back.

He said that he had placed a flower and a letter in Arwyn's car and that he had fitted a tracker, but he had not followed her, he had looked for her location on one evening as she had not returned home for three nights when he found the car was by the house of Raymond he did not look more. He wrote that he had written around twenty letters to Arwyn, pleading with her to stay with Douglas. He confessed that on occasions, over the past weeks, when Arwyn had been at home he had hovered about her and had not wanted to leave her out of sight.

He wrote that one day he had felt so low when she had told him that she would be away for the weekend, that he had driven to Arwyn's school on the Friday evening to see her before she went. He wrote that he saw Arwyn climb into a car with Raymond and at that moment Arwyn had caught sight of Douglas and he drove home.

Later Douglas came to regret writing these things down because, stupidly, he thought if he was open and honest he might be forgiven. He pressed the call button when he had finished re-reading his work and he gave the paper to the custody person. He said this is all that I have done. Nothing more and nothing less. Please give it to whoever is in charge.

"Naiveté at it's grandest," said the duty solicitor, "What were you thinking? You told me that this police officer works here. Why would you give the police such a 'confession'? Look at the charge sheet there is nothing of all that here, all it says here is that you put a flower in her car, you send her lots of letters, and you turned up at her school. Oh and the big one the camera. You say you did not put that in your 'confession'. "

Douglas stammered. "It was a camera, I put a camera outside the bedroom. It would not work."

The solicitor said. "It makes little odds for they say it was in the bedroom, your word against hers."

Douglas snapped back. "I did not."

The solicitor continued. "Putting tracking devices, used or not, is not allowed, interfering with telephones is not allowed. Putting cameras up in your house is allowed for security purposes. She claims you put it in her bedroom, and that will be considered as perverted. You say you put it outside the bedroom. It is her word against yours. I suggest during the interview, you will have later with the police, you emphasise the word security."

Douglas looked bewildered. "I thought you were here to be on my side." he said.

The solicitor said. "Of course but you need to be aware of the situation in which you are now. We do not yet know what the CPS will say, they could very well charge you with voyeurism, in which case you will receive a very heavy sentence and for the rest of your life you will be found on the sexual offences register. I think you understand what that would mean."

Douglas was agoraphobic.

"The cameras were put there because Raymond told me he had been in the house, he told me that I should be smarter and make sure I knew what was going on under my own roof. The cameras did not work anyway; I could not get them to function. There was something wrong with the software or something. I did not put the cameras to see Arwyn naked, I used to sleep in the bed in that room, I know what she looks like naked and I remember what she looked like naked when she was seventeen. I love Arwyn. She never made it clear to me that she no longer wanted me. She has not told me that she has been seeing Raymond. For all I know he has taken over her mind or something and is controlling her, things like that happen."

The solicitor said. "On television may be. Its says here that at Easter Arwyn told you that her relationship was over, it says you took it badly and have been harassing her ever since."

Douglas was engulfed in an imaginary funk, he actually knew that this stench was the smell of lies, Douglas said to the solicitor.

"Easter was in April, the first I knew of Raymond was in the middle of May. Arwyn has never told me that it was all over. When you say harassing, we lived under the same roof, our roof, a house we jointly own, a house where I care for her parents. I gave her space to get over her former partner, Gavin. I told her that if she had to have an affair with Raymond I would understand. Only two days ago she was upset, because she had argued with her son, she came to me and wanted me to give her a cuddle, and for me to listen whilst she told me the story. You know he, Raymond, works in this police station, it is likely that the person who interviews me will be a friend of Raymond."

The solicitor spoke. "Well even if he is that should not affect the situation, or how you are dealt with, I will ask the person who interviews you if they have a relationship."

This part of the time that Douglas was in custody was an easier bit, for it was not just four dismal walls and a door trapping him in. The solicitor and he were in another room so the claustrophobia had abated. Then the solicitor left, he said he would return for the interview, hopefully, later on that day. Then horror, upon horror, Douglas found himself back in the cell once more the toilet leaking in a slow but steady stream from somewhere in it's concrete box.

The cell door was opened and a person claiming to be a health worker came in he enquired after Douglas's mental health, but before Douglas could respond the custody person called him away to an urgent situation. Douglas felt the door lock once more upon him. He thought that a day must have just about gone by. He should have been working today what would they think? He was always reliable now he was not even able to say that he was not coming. They do not really care about the state of my mental health; they just do not want me to commit suicide in here. They can tell the outside world that I was seen by a mental health specialist, so they have done their duty.

The custody people had been good about the phone call; it was Douglas's right to make. Of course people no longer remember phone numbers, because mobiles store the numbers beneath the name. The custody people did their best to locate Douglas's sister. Douglas thought that he would be allowed to speak to her, but no, that was not allowed, the custody people would pass on a short message but nothing more. So Douglas asked her to contact the people he was supposed to work for and make some excuse, which did not include his current predicament.

These bursts of little things to break up the monotony were things that kept Douglas almost sane. He thought a lot about how he could kill himself right there and right then. Then the faces of his children came to him and he realised that it was not a possible action. That does not mean that the sea of black had gone away, no, no, it was more that this huge ocean was now in full storm.

The custody people told him that it was possible for Douglas to stretch his legs in the courtyard. He pressed the call button and made that request. The courtyard turned out to be another cell but without a roof and nowhere to sit down.

Meals were offered, something described as 'Lasagne' was brought to him, he asked for salt but that was not allowed. It was a soggy mass of goo, which had been put into a microwave and served piping hot.

The person dealing with mental health never did return, although he had said he would.

The there was the nurse who fussed about medication. She sat so intently watching as Douglas consumed his regular pills. The cell door was ajar, Douglas thought so she could escape if she wanted too. She noted everything that happened.

Douglas was so happy for these small interventions in the drudgery of the hours and hours he spent with nothing to do, nothing to distract his brain, nothing shielded him from the pain of what Arwyn and her policeman friend had done, nothing to hide Douglas from the fear that at any moment that very policeman might appear in the doorway of that cell and beat Douglas.

The time stretched and it stretched and it got longer and longer. Douglas had the sense that time travel was available, because time had never felt longer, nor heavier, than it was at this point in his life. The worst of it was that he could not even practice the piano in his head, such was his distraction.

Then the custody person gave Douglas a book to read, it was like a cool drink on a thirsty hot day, but as he read the first paragraph he remembered that it was a book he had read the most of some years before, he had not enjoyed it then and he did not enjoy it now, although he tried.

Then the cell door opened and Douglas was ushered to a small, dimly lit room, he did not mind the dim light, for the light in the cell remained bright twenty four hours, making sleep even more impossible, as if the racing in his brain were not enough, as if the fear of Arwyn's policeman, as if the thought of having to stay in a prison for a second longer were not enough, to fill his head with a desire for death. Or maybe the desire for the death of Raymond.

The custody person left the room as the duty solicitor entered and shook Douglas's hand, a small, a simple gesture, which filled Douglas with hope, for this was human, in the midst of something that seemed to Douglas to be the most alien situation in which he had ever been. Here was St. Leonard, the 'Patron Saint of Prisoners', in the form of the Duty Solicitor and Douglas suddenly realised what 'Advocate' meant, and how vital it was, at this moment, in preserving his sanity.

CHAPTER 16
Arwyn the People's Friend

I n some ways Arwyn was in as much of a state as was Douglas. On the one hand she was enjoying the ride, being swept along by Raymond and his ambitions, on the other there was something within her that was flashing off and on, like some warning flooding and emptying her mind with red light. Should she have done all of this to a man she knew had loved her? Douglas had surely given her more than anyone, he was actually amazing in so many ways, and she had not wanted him to be arrested, she just wanted to frighten him. Well that's what she said to her herself over and over. Then she could not understand why she had wanted to do, even, that. She wanted Raymond, she wanted his sex, and she wanted the feeling that she was a bit above Raymond. She was worried about what would happen next. Raymond had told her what to say; he said that the victim impact statement would be the most important thing, regardless of the charges she had made. So she told the policewoman, that although Douglas had not been violent, he had frightened Arwyn, and Arwyn laid that on thick, just as Raymond had suggested. Arwyn could not say that Douglas tried to control her, he never did, Raymond told her to say Douglas was controlling, but Douglas was not, Raymond was, she knew he was, but she did not mind; for it made her life easier, it was like having her mother there, it meant there were less decisions to make. Arwyn gave a potted history of the years she had been involved with Douglas, conveniently précising much, editing out the good bits, and making up the bits she really did not know, in answer to the questions.

Raymond had told her. "You are my woman now, they know that, they know me, so they will believe whatever you have to say. Soon Douglas will be in your past and we will have the future for us." Raymond really was not that poetic but that was the flow.

Arwyn asked. "What will he do? He won't have any place to live."

Raymond gave a cold stare and questioned, bluntly.

"So? That bastard is lucky to be alive, it would be better if he were dead. May be I should arrange that."

Raymond frightened Arwyn with these words, they made her feel unsteady, It was as if she had drunk too much wine and wanted to be sick.

Arwyn now had to impress upon friends and family that she had done the right thing. For she knew too that Douglas had been good to each of them. Arwyn had a gift of justification; she had a 'Degree' in it. Now with Raymond in control, which he was, in a way Douglas just never knew how, Arwyn's resolve was strengthened. She found it easy to exaggerate the things that Douglas had done. She emphasised the impact that all the accumulated happenings had had upon her well-being. Even when Susan, Arwyn's sister, questioned Arwyn's story Arwyn was able to justify and embellish convincingly. Gwyn said.

"I am sorry Arwyn, but this is a load of tosh, Douglas could not frighten you, he just does not possess those sorts of genes. He is the best man you have ever known, you know it, everyone knows it and you would do this to him, and throw him out for this policeman. I am sorry sis, I love you, you are my big sister, but I tell you now you are being a fool. You know lying to the police is more serious than anything that has happened between you and Douglas, if they find out it will be you in prison not him."

Arwyn did not listen to her brother, she could see only her life with Raymond, in the house which Douglas had provided, in a little while her parents would die, her boys would move to their own homes. Raymond would give her good sex, when she wanted it, and he would relieve her of all the decisions that she hated having to make. Although she desired to be in charge, she had spent so many years not being in charge, it was just easier to hand the controls to Raymond. Raymond would never confront her with philosophy, or the politics of the day, he would never quote passages from books. If that was a cost for Douglas well that was a price Douglas would have to pay. Arwyn knew that she had damaged Douglas until he had had a break down, but that was his own silly fault. Before long Arwyn convinced herself that she had told Douglas about Raymond three weeks before she had actually met Raymond, she convinced herself that Douglas had frightened her so when the policewomen had asked the impact assessment was not a lie, it was what she convinced herself was the truth.

Raymond smiled at her across the dinner table and Arwyn did not realise that she paid for the dinner, Raymond had that effect upon her. Douglas seldom let her pay, she actually never thought about paying when Douglas was with her. She and Raymond went back to Arwyn's house, for it was hers now, and Raymond fucked her, Raymond never once 'made love' to Arwyn, he did not know how to, Raymond never loved Arwyn, he never wanted to, but he knew that Arwyn thought he did, and he knew that she thought the sex he did with her was making love. Raymond thought that that was all right for he was getting what he wanted and Arwyn was getting what she wanted.

'Raymond controls' Arwyn thought 'so there are endless possibilities to moan.' Arwyn saw the face of her mother in the midst of all these thoughts for her mother was the controller general of them all, and she had controlled because it was her way of showing that she loved Arwyn, and wanted no mishap to come upon Arwyn. Thus Arwyn had learned of love and Raymond almost matched her mother in these abilities. So, for the first time since childhood, Arwyn felt in control because Raymond was in control, Arwyn found herself back home where life was predictable. That was the problem with Douglas, he never wanted to put up barriers, he said people are what they are, they cannot be changed so enjoy them for what they are, and work around them. That was to lose for Arwyn, and that was why Raymond was great, and Douglas was where he should be, behind bars, she had all his money, and she had his house, which she believed was hers.

These feelings were, of course like waves on the ocean, they came and went but it was an incoming tide and fresh salty water only peppered up the notions and let them be stronger and stronger.

Besides Raymond was good with sex and sex was important.

The Interview

There was more light in the police interview room. The duty solicitor sat at a desk behind Douglas and to his left. The policeman in charge of the interview sat in front. The policeman explained that the interview would be recorded on a video camera and that he wanted truthful answers to his questions. The policeman pointed out that the paper that Douglas had written in the police cell had been read and that it amounted to a confession of more misdemeanours than Arwyn had complained about. The Policeman said to Douglas that he found it quite bizarre to have such a list. Douglas heard the policeman go through all the items and Douglas realised that most of what was put to him was really nothing. He realised that there was only one thing that the policeman was actually really concerned about.

Douglas said that he wanted to answer all truthfully and he said that he thought that by making everything he had done open and available the whole situation might be quickly resolved. However, beyond these fine words and inside his head Douglas was more frightened than he had ever been. He wondered if Arwyn's policeman was this policeman's friend. He wondered if Arwyn's policeman was behind the door, he wondered if Arwyn's policeman was observing all of this on a video link.

The duty solicitor spoke. "My client is concerned that the man who is at the centre of the story, the man my client's partner has been having a relationship with, and who has been a party in the situation my client now finds himself in, is a policeman. My client is further concerned that this policeman, whom he thinks is called Raymond, may work at this police station, and that he may be an acquaintance of yours, or that you could even be a friend of his."

The policeman looked somewhat uncomfortable and said. "I am not at liberty to comment upon other officer's at this or any police station. Now let us move on to the camera which is not included in your list Douglas."

Douglas was cold inside; his brain was leaping from point to point. He must say it was for security. It was his word against theirs, and theirs was the word of a 'wronged woman and a policeman'. How much could, or should, he say about the cameras? Should he say that Raymond had given him the idea? Should he say that Raymond had even told him the make of camera that would be the best? That Raymond had given him a business card of an expert in this field? Maybe if Douglas had used the expert's services the cameras would have been undetected, and may be they would have worked. Should Douglas say that Raymond had slept in, and had sex, with Arwyn in Douglas and Arwyn's bed? Should he say that it was Raymond who had told him to put a camera in the bedroom, but that he had it put in the hall beside the bedroom? Douglas was dry in the mouth; he could feel the halitosis and hoped that the policeman could not smell it. Douglas knew that his face was being recorded, he knew that they could study the body language, could they understand that he had told the truth, would they workout what this anxiety was, which was now pouring from all his sweat glands, would they think he was hiding something or would that interpret as guilt? He and 'confessed' already to many things. If he said it was Raymond would he find himself subject of a beating in the cells later that day? Douglas could not decide.

The policeman said. "Douglas why did you put the camera in the bedroom?"

Douglas knew that he had not put the camera in the bedroom. His head felt like a fire station in the middle of the night as half slumbering fire fighters are roused from somnolence by sirens. Douglas then understood the voyeurism label written by his name in the custody suite, in the office behind the giant counter, in the custody suite. Was that counter so high? Or was it just the height of a pub bar. Did he put the camera in the room, or are they just saying that. The mental breakdown surrounded him, it was beneath and above. He could not find words, his mouth was so dry, he could not speak, and his throat, his throat felt as if it would never sing again. Then he, in his mind heard the duty solicitor explaining that a charge of voyeurism would see his name added to the sex offender's register, which would be much the same as a death sentence. Something that would haunt every moment of life until death. Douglas knew that he was not such an offender but what to say? How to say it? Was Raymond a part of this interview, and had the police already decided what the outcome of all this was going to be.

Then, from somewhere in the primeval, reptilian, part of his brain the thought of self-preservation erupted burning though all this as a stream of molten metal into a mould. He could not control its path and it bought these words with it.

"Raymond told me he had slept with Arwyn, in the bed I had purchased for Arwyn and I, Raymond told me that I, I should have security cameras up, I took his advice. I, I thought that he might harm her."

Before Douglas could say that the camera was mounted outside the bedroom the policeman cut Douglas short.

"You are trying telling me that you thought a serving police officer" and as he said that Douglas knew, as did the duty solicitor, that Raymond was surely a part of the police force in this station, "that you thought a serving police officer would harm someone.... Bizarre!"

Douglas had read newspapers of corrupt police officers. No he never expected to be involved with one but he knew for certain that he was joined by the hip to one at this moment.

Both Douglas and the duty solicitor knew that this was not good. They could feel the atmosphere. It was the end of the interview and Douglas was taken back to the cells. Where he complained that the leaking toilet was really unpleasant now. He was shown to another cell, which was the same, but without the leak. He knew that there was a limited time they could keep him here, but the paper with his rights was now in the old cell and he could no longer read it, he asked for it, but it was not brought to him. The time stretched out once more and Douglas replayed the interview around in circles again an again. The cell door opened.

The policeman who had conducted Douglas's interview came in. The door of the cell was open but not as open as when other people came in. He stood looking down on Douglas who sat on the edge of the blue plastic covered mattress. The policeman stood with his back to the video camera. He bowed his head and became very softly spoken.

"The CPS *(Criminal Prosecution Service)* have come back to me now, they have reviewed your interview and other evidence. I have to tell you that you will be retained here for a further twenty four hours and you will then go before the Magistrate's tomorrow. In a short while you will be charged. Here I have a choice for you, off the record Douglas, listen carefully, I know that you are upset, and I know that you want this over and done with a soon as possible, so I have a choice for you. This voyeurism charge it is a big one, I think you know that, and something tells me that you would fight that, but you know they would put you on remand and so, effectively, you will go to prison, not a good place for sex offenders, I am sure you have some idea of what happy moments that might lead you to." At this the policeman smiled in the way that a Nazi officer might in an old war movie. "On the brighter side I am sure that if you were to agree to accepting and pleading guilty to charge of Harassment this whole thing could be over and done with, and as a little bonus I will over look the accusations you made. I cannot understand Douglas why an intelligent man would resort to trying to implicate a serving police officer. Maybe you just got over nervous. So what do you say?"

Later Douglas began to understand that thing he had seen on television cop shows where the accused says 'No Comment'. Later he realised that the right not to make a comment was something quiet fabulous, for in the middle of something like this, even with an Advocate, no one is in a stable enough state to make the correct decisions under these circumstances. Later Douglas thought that he should have made no comment to everything until he had actually really got control of his mind. However, time was used to pressure him for an answer and later he realised that the whole system of, so called, justice in England is governed by time and money, and that there is such a shortage of both, these fundamental elements that justice is impossible, at least for those who have no funds, Douglas further realised that it probably did not matter much; for when the members English society called for justice what they were looking for is revenge, and many who sought revenge had never been wronged, they just enjoyed watching the punishments, and wished that people were still put in the Stocks so they could throw things at them. Oh that thought had come to him before, and it would repeat and repeat as a bad breakfast.

Douglas's response to the policeman came in the form of relief, he had to get out of here and if accepting harassment as a charge, even if he did not think he was guilty was obviously a better offer than the sex offenders register. So like any good salesman 'product', 'feature', 'benefit' the policemen had what he wanted, after all, targets are targets, and if you can stop the target moving why would you not? Money in your own pocket is a lot more valuable than many in someone else's bank account.

The policeman, like any good salesman, once he had made the sale, failed to go into the fine details of the contract. He failed to say to Douglas that pleading guilty to this charge gave no guaranteed outcome. If the Magistrate decided a custodial sentence was appropriate that is what would happen, nothing to do with the policeman. The policeman failed to point out all the other disadvantages of pleading guilty, but some of those will be made plain later in this story. Something the policeman did mention was that should Douglas sleep on this idea, and have second thoughts, it really would not be much of a problem to update the charges to ensure a lifetime on the sex offenders register.

Douglas could not believe that 'offending' and 'sex' were mentioned around his name. He had truly been sexually attracted to very few women in his entire life. For years he had been in a sexless marriage and had remained faithful. Douglas was a man who wanted love, yes he liked sex but he would not want it with every woman that passed him in the street. He had known men who would ogle at most of the women on a high street. Douglas was not this. Yet he was, even though he did not know it, being pushed into a group who were labelled, and whom others would shun. Douglas had forgotten that people, for the most part, do not see fine lines, and have no time for distinction of 'this' verses 'that', if you are close to that football crowd you are one of it.

CHAPTER 17
Turmoil Back Home

The overriding, over powering, thoughts for Douglas were he had stolen nothing, and he had harmed no one, and yet he was here in prison, and he had no idea at all what would happen next, and frankly, even if they had told him he would not really have understood, because those telling him had never been on his side in all of this. Many times he had heard people talking about 'criminals', and how punishments were insufficient to be a deterrent. As far as Douglas could see he had never thought that he was breaking the law, and he knew already that the punishment thus far was enough to keep him away from any further thought of chivalry, or trying to protect his woman.

He had seen so many movies where the star had fought to keep his girl, or get her back; he had never thought that to fight for something was wrong. It was without any doubt the most awful predicament in which he had ever found himself. He looked about the cell and wondered if he would be sent to prison. Claustrophobia had never been apart of Douglas's life until now. He had missed two engagements, and, therefore, the money for those, and what of is reputation? He had never missed bookings before, would they book him again? What excuse could he make for his absence?

A different duty solicitor arrived; the previous one had had to attend to other business. So Douglas had to go through the entire story with the new solicitor, only moments before the hearing in the Magistrates Court. Douglas knew that the poor man had had little time to prepare; the previous solicitor had had a good few hours to digest the story Douglas had put forward. The new man had had only minutes. To Douglas this was catastrophic. Douglas was not so comfortable with this new duty solicitor; if the other one had come Douglas might have said something about the whispered conversation in the police cell. Nothing to be done it was time and Douglas was lead through the custody suit and greeted at the court door by a bailiff who hand cuffed Douglas to him and led him into a room. Nothing much, if anything, was said. Douglas did not think it was good to be handcuffed, he had not realised there were further depths into which he would be plunged and then he was told to enter a room, you might say a broom cupboard. The handcuffs were freed and Douglas was told to sit on the bench. A door came towards Douglas and slammed firmly shut in his face. The space was dimly lit and more claustrophobically full than anything he had yet encountered. When you read slammed...in his face. That is exactly what it did the room was so small nothing else was possible. He had thought the 'innocent until proven guilty' was the mainstay of English law. Obviously not, again this thought, but then he had said that he was guilty, so may be it was right that they had put him in here.

Douglas was not clear about breathing and he felt that he needed to go to the toilet but the bell push failed to bring aid. He thought suppose they leave me here? May be they do this, may be…. because the fear had muddled Douglas's mind so much now he was in room one-o-one, and George Orwell was breathing down his neck, and he felt that he was Winston and the rats were coming for him, and what had Douglas done to deserve all of this?

For more than fifty years Douglas had paid all his taxes, never cheated a penny, he had given to charity, he had helped anyone that he could. He had never shirked responsibilities even those he had not chosen. He had loved his children and had accepted humiliations and above all he had been such a kind person, in so many ways, to so many people. You would have been unable to find anyone, except Raymond and Arwyn, who would have had a bad word to say of him, not even his former wives, or his agent.

Insanity had long been vanquished in Douglas's fears. The humming background of the mental break down, which he had been going through, was louder and louder. If there had been a cliff he would have jumped, if he had had a belt he would have hung himself, and no thought that his friends and family would be devastated would have stopped him. For the ocean of black was so wide and so deep he wondered how he could kill himself within this little, dirty broom cupboard.

The door opened and the face of the 'handcuff man' was before him. Douglas noticed how smartly dressed were these courtroom employees, starch in their crisp white shirts and ironed trousers. Douglas had been in the same, casual, clothes for seventy-two hours. He had not showered, or shaved, or been allowed to brush his teeth. Douglas stood and was once again handcuffed to his jailor. They walked side by side down a corridor and into the court. Douglas was told to enter into a glass cabinet, the handcuff was removed and a different court usher indicated that Douglas should sit whilst the usher sat next to him, but just a little behind him.

On the television they always make it look as if everybody knows what is going on. Douglas did not, indeed, later, he was unable to recall exactly what was asked of him, and exactly what was said until the moment the Crown Prosecutor started outlining the story of Douglas's life. At this point Douglas engaged, and he tried to speak, but the usher stopped him, whispering under his breath

"It's Ok."

Indicating with his hand for Douglas to keep quiet. Whoever the Crown Prosecutor had described it was someone who was not Douglas. It was a compete fiction. Douglas knew that his solicitor would be unable to counter what had been said for they had only just met.

The Crown Prosecutor continued his fictional rant saying. "The defendant was given sanctuary by the plaintiff's family, when he was made homeless after the breakdown of his previous marriage."

Douglas whispered to the usher. "That is not true."

The usher whispered. "Shush, it will make no difference."

To give him his due the duty solicitor did quite well with very little knowledge of the whole story. Then came a discussion about bail. The Crown Prosecutor laid the margarine on in a thick dollop. He tried to suggest that Arwyn was in true danger if Douglas were allowed to stay in the county. The duty solicitor managed to counter that, over the top, assessment. It was agreed that Douglas would appear before the bench in six weeks time. He would be subjected to probation reports and under the penalty of prison. He would not be allowed to go to his home except, with police, to collect belongings and his car. It was agreed that he would lodge with his sister, Mary, however, Douglas had made no arrangement with her, and did not know if she could have him stay. As the proceedings came to an end the usher said.

"Its ok you can leave now, there was no point in making a fuss about details. Go through there and your solicitor will see you."

Douglas had left his jumper back in the police cell, he never saw it again, and did not ask if he could get it.

He said to the solicitor. "Bail? How much money do I need for bail?"

The solicitor half laughed and said. "This is not America."

Douglas said. "You see I have spent just about all my money, the house and legal expenses, It has been so expensive with Arwyn and I have had to provide money for my children etc. etc., the coffers are empty," Douglas paused in his daze.

"What about all those things that man said in there, none of it was true. It was a complete fabrication. Who told him to say all of that? He made it sound as if I was sponging off Arwyn's family. It is my money in that house; half of it belongs to me. It was as if he had never heard of me."

The solicitor said. "I think that it is good that he did not introduce your professional life to the story, that would bring all this to the attention of the press, I think you would be wise to keep all of professional life as quiet as you can."

"The policeman knew, the Custody Sergeant, he sneered, I remember now, but they all know because they know this man that Arwyn is now with." Said Douglas.

The solicitors mind was not on what had happened in the court, having heard what Douglas had just said he was searching his briefcase for a legal aid form. From there on in the solicitor's only interest was in filling out the form for Legal Aid. He needed to be paid and he repeated, several times, that the money from legal aid was so thin that it was hardly worth his while. Once he was satisfied that the form was complete he turned to what Douglas had to do next, the solicitor repeated the rules of Douglas's bail and then asked Douglas what he would do that evening.

Douglas said "Well I need a police person to come with me to my house so I can get my car and things, I have no money and I have been wearing these clothes for three days. They would not allow me to shower; I have not brushed my teeth. I apologise if I am unpleasant to be close to."

The solicitor called the police, on his mobile phone. He explained the situation, their response was, that such appointments had to be made in advance and the next appointment available was at nine o'clock on the following morning. The solicitor scoffed at that and reiterated the saga.

Having failed a second time he asked to speak to a superior person. At this time the caretaker of the court building opened the door to ask how much longer the solicitor would be, he pointed out that he should have locked up sometime before. The solicitor made an agreement that Douglas would wait outside the court and when a police car, and an officer, became available they would take him to his house to collect his things. The solicitor said you might have to wait some time.

It was not too long, but Douglas had no watch and there was no clock to see in the street. Traffic whizzed by in an endless stream and Douglas paced up and down, it was not cold but it was not warm, he would have liked the jumper to cover his shirt, but it was still under lock and key. He had not eaten, nor had he drunk for a long time. He felt empty, relieved, scared, lonely, and unhappy, the street he was on was full of car exhaust and litter and nothingness. Hardly any people walked by him and then a police car pulled up and the policeman in it called out

"Douglas?"

Off they sped, it seemed that all policemen drive at breakneck speed. When they arrived at the house the policeman told Douglas to sit in the car whilst he knocked on the door. Then he told Douglas to go and collect his things, Douglas said.

"I will need to go into one of the rooms upstairs as well, if you could make that possible."

It was a dash, and run, and a sweat to put as much stuff in his car as he could. He knew not when he would be able to collect the rest or where he could put it all. As he opened the door to his study and he could see no computers, the police had obviously taken them. Douglas remembered that, during his interview, he had been asked if the police would find anything that they should not on his computers. Douglas had replied.

"Of course not."

He also remembered that he had told the policeman that the cameras had not functioned; he had been unable to make them work. This was true. It might be thought that that is the first thing Douglas would have said to the police about all of this, but it was not, his brain was in such turmoil he had not thought of it, or had he? There was one thing for sure in Douglas's head he was in a fog of confusion. Many months later he described it as he found himself hedgehog like rolled so tightly in a ball he could not see the light.

Now Douglas wondered what he would do with no computer to run his business and how long would it be before the computers were returned. Would the police leave some Trojan programme on his laptop so that they could monitor Douglas henceforth.

Douglas was long and deep in 'Wonderland' now and if a white rabbit had popped up to tell him the time he would have just accepted it as normal and 'par for the course'. The policeman pressed Douglas to finish up, Douglas did not respond. Then all that could be got into the car had gone into the car. The policeman reminded Douglas that he was not to return to the house without a police presence and that he should arrange with the police station a suitable time at which to collect the rest of his stuff. The policeman then said.

"Drive in front of me now and I will leave you once you are on the motorway slip road. Please be aware that the are PNC cameras all around this area if your car is found to be near this house you will be challenged you may then be arrested which would make things infinitely worse."

Douglas wondered about this and many other things he had been told by those enforcing laws in the past few days. Spontaneously he started singing '*My old man said follow the van and don't dilly dally on the way...*'

It struck Douglas that many of these people had 'Off the Record' comments to make to him, and Douglas wondered if they were not as guilty, as anyone could be, for breaking various rules and regulations in what is, or is not, the correct thing to say at this or that time. Then what could Douglas do about that? He was on the motorway now, and he felt very glad that he was no longer with any police person; he felt too that he would never trust another police person, and that his whole thought about the country, in which he lived, was altered. He did not feel free but it was better to be alone in his own car than to be alone and locked in a police cell. Then he wondered if he should be grateful that he had been met with English justice rather than Indonesian or American justice, he had know way of knowing if justice was different there or different anywhere.

What Douglas really needed at this moment was some love from someone who really loved and cared about him. He was heading for his brother's house. He did not know that his sister had spoken with his brother, Douglas did not know if he could stay at his sister's house. He did not know if the police would call to see if he was there or not, something said that as it was a different area, maybe such coordination, between two police forces, was unlikely, over such a small person as himself. After all murders go unsolved sometimes, because different police forces fail to communicate. He was already outside his brother's house. He felt unkempt and dirty. His sister in law kept a very clean and tidy, modern, home. Mud on shoes was certainly not welcome here and Douglas looked down at his shoe for he felt sure he could smell dog waste.

It was his sister in law, Ulrika, who answered the door, she seemed surprised to see him, but then again it seemed that she was expecting him. As soon as Douglas was inside, and the door was closed behind him she got on her high horse and let fly. She seemed to know a lot about what had gone on, Douglas guessed that the police had been more chatty with his sister than he had thought and that what the police had said was now being topped up with imagination. Or may be it was all imagination. Within a few moments Douglas was feeling at least as bad as had had done when the policeman had interviewed him, and actually a little worse. For, although he had known his brother's wife for many years, he did not really know her, and actually he knew very little about her, they were acquaintances, certainly not friends, although presents were exchanged over Christmas and sometimes at birthdays and there were meetings and dinners and family occasions. Here she was now tearing into Douglas, with guard dog teeth ripping more chunks of his raw flesh, from the meagre bones, of his crumbled life. He did not hear all she said, although it was loud enough, and when the fury had died he remembered even less. The parts that stuck were.

"Think of your Mum and Dad, up in heaven, looking down on you now, what must they be thinking? It is time to pull yourself together. You had a good marriage and you threw it all away for a woman, who anyone could see was a user, all she wanted was your money and now she has thrown you away. Now we will help you but you have to help yourself."

With that the door opened and Douglas's brother, Wesley, stepped into the hallway, the expression he carried was that he had been waiting in the kitchen and now, as an actor, he had come on stage to his cue. What Douglas needed was a hug and some sympathy. They were then kind to him, Douglas thought later, they took him to a restaurant and paid for a meal and watched him eat it. They checked him in to a hotel and Douglas's brother paid. Douglas had hoped for a place on their sofa, but that was not on offer, he would have liked to be loved that night, no he could not complain but he realised this was a one night only solution to his next problem which was, actually, homelessness. In a conversation on the phone with his sister, Mary, he detected a cold draft, just what had the police said to her? Certainly his brother, his brother's wife and his sister made no attempt to quiz him about what had happened, they seemed to think they knew everything there was to know. Douglas got the feeling that their involvement was going to be light. His sister said to Douglas,

"I am sorry Douglas, but I have not got room for you here. You will have to find somewhere else."

Three brothers, and two sisters, could, or maybe would, not provide a roof for Douglas.

Douglas asked for a morning call from the hotel reception and fell into the sleep of the exhausted.

He slept until the bedside phone clanged into life. He showered and got ready then he climbed into his car and drove to the venue for his show. He was in good time, and now that he had his phone, and it was fully charged he made some phone calls. His sister Margaret had engaged the help of Douglas's other brother Luke, and he had actually managed to get a message to one of the venues who had been expecting Douglas, whist Douglas had been in custody. The excuse of food poisoning, and a hospital admission were the lies used to dampen the anger of let down employers, and so Douglas continued those lies with his apologies, as he grovelled his way through awkward conversations of possible alternative dates for free performances to make up.

Then it was where am I to sleep tonight? In the car? Douglas called several friends who all had good excuses not to take him in. Then he was out of time. The show had to go on and it did. It went well and Douglas felt that whatever else may have happened he had his work. He was good at it and it brought joy to people. Douglas and arrived with his cheery smile, and his Joppy fingers, and an hour or more disappeared so happily.

After the show he realised he was quite near to the house of one of his closest friends. Who, without blinking, on hearing Douglas's tale, showed him into the house and up to a lovely room, with a view of the garden and a shower beside.

"Make yourself comfortable here for as long as you need. I will be back about six we will have dinner then."

Douglas knew that there was still love in the world he felt safe.

The hours spent in the police cell had given Douglas time to fantasise murder scenarios. The death of Raymond, at Douglas's hand, had been an epic, cinema graphic, technicolor feature, with panoramic screen and full dobly surround sound, and a dozen different scripts. In one; a huge argument followed by a fist fight, Douglas had a cut eye, but one huge punch had knocked Raymond off his feet and as he fell his head hit a sharp corner and he was finished. Another involved a police car chase, which Douglas only watched as a bystander, but as Raymond's colleagues realised that Raymond was a corrupt, lying thief. Raymond had fled to his Yellow TR7 and after many miles had crashed through a barrier of road works, to make a spectacular crash from the end of an unfinished road bridge. The most brutal Douglas held an ordinary kitchen carving knife which plunged into Raymond's chest, and in one really mad episode into Arwyn's too. Here in this beautiful room, now free-ish Douglas no longer replayed these nightmares, he felt calm, he felt safe.

The room was light with windows across the complete wall facing the garden. Pastel blues on the walls contrasted by a brightly coloured duvet cover with jagged, irregular patterns across it. It was big, open and fresh smelling, the opposite of the police cell, and in many ways better than the house to which he knew he would never return. He started to make himself at home, he wondered how long 'as long as you like' would be, the court hearing of the case would be in six weeks. Douglas telephoned the solicitor and explained that he could not stay with his sister, the solicitor's secretary said that they would send a letter to the court telling them what Douglas had said. A few days later a letter arrived telling Douglas that this arrangement was acceptable. Another few days later a letter with an appointment with somebody at the local probation office arrived.

Douglas had a computer that he used in his show; it had been in a bag in the car so it had not been seized by the police. So Douglas got his things in some sort of order. He did ask the solicitor to ask the police when his seized computers would be returned, it took about a week, and Douglas had to travel to a police station to get them. They were all wrapped up in plastic with stickers on which was written 'evidence'. Douglas also asked the solicitor if he could pay for a couple of hours, outside the 'legal aid' to make sure that Douglas's side of the story was fully in the solicitors mind before the court hearing. Douglas was, by now, uncertain of what he had agreed to in the police station and he was beginning to think that he should have other options than the ones offered and the one accepted. Douglas said.

"I could play you a tune on my piano that I had learned today, but until I have performed it to an audience, a few times, I do not really know it. I can see that this applies to solicitors in court they do not really know the story, and so the story reflects only a shade of the reality. Try as he might Douglas could not make that happen.

So for the next few weeks he was living far away from most of the places he had to do his shows and so there were many extra hours of driving and much extra cost involved. Douglas just got on and did what he had to do although, at times, his emotions got the better of him, and tears filled his eyes and dribbled down his face as he sobbed.

Douglas had to cancel a show to meet with the Probation Officer. Although not the same as the police station, it was the same as the police station. That element of reminding criminals just who they are is quite breathable in police stations, courts, and in this rundown facility. Douglas wondered if such facilities in other European countries were as drab. Or was this décor here deliberately to depress people?

Douglas, always dressed smartly, he had made an extra effort today and felt quite out of place as he watched other poor souls in the waiting room. Should he start a conversation? How would he? 'So what are you doing here?' Maybe not. 'I am here because the woman I loved went off with a policeman and I had a break down…' Maybe not. May be that is what the other's, all younger than he were thinking, in their hoodies and trainers. Then there was the Caribbean girl, she was different from the others, with dreadlocks in her hair, but thin, so thin, and she looked as though she needed several good meals. What did all these under thirties, mostly under twenties, make of Douglas in his suit, white shirt, tie and shining shoes. What did they think of this old man, and why would he be here? Then Douglas realised that such thoughts were complete vanity for, probably, like him, they were all worried out of their minds about what was going to happen next in their own lives, why would they have even a second to waste worrying about him when surely they had enough to worry about. Douglas glanced about and captured a little memory photograph of this seen, such young faces whom you could never think would be messed up in the law, but they must be, for no one would come here, unless coerced, unless it was for their employment. Douglas watched as each person in turn was greeted, usually by, what he assumed was their probation officer, their forename and a pleasantry about the weather, or some other innocuous thing. Then they were led away, never to be seen again.

Douglas had arrived early, afraid of being late. He had time to consider this although he had been through some pretty scary things in his life, and he had survived, he had always been scared of breaking the law, he had always been scared that he would be made homeless. For the most part he had been very brave in life, he had taken some risks, and sometimes he had won. Now as he waited he realised he was more scared than he had ever been before, and he was unsure if he could ever be this scared again. He knew that if the Magistrate decided to send him to prison, that is where he would have to go, and his idea of prison was something worse than anything he could contemplate as he sat. Of course your experience of the world may well be broader than Douglas's, but this is not a story about your experiences.

Then the probation officer called Douglas's name, and Douglas thought why did he call out my full name? Why did he call it out so loudly? Suppose someone recognised me? Then he thought who in the world will recognise me here?

The probation officer sported a 'fashionable' greying beard, fashionable to a point, in that his grooming could have been more thorough, his clothes could have been more kempt, and next to Douglas he looked scruffy. Douglas realised, immediately, that this made the probation officer uneasy and so Douglas thought 'this has not got off to the greatest of starts'. Douglas's view was confirmed by the aggression in the questions, which were more probing than those of the policeman, and the complete lack of empathy, which culminated in a statement.

"Well that is all very well, but if you put a camera in a woman's bedroom what is anyone to think? You say there was nothing sexual in your motivation, but no one will ever really know. Of course I have heard that you say that you did not put the camera in the bedroom but she says you did, I know who I would prefer to believe. I know you have accepted the lesser of two charges, and that speaks volumes to me. I think at best you are looking at community service for about one hundred and eighty hours, but frankly you could easily find yourself in prison for several years. That's where I would send you."

This stunned Douglas, even though he knew it was true. The solicitor had said that with any luck it would be a suspended sentence. Douglas realised that this is probably all part of the system to grind offenders into submission and make them feel as bad as possible. Douglas thought 'well thank goodness you are not the Magistrate.' Then he wondered had he spoken this out loud. Probably not for the probation officer just kept spewing his endless rhetoric. 'Oh God' thought Douglas, 'what was that he said?'

Douglas left the Probation Office and wandered, zombie like, along the pavement. He crossed the traffic lights and was nearly hit by a car. He wished he had been, for dead, or alive, the pain could not have been as excruciating. He walked through the shopping 'pedestrian only' cobble street. He felt sweaty and cold and hot, his mouth was dry and he wanted a drink. There were Costa Coffee and Nero; there was a normal high street café, and a Methodist Church, with a board advertising coffee and cake. Douglas fell through the doors and found that he had need of the toilet. His eyes were full of tears and his mind was full of emotion and he did not want people to see the tears, and then he managed to make out the sign, and so was able to find a little bit of privacy. He did what he could to straighten himself up; he dried his eyes, rinsed out his mouth and combed his black hair. He had not gone grey, as many men of his age, and he still had a full head of it, but it was cut short these days. He pulled himself together and then entered the Church Café. His coffee was weak and lifeless; he wondered what Italians or Austrian's would make of this anaemic liquid, he remembered what Arwyn had said, could it really have been nearly forty years before? When they drank that superb coffee, in that pretty Paris Boulevard. Or what would sophisticates from the neighbouring countries in the rest of Europe make of a café in an ancient run down church. He managed to imbibe the liquid and was about to depart when a man dressed in a cassock sat down at his table. The cleric was a nice person, with a kindly disposition, and Douglas wanted to tell him all that had gone on and ask for absolution, but why absolution? Was Douglas the guilty one or was it Arwyn? Mix yourself with enough policemen and probation officers and you might not be able to give an answer either. Instead he asked the Minister how long he had been in charge of the parish, and told him how wonderful this café was. He shared the information that he was the son of a Methodist Minister, but he did not say that it was a long time since the church had filled him with a desire to attend. Then Douglas realised that he was attending church now. What would his old Dad, named after John Wesley, make of all this? The Minister knew, of course, that it had been many Sundays since Douglas had been inside a church.

Then Douglas left, and tears flooded his eyes once more, and the emotion overwhelmed him. He climbed the concrete stairs of the multi-story car park, to return to his car. On one landing he turned to look through the gap where, presumably a window could have been fitted. The scene was the back garden of a pub. In the pub stood a fine Tulip tree, Douglas liked Tulip trees. He found his car and sat in it, he felt that the world had come to an end.

CHAPTER 18
The Reality

T hings have a cycle. A couple meet and there is a spark of sexual excitement, consummation, gratification and satisfaction. Hang on, and around, for a while to see if there is more. Every salesman knows that it is easier to keep a customer than to find a new one.

Sometimes these early moments of a relationship are peppered by the word 'love', but that is not what it is. In these early stages it is all chemical reaction and relief that at last someone finds the other non-repugnant enough to allow physical joining of bodies, and the great dam of 'hormonic' sap is released. For deep down most people know that not everyone takes their fancy, and that it is not so easy to find that double coincidence of wants. Just like barter if you can find nobody who wants your sack of potato's for the trousers you need no deal will be done.

One of the reasons people are glued by romantic fiction, and by the romance in Hollywood movies, is that love is hard to find, harder to find than sex, but it is not easy to find sex either. It would be easy to give examples of various Casanovas and Nymphomaniacs but that would miss the point for great swathes of population.

The news media reflects the heavenly, and hellish acts, of society mostly avoiding the humdrum of every day life, or most persons.

After a while the sex caves into everyday life, and life has to be lived, so all the stuff people have to do has to be done. Lucky couples may then fall in love, real love, the love that accepts that the dishes must be washed, and the mortgage must be paid. It is a long haul operation and sex is not the top of the agenda, it takes on a different role, which, when healthy, and good, and equal to each partner, glues a couple together and the sex becomes an expression of the love. People remember the time they experienced their greatest orgasm, and although they would like to have that one again, and again, they accept what was, and enjoy what they now have.

Everyone is different, and everyone is the same. One thing is for sure people do things because they have a desire to do so. Sometimes that desire is a free choice, sometimes it is the result of the circumstances and events that engulf a person, or it is the pressures exerted by other people that spur them on.

Arwyn was distressed by the arrest of Douglas. Sure she knew that it was what Raymond wanted, but she was unsure if that is actually what should have happened, after all, the claim that the camera was installed in the bedroom was not truthful, but she could not go back on that now. She knew that Douglas had been the person who had done more for her than any other. She had been happy that he took on responsibility for her parents and that he had helped her girl and boys. She knew that she had upset Douglas in the most terrible of ways, and she knew that sex had the better of her, and that Raymond gave her something she wanted in this respect, but he did not respect her.

She had listened to Raymond so much that his words melted into her words, and his ideas seemed to become hers, she was confused, and sad, and happy. She wanted Douglas out of the way so she could pursue her relationship with Raymond, but she also thought things had gone a bit too far. The last thing on earth Douglas was, was a voyeur. However, she knew that, that train had left the station and now she had to make sure that no one could accuse her of perjury, for that would be all the worse for her.

Another thought glanced through her mind too. She knew that if anything did go wrong with all this Raymond would not be anywhere close to catch her fall, and she also knew that he would not fall. She found herself in a vortex, she had just ruined the life the kindest man she had ever known, and exchanged him for a man she hardly knew, and about whom she was just beginning to have second thoughts. Now for the sake of saving herself, and her face, she had to emphasise to all friends, colleagues and family that Douglas was the guilty party, Douglas was the horror, she was the innocent, she was the victim, and that Raymond was her knight in shining armour, who had rescued her in stylish fashion.

She dare not give out any other idea for if she did she knew that she too could be arrested. So fear and sex led Arwyn onward down a darkened corridor to where, she did not really know. Raymond told her it would be a life of bliss, where Douglas would never trouble her again, and Raymond and Arwyn would lay on a bed of thorn less roses.

Arwyn pursued her closest allies for coffee, whenever she could, during the next weeks. She called family members and re-enforced the horror of what she had been through, reciting the claims of her 'Victim Statement', so carefully schooled by Raymond, until she felt that all her nearest, and dearest, were on board. Her precarious rowing boat heading somewhere up the Zambezi of Raymond's scheme.

It was Raymond's intention to keep with Arwyn, evict her parents, sons and daughter, from the house in which she lived and, over time, take over the ownership of the property, rid himself of the property which was mortgaged to him and secure his retirement. He realised it was not going to be easy, but he was prepared to play the long game. He was fully aware that Douglas's position would never allow a return to the house he owned with Arwyn. So that was a part of the journey over. He knew also that

Arwyn had lied in her statements, to the police, and that he had schooled her in what to say to the police. He had shown her how to emphasise her complaints about Douglas, and he knew too, that he could use that against her for the rest of Arwyn's life.

Raymond was happy to have sex with Arwyn, and happy with the possibility of taking her home from her. He would be happy if she stayed and not unhappy if she went, for there were plenty of women in their fifties, who would scrub up well, and be happy to move into the house of a real man who owned his own home.

Raymond could see no fault in the situation he was setting up for himself. Love, he had never received it, and he could, therefore, never give it, but he had the gift for making people think he could. Raymond's strongest suit was manipulation; years of meeting police targets had made him a master of it.

Douglas felt alone and isolated he made a list of family, friends and acquaintances. He contacted each in turn. He wanted to grab on to some reality. He wanted to confirm that he was not an awful criminal and that he had led a good and decent life before all these terrible, recent, events. The thing he found the hardest to understand was that he had done such good for Arwyn, he had never thrust the good upon her, anything he had done for her was with her consent. He had never forced her into anything. He had understood her and backed off whenever he felt she needed time and space for herself. None of what had recently happened had any precedent in his own history, or in the stories he was familiar with, from experience or literature, never had any of his family or friends treated anyone like he had been treated, nor had any of them ever been treated like he had been.

All his friends and family supported him and reminded him of the good life he had lived but Douglas still had doubts.

Douglas had to somehow keep a grip on everything for he needed money so he had to get along with is work despite of the hollow inside him. This is where professionalism has it's chance to shine, for not one member of any audience he saw, during this time, knew anything of what had happened.

He could not compose now, his heart was shattered, and without the heart you cannot create music, even if it is 'only' Jazz.

Despite Douglas's solicitor's constant moaning about how little money was available from legal aid, he did not respond to Douglas's request for a couple of hours work, paid for by Douglas, to ensure that the solicitor really understood what had gone on. For the weeks that had passed between Douglas's arrest, the treats from the police, and their offer of accepting guilt for this crime or we will charge you with something worse, and the up, and coming, court case had given time for Douglas to think. The more he thought, the more wrong he found the situation to be. Douglas knew that he had had a mental breakdown, and he knew that some things he had done were considered to be wrong, although he had not realised that when he had done them. He just thought that he was trying to get his woman back, to save her from the mistake he thought she was making. The solicitor had told him

"If a woman says the relationship is finished you may respond—oh come on darling—anything more is then harassment."

The solicitor told him that putting a flower in her car, although technically Douglas's car was tantamount to stalking. The solicitor told him that messing with other people's mobile phones was not allowed, and Douglas asked him.

"If it were your wife? Are you going to tell me that you would not look at her phone? Is there a man on the planet who would not look at his partners phone, if he thought he were the cuckold?"

Douglas arrived at the St George's Road Magistrates Court in good time. It was a fine Cheltenham morning. There was no racing of horses today, so the traffic was easier than it might have been. He found a free place to park his car, but there was a shield that said the parking was free until 16:00 each weekday. As the case was scheduled for 11:00 he did not think that was a problem. The horror did cross his mind that he could be sent to prison what would happen to the car then? He could not work it out, for fear gripped the inside of his stomach at the thought, for that thought was actually too, too, too much to bear.

The surroundings of the court were dismal, litter everywhere, chipped paint and dowdy. Beyond the gate he could see one of those vans which are used for transporting people to prison, and again he was filled with horror.

He was not the only person appearing in court that day, of course, and he had a lot of time on his hands. He overheard conversations between various persons, and really found it hard to understand why such trivial matters had come all the way to court. Of course he also realised he was hearing only one side of a story.

The reception desk was 'woman-manned' by a particularly unpleasant, and harsh person, whom Douglas thought must have him down for guilty even before the court had tried the case.

Of course he was guilty, he had made that plea, but he knew he was guilty of only one thing…total love for Arwyn. A love that now lay in a shattered pile. He had also had time to think through all that had happened, but the solicitor was not available to help him. For now

Douglas wanted to say that the camera was not in the room but outside, but who would believe that now. The Probation officer had not.

Douglas heard his name being shouted from the reception desk, he did not want everyone to know his name, but he somehow realised that privacy was not of great concern to the receptionist. She said.

"Your solicitor called he is going to be late, the Magistrate is not happy about this."

Douglas waited and waited. Wandering around the dingy inside space and then to the dingy outside space. Wishing that he had refused to accept the offer of a lesser crime, and wishing that he had protested his innocence and argued his case.

All those weeks before he had been a broken man, who would have done anything to get released from the incarceration. Now he was a terrified man contemplating the consequences of his acceptance of the terms foisted upon him in his darkest hour.

He wondered if changing his mind might lead him further into these deep waters. That policeman had threatened the worse crime and Douglas felt of all the things he had heard from all the people involved this was the one truth he could rely on. For one thing he had learned was that nobody told him the truth about what would happen next, and no one told him what the whole story would be when the police arrested him.

You can watch the cop shows and see a prisoner in a bare cell but until it is you, you will never understand the horror, the terror and the awfulness of it all. Douglas was still to learn that the consequences of all of this would not leave him, even after his death. For these things, not all the wonderful things he had done, would be the things that would get attention. Why? It is because people live in fear, and they collect vast catalogues of things that might hurt them. The hunter-gatherers had to know what plants would make them sick, and which snakes could bite them to their death. Evolution now requires human kind to watch the television news and catalogue all the bad things presented, even if the chance of it happening to you are a zillion to one. The message avoid terrors at all costs, and of course they do not want anyone else to have to suffer in the same way. (Well that is what they always say) They try to justify, and try to cover up, that which is simply revenge.

Douglas was sitting on an uncomfortable, plastic chair that had been designed to stack with other chairs. He thought 'I wonder how the chair would have been designed if only the designer had considered a person sitting on it, rather than to design a chair so that it could be hidden away'.

Douglas waited and waited and then it seemed there was some sort of lunch break, he could not think of eating. Timidly he approached the, unapproachable, receptionist, and timidly asked for any news of his solicitor. He was told that his case had been shifted, much to the annoyance of the Magistrate, to the afternoon.

Then he asked. "What if the solicitor fails to arrive?"

She said "Well you will be all alone in there!"

Douglas felt the tide of the black sea he had been keeping at bay for weeks now lapping at his feet. His chest was tight; there was perspiration upon his forehead. He went into the smelly, unkempt toilets. He used the lavatory and then washed his face in running cold water that drained into the dirty sink. The smell was not good, like most toilets in this awful country, he thought to himself. Then he thought I hope I did not say that out loud for I am sure that would give me an even more hostile sentence. He dried his face with a tissue he had bought with him, and combed his hair. For the first time he saw a couple of grey hairs amongst the black. He saw the Crows Feet around his eyes, more like Alligator feet he thought, as he looked into the mirror. For a moment he thought he saw the reflection that was him, but then he saw a good man, broken by the woman he had loved, and her lover. He saw that broken man further broken by a blunt instrument legal system. He would have rather fallen into quicksand.

When the solicitor, finally, arrived there was just thirty minutes before the rescheduled hearing. The solicitor and Douglas went into a private room, but Douglas wondered if it was bugged by some microphone, then he had second thoughts how would they afford that when they cannot even give the filthy place a lick of paint?

The solicitor was intent on ploughing through the probation officer's report. Douglas said.

"I would really rather try and make you understand that this story is not as simple as everyone tries to make out. I accept that I have agreed to plead guilty rather than accept a heavier charge, but I do not want to end up in prison."

The solicitor carried blindly on saying. "With any luck they will give you a suspended sentence and you will walk away from this today."

What Douglas heard from the probation report was 'he would be able to cope with a custodial sentence'. These words hit him like an iceberg and the horror made him say loudly.

"Stop and listen to me, we have ten minutes before we are in court. All this is completely wrong."

Douglas précised what he wanted to say and saw the light of recognition on the solicitor's face, but he knew it was too late, the solicitor could not internalise this information quickly enough to make it come out, in a coherent way, before the Magistrate, it would take the solicitor days to work all that through his dendrites. So they left the private room and as they did so the court probation officer approached Douglas.

"I have read the notes on this case and I know what my recommendation will be. I will recommend a severe sentence, and I will recommend that you are never again allowed anywhere near that poor woman again, just so you know, I know Raymond, and I know everything."

Douglas did not understand, how any such conversation could be allowed, this was supposed to be British justice in a court of law for Her Majesty the Queen, law provided by the Mother of Parliaments. He could see that the probation officer was full of his own self-importance. It lowered the temperature even more than the previous iceberg. Douglas realised that eighty percent of this story was beneath the sea and that everyone involved would only be looking at one side of this iceberg, and he realised that his name had just changed to 'Douglas Titanic'. He was led into a glass box, he was grateful for the fact that no handcuffs were involved this time, but the door was locked and he sat alone understanding fishes better.

He sat and listened to his life story, as served up by the prosecution, as in the previous court it was a fantasy. He said to himself 'well may be that is not so bad who will know that is me from that fabrication?'

Douglas looked around the court there were three Magistrates set up higher than everyone else, a huge coat of arms on the wall behind them. There were his solicitor and the prosecuting solicitor, the probation officer, The Clerk of he Court and two other people sitting to Douglas's right and they were taking notes of the proceedings. Douglas wondered who they were but there was no one he could ask.

The prosecutor, having belittled all of Douglas's previous half century continued to drone on about the alleged misdemeanours, and then went on to say, although no violence took place, and no threats were made, Arwyn had been terrified of Douglas. Douglas found that impossible and wanted to call out. Of course he knew that Raymond had told her to say that, but how could she possibly have repeated it. Terrified of me? Douglas asked himself in rhetorical fashion.

It was one of those times when everything took forever, and yet it was all over in seconds. The Magistrates left the court and Douglas went over what his solicitor had said to them. Douglas thought 'well considering he had not long cottoned on that there was far more to this story than had been expressed so far'. Douglas could hear his solicitor and the prosecuting solicitor sharing anecdotes and stories about bicycling, and a dinner they had both attended a week before. Douglas knew from this that they were old pals and this was their job, it was nothing to do with who won or lost, it was nothing to do with guilt and innocence, this is how they earned the money that they needed to pay their bills, and their performance mattered not one jot, for tomorrow it would be another stupid boso in the dock, and they would only need to bend their script a little to fit, and then it would be home time. Although this was only legal aid work there were other clients who could really afford the services of a good solicitor. Getting a drug dealer of the hook that was always a well paying job, enough to share between the two solicitors, 'you go easy, I'll go hard'. Justice will never be done.

The defendant will be done though, and all in the court stood to welcome back the three grey, stern, Magistrates who had deliberated for five minutes and then had a cup of coffee and a slice of cake. Everyone but Douglas sat down. The Magistrate in the centre started ripping into Douglas with words, and in away one might have thought a naughty teenager would experience. May be this was what it felt like to be dressed down by an army sergeant because the soldier's boots had not been polished as well as it was possible to polish them. Whatever, Douglas was trembling. The Magistrate told Douglas that he would have to do two hundred and twenty five hours of community service and that he must have no contact with Arwyn, nor go to her house for two complete years. If he did so Douglas would be arrested and would serve a minimum of six years in prison, and be liable to a fine of five thousand pounds. Further Douglas was required to pay an amount for the victim surcharge and other costs, a sum not much short of one hundred and fifty pounds. It would be possible for a representative to go to the house to collect the remainder of Douglas's possessions.

It is important to understand, at this point, that in the court room no reference was made to the address at which Douglas would reside, shouls he not be imprisoned, once he left the court, only three people knew that, Douglas, his solicitor and after the court proceedings the probation officer. Remember that for it will arise as an issue a few pages from now.

Douglas thought that the sentence was harsh, far more than the first probation officer had intimated and far, far, more than his solicitor had suggested. Douglas was thankful that he was not now being escorted to the prison van behind the courthouse. Strange how the withdrawal of a horrid threat brings a kind of joy and relief, making one feel grateful to all those who have just hurt you.

Douglas wondered what Arwyn would think, would she be happy, would she think the sentence too tough or too lenient, any way Raymond would put her straight on that. Then he started to realise that he was now a convicted criminal, he was not sure what that would mean but he was about to find out.

He was led back into the room he had been in with his solicitor before the court appearance. The short, bespectacled solicitor, with his monk like hair and shabby tweed jacket said.

"Well it could have been worse. You could appeal against the sentence, but as you pleaded guilty the chances are that they would give you an even heftier one for wasting their time. Now to do your sentence and move on. Put all this behind you."

Then the probation officer came in with forms to fill, he asked for Douglas's address, so this is the moment that the probation officer learned Douglas's address. He was a thin gangly man who converted an expression of one straining upon a toilet into the one expression he could manage. Douglas could not believe how this man spoke to him. Apart from the instructions he had to say.

"If I were the Magistrate you'd be on your way to the jail now."

Douglas thought that this was poor practice but had no idea how, in this situation, he could make a complaint. The door opened and the probation officer was called away Douglas caught a glimpse of the clock through the door and realised that it was just a few minutes to four o'clock and his car had to be moved before it got a parking ticket. He left the courtroom and ran out of the door down the steps and up the road to his car.

It was a good job that the car had to be moved for the feelings under his skull were similar to those in the stomach after food poisoning. Having to do something give a little respite from the flames he had just experienced. The people in the courtroom had no idea of the real story of this, the worst episode in Douglas's life.

Douglas had dealt with many things, over the years, and had managed to keep life together. Arwyn's betrayal was that mountain too far, and now he was a criminal.

If Douglas had known the next part of his story in this book there would have probably been an accident, fortunately he did not. He managed to enter the car, start the engine, look over his shoulder, indicate, check the mirrors and move off. He indicated to turn left and joined the flow of traffic on the main road. He drove and he drove trying to keep the clattering thoughts of all that had happened at bay. He did that successfully until he came to the place he was staying.

He climbed the stairs and opened the door of his room. He lay down on the bed and the faces of the awful Magistrate, Arwyn, Raymond the two Probation officers, his sister in law, and the solicitors, and the receptionist at the court, and the face of the driver of the prison van which could so easily have claimed Douglas that day. So filled with horror the thought that he was more or less free sent him into an unconscious sleep.

In this sleep he dreamed about all the good things he had done in his life, the places he had been, his friends and his family and his wonderful children. Like the Iban's of Borneo, and their ideas of the 'Dream Wanderer', he wandered up and down the ally ways, in and around the grand plazas, there were many. Glittering lights of Hong Kong Streets at night, high alpine mountains, and ocean voyages. When he woke he was in a dark narrow tunnel, which seemed to have no exit and he wanted only to get back into his dreams.

CHAPTER 19
A Flash of Raymond

A little while before Douglas's trial Raymond was extremely pleased, he could have been more pleased, but how harsh a sentence Douglas would get Raymond could not know, he knew that the knockon effect in Douglas's life would actually be the end of Douglas's life as Douglas had known it. Raymond wanted to make sure the damage was catastrophic and unrecoverable. So to make sure of that he, Raymond, had to really make sure that Douglas's life was ruined absolutely, and completely, so he pushed Arwyn along to the next part of his plot.

"Ok so this woman you know, who works for the paper, it is time to let her know. You need to speak with her and tell her about Douglas, and make sure they have a reporter at his trial to cover the case." Said Raymond.

Arwyn said. "I am not sure I can. I just do not know I can."

Raymond lifted her head by using three fingers under Arwyn's chin, he said. "Ok you call her and then I will talk to her." Raymond did and he laid the story on thick and he said, "you will have a front page out of this."

Arwyn said to Raymond. "What about this letter from Douglas's solicitor?"

Raymond said. "What about it? Douglas will be in court next week with any luck they will put him away."

Arwyn said. "With any luck, but it is not right is it? You know, and I know, where he had the camera put and you and I know I lied."

Raymond pulled her towards him. "Hey it's ok. It's your word against his, no one could ever find out. His solicitor, so what. No one is going to turf your folks out of here, but just to make sure I have written this letter to the Land Registry it says that half of the house belongs to your Dad, just get him to sign it."

Arwyn looked horrified. "That is not true the house belongs to Douglas and me, my Dad loaned money to me to buy my share in exchange they can live here for the rest of their lives."

Raymond said. "Is that written down anywhere?"

Arwyn looked astonished. "That they can live here until they die, no, but Douglas, or I, would never throw them out. My Dad and I made a contract over the money, we went to his solicitor and we both signed."

Raymond questioned. "Does Douglas know about that contract?"

Arwyn said. "Yes my Dad gave him a copy, I told him not to. Douglas said he would not leave the old house, where the ownership was clearly his, into a vague situation. Apparently the solicitor who did the conveyance had to have proof of the source of funds, so there is no money laundering. Douglas said the only way he would move to this house was if it were a fifty-fifty split between he and me."

Raymond said. "Well I do not see that that changes anything, get your Dad to sign this letter and I will send it off, sooner the better, you must be able to show that your father paid that money, if he paid the money he must own something of the house."

Raymond said. "Enough said then! Sex?"

Raymond always knew what he wanted; Arwyn was often not quiet sure. Of course there were some things to which she would never say no. Sex with Raymond was one of them.

The next letter from Douglas's solicitor contained a reminder of his demand that the house be sold and a notice which said that the car, Arwyn had been driving, was actually financed to Douglas, and that, although, he had asked the finance company, if Arwyn could keep the car, the finance company had refused to allow this. The car would be collected on Thursday morning. There was a request for the car to be made ready, and that any possessions that belonged to Arwyn should be removed from the vehicle.

This letter made Arwyn mad. How would she manage, there was no bus, no train, and taxis would cost a fortune. How would she move her parents about? The stress of the lies she had told about Douglas and the pressure put on her by Raymond overwhelmed her for a few minutes and something made her pick up the scouring pad, she had been using to wash up the dishes, and she went out to the car and deliberately placed the scouring pad on the bonnet of the car. Then pressing down as hard as she could, all the tension of the past weeks forced it's way into her palm and fingers and she rubbed hard, and fast, and furious until there were deep scratch marks in the shiny red paint work, right across the bonnet leaving the words, clearly visible. 'FUCK YOU'.

She opened the car and took out a few things, she lay the keys upon the driver's seat and shut the door without locking it. 'If it gets stolen in the night what do I care.' she said under her breath. It was Wednesday evening; she never saw the car again. Raymond did, that evening when he got back from work; he had to smile 'what a wind up.' He snorted; he went into the house but said nothing to Arwyn.

Douglas's agonies were getting deeper and darker. After the ordeal in the court was the ordeal of another Probation Office. Another dingy building, another dingy room with cobwebs, and pealing paint that had dried many years before, and was covered in bits of poster, blue tack, and even a bit of Christmas decoration way up in the far eastern corner, from some Christmas long before this place became a probation office, thought Douglas. A bare light bulb for a sun, and a dark ring from the days when smoking had been allowed in the building. It was stuffy, and the room was full, full of criminals? 'Yes.' Said Douglas to himself and you are one of them, much older than any of the others and 'Douglas.' He said to himself 'you are the only person here wearing a suit, you made that mistake last time, will you never learn!' Another voice, which was not Douglas's but it did come from somewhere within him 'Do you really think that wearing a suit to this, in this day and age, will count for anything? You are crazy.'

Douglas found himself in another, similarly decorated room, there was a desk between him and a flustered woman, who wore thick, black rimmed, spectacles an ill fitting summer dress and a cardigan. She was less then half of Douglas's age, but looked far more worn than that. When she spoke to Douglas he felt as if he were back in the school classroom. It seemed to him that she was a bit scared of Douglas. She seemed to be totally suspicious of him and each time he spoke to her he felt that he was not being believed. Douglas thought that this women must think that he was some sort of pervert, she had obviously read all that paper work from the court. Now it was her job to lash out the punishment. To his surprise she said.

"Well at least I have someone, at last, I can send to the charity shop. I have had nobody suitable for several weeks, but you are smart enough, I think." She had the arm of her spectacles hanging in the right corner of her mouth now.

She paused. "I hope that I am right. This is not an easy ride, you will present yourself each Sunday morning at the address I am writing on this card. Report to the manager and at the end of your shift ask her to sign the card in the appropriate space."

The woman then switched tack, Douglas had observed several Probation officers now, and had also experienced it with the police, and others, in the so-called 'Criminal Justice System'. It was a kind of mock friendliness, a 'joke-y' camaraderie, which was far from sincere, but gave the air of some sort of compassion, if you were foolish enough to let it. Then the woman said.

"You have served one hour of your sentence by being present at this meeting today. Please remember that failure to comply with our agreement today will lead to your further arrest, and further, and possibly, more severe consequences, I am sure you understand. You are allowed to take holidays from your punishment, should it be that there is a Sunday, or Sunday's, for which you are unable to attend. These are under the guidance of another officer, this is his number, and you must keep him informed."

So Douglas left the dismal premises and on the Sunday following he found that the Charity shop did not open until ten o'clock. So he had been there for two hours before the assistant manager turned up. He was set to work emptying dozens of black plastic sacks of donated clothes. For every bag he opened there were three more delivered. He discovered that most of the stuff was not sellable in the shop. Some could go to what would have been the 'Rag-a-bone-man' when Douglas had been a boy. The vast majority was destined for landfill. Items that were clean, not all items were. Douglas had a shock to find a, used, dry, sanitary towel attached to a pair of women's knickers; he determined to bring a pair of rubber gloves for future work sessions. Items of good quality, that were clean, and undamaged, had to be hung on a hanger and then on a rack, in the proper place for the size of the garment. If an item was 'Gift Aided' the item had to be recorded in a ledger and then on the computer, and then clearly marked with a special label, which was attached to the item with a kind of gun that shot a nylon tag through the weave and the hole which was especially punched into the cardboard label. Douglas was bemused by this, finicky, time wasting, exercise. Each, and every item, marked, thousands of bits of second hand clothing, treated with more care than the items in H&M's or Marks & Spencer's, all so the Government would not over pay the 'Gift Aid' payment.

Trips to the bins, along way down the road, broke up the time a little. Douglas felt sweaty and exhausted by the end of the day. Six hours with no breaks. He was thirsty and aching and then cross, for the two hours he had spent from eight until ten, were not counted on his card. This meant that there were going to be more weeks of this than he had calculated. Then the assistant manager said.

"I am sure if you have a word with the manager you will be able to do some extra shifts in the week and get this out of the way quicker. That is up to her of course, but I will tell her you have done a good day's work today."

Douglas had always worked for himself, and he had never experienced being patronised, in this sort of way before. He was not used to it, and thought he never wanted to be used to it.

There were other people working in the shop, Douglas wondered if any of them were working on a similar basis to himself, or were they all just good upstanding citizens working voluntarily?

*

One of Douglas's friends had been encouraging Douglas to move on in his life.

"Look this has happened and it was a terrible thing to go through. I know and you know that you have been badly treated, but what is done is done. So come on, get out there get yourself a date, take some nice woman out for a drink, and forget all this horrid stuff, move on, life is too short."

Many other platitudes were expressed. Douglas asked how he would meet a woman to take for a drink, after all who would come out with a criminal?

His friend said. "Well you would not want to use that in your opening line! You are only looking to go out with someone for a drink, and if it goes further than that you will find the words to tell the woman, and she can make up her mind if it is ok or not. Cross bridges when you come to them. You get on your computer and go to this web site."

Douglas was a professional man, who had made decisions all his adult life, and now here he was doing what other people suggested he do. Well life was crazy at this time.

Douglas was in no fit state to start thinking about dating women. He was far too damaged and fragile. His friend had never been close enough to real love to know what Douglas had been through. Neither was he sensitive enough to understand that looking for a new partner, even if it were only for a drink, was the worst possible course for Douglas at this time.

So that evening, when all had been done that had to be done, Douglas switched on his machine and it hummed and the screen flashed, and Apple welcomed him, and asked for his password.

He glanced at the pictures before him. Yes there were some pretty woman there, but in all his life, you have read it before, Douglas had only been attracted by a small number of women. The three he had become really involved with had all let him down, in fearsome ways, and Arwyn had nearly killed him. Did he really want to go on a date with any of these women? How did Douglas know if they would be nice, or nasty, he had just come to the conclusion that he did not want to take chance when, as he clicked the mouse and looked at the screen there was Arwyn!

The best photograph he had ever taken of her, the only photograph of her that she had actually liked. There she was advertising herself 'for sale'. Douglas read the profile and the pitch.

"I am here for fun times and a serious relationship."

Douglas felt like a wrought iron railing, he wanted someone to cut him down, as in the war, to melt him down to make bombs or bullets. He thought he had been through a lot in these past months, but this, how much more was there? There could not be more, could there? Douglas clicked to the home page and changed the preferences, instead of looking for the woman of his dreams in asked to see the man of his dreams, and changed the filters until Raymond was staring from the screen right up Douglas's nose. Douglas read.

"Sorry ladies, it has been great fun dating you but I have found a partner who suits me so I am no longer on the market."

The missal was dated, and Douglas's internal calculator quickly computed that that was a short while after the thump on his chest, in bed, from Arwyn, that bitter night. All that was subsequent, resonated with this new date data. Zero's and One's were all that were needed to compute anything. Douglas cuckold extraordinaire!

"Step up and collect your medal." Said, Her Majesty the Queen, in Douglas's delirium.

Douglas was at a point where he thought he knew how a murderer might feel. He had always felt that he could never kill another human but 'may be, how far must one be pushed before one could?' He asked himself. Who would he kill Arwyn of Raymond?

Douglas woke next morning with a headache, this was very unusual. Had he really seen that, on his computer, the night before, or was it just a ghastly, ghoulish, nightmare? As the computer wiped the sleep from it's eyes Douglas saw a news alert flash on the screen.

He clicked and the screen was full of the front page of a newspaper and the picture, full centre and covering most of the space was of Douglas. Douglas stopped breathing for a moment. It was a picture of him leaving the Court after the trial, he was in amongst a group of people, it almost looked as if he were leading a charge! He had remembered not to wear a suit to the court, he was wearing light grey trousers, and a red and black Cheltenham Tigers training top; as the picture had other people's faces in it the picture editor, of the paper, had put a lighter circle around Douglas's head, and had blurred the other faces. It looked as though Douglas was running away. Douglas remembered his car on the yellow line; and then read the words of the journalist, who was obviously lying in wait for him outside the court. The article suggested that 'Evil Douglas' was running away from the courthouse in shame. The article exaggerated all that had gone on in the court, and then some.

The article included much information, which was not a part of the court proceedings. Much was untrue. It said that he had been a student at Cheltenham College, he had not. It said he was a member of the Cheltenham Tigers, he was not, he had never played rugby in his life, one of his friends had given him the shirt. It said that he had never been married, he had. It said that he had not children, he had. The article got one bit exactly right; it revealed the area in which Douglas intended to reside, after the trial, it was was clearly printed Charlton Kings. This only three people knew, Douglas, Douglas's 'Oh there is not much money in legal aid work solicitor' and the court probation officer.

As the paper had not contacted Douglas. The article gave details of Douglas's work, unfortunately this was correctly reported. There were details of Arwyn's life. Douglas thought she will not like that. There was nothing about Raymond, nothing about Douglas's generosity to Arwyn and her family. The article also said that Douglas lived in the house thanks to the generosity of Arwyn and her parents as they had taken him when Arwyn had found him busking, on a winter street, after Douglas had been made homeless!

Douglas's jaw had dropped as he read, and re-read what had been written. Douglas was a private man, he got on with his work and did it to the best of his ability, he loved to do his work because he knew he was able to make many people happy. As he read further he realised that apart from everything else he was on the cusp of loosing his profession.

He thought that what Arwyn and Raymond had done up until the newspaper story was the most reprehensible thing he had encountered. Now he read and re-read again. There were things written that only Arwyn knew, so what was reprehensible before was not any more, for this was lower that he thought anybody could stoop, unless that were a character from some awful movie.

Douglas knew that he would have a tough time surviving this. Would people recognise him in the street? Would that be the end of his career? What would he do to earn a living? Who employs a criminal? However, before all those things branded his brain he had thought about what his children, his family and his friends would think.

There was no hiding, this it was available for the whole world to see. Douglas did not much care about the personal aspect of this but for Arwyn, and more probably Raymond, to seek to destroy Douglas's only means of earning a living, that Douglas could not adjust to. He then noticed a bit of sticky tape, on the edge of his computer, and his heart was full of horror, once more, as his brain tripped him into the memory of the police seizing his computers and going through them, as if he were some sort of pervert. He was not, he never had been. He had loved three women in his life and given all he could to them, more to Arwyn that anyone. How could she have been capable of hurting Douglas so comprehensively? Douglas had no answer.

In the meantime Raymond was feeling very smug, He had harmed many people in his life, there were a good number for fine people in prison because of his lies, but to have destroyed Douglas so completely was like hitting six sixes in a test cricket match. Raymond was so pumped the newspaper had written, more or less exactly what he had told them.

Arwyn was not very happy that the newspaper had mentioned her quite so much. She was very unhappy that so many details had been revealed. Raymond told her that it was just a part of the price of making sure that Douglas would never bother them again.

Raymond then turned his thoughts to ridding Arwyn's house of her parents, daugter, and sons. For Arwyn's house was a house somewhat bigger and better than his own. He knew that he would have to act gently for he wanted no one to suspect he had a plan. This plan had recently acquired another dimension for he had recently started to think that Arwyn was not so much the woman of his dreams, in fact he realised that he was growing increasingly tired of her depressions, and her dissatisfactions. He was niggled by her criticisms. He had actually changed his dating site profile, and put himself back on the market and had had sex with a few women, behind Arwyn's back, just recently. Raymond realised that he had to be careful for the opportunity to take over the ownership of Arwyn's house, and to rid himself of his own mortgage, was hardly an opportunity that would repeat itself. Until recently his plan had included keeping Arwyn on as his sex partner, but all in all, he thought that a life time of her moans and dissatisfaction would be more than he wanted to bare. He wondered now how Douglas had managed to put up with it.

As for Arwyn she was in a state of confusion. She had not enjoyed the newspaper featuring her, and her life, front and centre. She had noticed that Raymond did nothing to ease the burden of her parents and showed but little sympathy for her trails and struggles with her daughter and sons. She was also getting a little bored with the way Raymond demanded sex, it felt a bit like a hammer beating her on the side of the head, not too hard but there was an annoying regularity and it was always the same way. What Arwyn wanted was a bit more lust and a lot more excitement. She had not looked on the dating site since Raymond had jumped out of the screen at her, but she had thought about looking. As for Douglas well she was actually still worried for she knew that the house, in which she lived, was owned fifty percent by her and fifty percent by Douglas. She knew that that is what she had agreed. Raymond saying that a letter to the land registry would change all that was not convincing. Now she had a letter saying that Douglas would be taking her to court to enforce his rights in the property. 'What if he succeeds and I have nowhere to live?' she asked herself. Raymond tried to reassure her but she was not convinced. In fact something in his fervour disturbed her and she felt a whisper of discomfort, she tried to dismiss it but could not dislodge the thought.

Douglas did have many problems now. Many engagements he had had lined up had been cancelled; none of those who cancelled cared a jot when he tried to explain the situation. Some of those to whom he tried to explain had known him for many years, and all those years now were as nothing. In desperation Douglas said to one.

"What happened, happened, it is over and I have been punished, most severely, you have no right to punish me further." That made no difference whatsoever.

Short of money Douglas asked for some assistance from the 'Welfare State' he soon realized that the words 'Welfare State' may have some significance to some people but there was not help for him from it. He had seen stories about folk who benefit by thousands of pounds each year from Government hand outs but then he had read a pages of lies about himself in newspapers recently, so now he found that the Welfare State was just another lie. They told him to try his local council for housing benefit but their response was.

"You own a house, therefore, we have nothing to give you."

Douglas said. "I do own half of a house, but circumstances mean that I have no opportunity to live in it right now. It will be sold, in the not too distant future. In the meantime could you possibly help me with my rented room? I will repay you when the property is sold."

The 'nice' lady who worked in the council offices replied. "No."

The story in the newspaper of Douglas's court appearance had many effects on Douglas's life. Having seen the story, the manager of the Charity Shop, were Douglas had worked a couple of Sundays, had called Douglas's Probation Officer and told him that she did not want Douglas to return. She told him that Douglas was an excellent worker; indeed, he had achieved more in the hours he had put in than any other person who had worked for her. Never had she had such a hard worker.

So the following Sunday Douglas reported to the Probation Office. There he met a gang of younger men who were being organised by two Probation Officers. One of them seemed to be an ex-sergeant major, who had not realised that he had retired. He barked orders this way and that, and made everyone in earshot feel extremely uncomfortable. By contrast the Probation Officer, to whom Douglas was attached, was a mild mannered man in his thirties. He was tall and somewhat overweight. Unlike his colleague his dress was lazy and his hair needed a comb. Some of the 'criminals' had been here for many weeks and knew the drill; a couple of others were, like Douglas, totally new to all of this. Douglas did not know if the other new men felt as uncomfortable as he. Douglas just wanted the ground to open up and swallow him. Douglas stood still and did not speak unless he had to. His stomach was in a knot, his head was pounding and his hatred of Raymond and Arwyn was as a red-hot poker burning in the centre of Douglas's brain.

The Probation Officer gave out brand new sets of boots and gloves, to nearly everyone of the men. Later Douglas saw a couple of them carefully change the new boots for older muddy pairs, which they had bought with them. Douglas realised that a new pair of boots, on Ebay, may well fetch a few pounds and a new pair of boots, every couple of weeks, from the Probation Service would be an easy thing to obtain, as no record was kept of who had been given what. Then there was a form to sign saying that Douglas was not afraid of meeting foxes or other wild animals. That he would not be distressed if he came upon faeces in some undergrowth in which he may have to work. There were lists of equipment and questions about could he work, and what he could do. There was a white mini bus. Piled in it's rear were various gardening tools, and bits of mud, and turf, and bits wood, bits of bark and other flotsam and jetsam. There was a tea urn and a bunch of plastic cups, and a puddle of milk, which should have been mopped up, and a dusting of sugar and biscuit crumbs.

The mini bus was far from clean and now full of the other men, the only place for Douglas was in the front, next to the driver, who was the tall, over weight, Probation Officer. The doors closed, the condensation wept from the windows, and radio one screeched from inadequate loud speakers, an inane dribble of Sunday morning disc jockey, and to Douglas, incomprehensible din, that some called music.

Douglas felt that it was torture. They drove through the countryside for half an hour to another pick up stop where there were more men waiting. The mini bus was full and the Probation Officer found himself in argument with the men who were told, that because they had turned up they had paid one hour of their sentence, but as no other mini bus was available, on this day, they would not be able to work. This caused much anger in the group outside the mini bus, for these men could not be rid of their sentences until all their work had been completed. Douglas learned that some of them had had to return to court because they had not completed their unpaid work hours within the time allowed, because there were not enough Probation Officers, or mini buses, to allow them to do so. Some, Douglas found out, after going to court for the second time, had had their unpaid work sentence cancelled, because the system lacked the capacity.

Douglas knew that that was not on the cards for him, but he realised that to get this sentence over and done with, he must make sure that he was bright and early, every Sunday morning, otherwise this would drag on, and on, and on.

The weeks went by Douglas sometimes despaired for there were weeks when he turned up but it was raining, so heavily, the ground was flooded and no work could be done. Then Christmas brought a halt to the sentence, which meant yet more weeks when he would have to live with an incomplete sentence. He just wanted it all to finish.

Back on this first week, with his new boots and gloves, which he would never have the balls to sell on Ebay, sitting in the front of the dirty mini bus, terrified by all that was happening, by the unknown of what was about to happen. The mini bus pulled into a petrol station. The Probation Officer got out and filled the mini bus with fuel, all the men got off the mini bus and went into the garage shop where they purchased food, and drinks, and sweets, and newspapers. Then several of them, including the probation officer, picked up a large number of the free advertising newspapers, which were on a stand outside the garage shop. These were neatly placed amongst the tools in the back of the van. Douglas bought a carton of milk and drank it. The journey took over an hour, loading the van had taken an hour, and now they had reached the place where they were to work it was time for a cup of tea from the urn, in the rear of the mini bus. After the tea came instructions from a new person, who seemed to be from the place in which they now, Douglas did not know where they were, he had never been here before, but it was pretty Cotswold country. It was the new man who told the crowd what they needed to do, and of a sudden all set too picking various tools, from the back of the mini bus. Douglas was still consumed by the fire of his thoughts, furiously angry that his liberty was not his now; flashes of the court and flashes of Arwyn and Raymond lit his mind like an ugly aurora borealis. Douglas was wrestling with this oxymoron when one of the other 'criminals' came up to shake hands with him. It woke Douglas from his day-mare and surprise engulfed him. The short, dark man puffed an e-cigarette and said.

"It's not so bad with this Probation Officer, just don't ever go with that other one, he is an absolute bastard. This guy is easy, as long as you play along, do what they tell you and we'll be home mid-afternoon with a full eight hours of your sentence complete, I'm Dave."

"Douglas." replied Douglas.

They lit a fire, using the free advertising papers, to burn the wood and foliage they cut down during their labours.

Dave was right; there was one week when the Probation Officer was sick and everyone got sent home, but there was another when the Probation Officer was on holiday. That was a bad week, for the woman who came in his stead was a stickler for details, and procedure, and a full eight-hour day was a very, very long, cold and wet one.

She was really unpleasant to herself, and everyone else. She had, tattooed on her right wrist, the word 'Absolute', and on her left wrist, the word 'Bitch'.

The local man was called Ben, something of a diamond; he was something to do with the local community council. He was well over weight, shorter than Douglas and two years younger, but he looked about ten years older. He wore a hi-vis jacket; his hair was streaked with grey, a bit greasy. He was a man of kind heart who loved his community. He often provided a bbq sausage, or at least some biscuits, from his own funds.

There were a couple of men who turned up in their own cars, they had finished their Community Service Sentences but came back to say hi and have a cup of tea with the group. The workload was quiet varied and as the weeks went by the group did many things around and about the area. Cleaning up a riverbank. Cutting back over grown hedgerows and dense bracken covered woodland. Douglas tended to work at the edge of the group. He was tougher than many of the younger men, and in a few weeks he became a 'trusted' member of the group. The group changed of course, new people came others went. Each sentence was a different length. Many short-term friendships evolved amongst the men, none continued once a sentence was completed. Some of the men were reckless. On two occasions trees were felled and Douglas was nearly crushed by them, for those cutting the trees down issued no warning. No women joined the group, although Ben said that sometimes there had been women.

On one Sunday a very large tree had fallen across a wide, fast flowing river. One of those on Community Service was a tree surgeon. This was fortunate for it was he who had the knowledge and the skills to cope with this extreme work. He shinnied and clambered cross the trunk cutting off branches with a chainsaw and flinging them back to the shore. Once across the river he cut the foliage away to free the main trunk. This was a good few hour's work. He climbed back on the trunk and chopped off some logs. Meanwhile the other men tied chains to the trunk and to a tractor and then pulled the trunk away from the river. Soon enough the whole tree was a pile of logs which were, magically whisked away, in various cars, by various local people, who were very grateful for the firewood.

On one, very cold, and snowy, day a fire was lit to burn some foliage and wood. On this day there was a particularly awkward man, who constantly drew attention to himself, the Probation Officer, and Ben, spoke to him and asked him to modify his behaviour, but he kept fooling about doing dangerous things with tools. Of a sudden he picked up the petrol canister, the fuel was used to start the fire; he opened it and threw some of the petrol towards the fire. The stream of petrol caught fire and exploded, suddenly, this idiot of a man, was on fire, like something Douglas had only seen on a television screen. Everyone, including the Probation Officer and Ben were frozen in inaction, horrified by what they saw. Douglas shouted.

"Roll on the floor." The idiot just jumped about in the flames, which were him. Douglas leaped forward and knocked the idiot to the floor and smothered the flames with his own body. Douglas was astonished that no one thanked him, or even mentioned what he had done. Later he thought well may be it was the shock, just imagine what would have happened if that man had died. Health and safety, there was not so much of that.

So the weeks rolled on it was not quite a year when it was all over and then there was a problem for the hours Douglas had done at the Charity Shop had not been recorded against Douglas's sentence and this took some sorting out.

Douglas bought a gift for the Probation Officer and for Ben, on his last Community Service shift. He bought some buns and drinks for the other men. They thanked Douglas and that was then end of that.

A few weeks later Douglas received a letter telling him that his sentence had been completed, within the required time, the reports on his work had been good, and that should Douglas require a reference one would be available from the Probation Office. Douglas smiled at this and wondered just how many jobs a reference from the probation service would get him?

Not all Douglas's clients had abandoned him, and he managed to scrape by through these months, it was far from easy, and he then understood that the sentence was not really over, for he needed to buy an insurance policy. On the insurance application forms question 5 was had he a criminal record? He realised that should a Criminal Records Bureaux check be required, it would show his conviction, bluntly, and without explanation.

He suffered terribly from Post Traumatic Stress Disorder. Horrible nightmares woke him until he was so tired he could not understand how to get along with his life. He regretted now that he had not fought the case, he understood why people have a right to remain silent, and he knew now that he should have kept his mouth closed, and made them prove that he had done what he was accused of. He now knew that the idea of innocent until proven guilty was a nonsense concept. For if he was innocent until proven guilty why did they lock him in a room with a leaking toilet? Why did they not allow him to brush his teeth, or have a shower, why would they not let him have some salt for the disgusting food they served up? Why had they handcuffed him and then locked him in a broom cupboard? He had been so frightened that they would send him to prison. Still there was no going back on all of that now, it was over, and now Douglas had to find a way of living the next part of his life.

He wanted the money from his house. For much as he knew that would make life difficult for Arwyn and her tribe, Douglas's own life was currently barely possible.

The Solicitor said to the Barrister

"I am surprise just how much damage has been done to our client. Jazz musicians, I thought they take drugs, and they often have chaotic lives. Then they bounce back, and people forget the courtroom appearances. Then who cares any more?" Said the barrister.

"I think Douglas is a unique member of his profession. Well maybe not unique, but he appears to be much more like a businessman, dare I say, like one of us. He always wears a suit. I am sure his tailor is better than yours Bernard. Douglas is a sensitive man, and he likes to do good. I am sure he has never taken drugs, and he has never been involved in any criminality, before all of this, not even a speeding fine. The way the newspapers tore into this, one moment he was an, obscure, Jazz musician, next minute he is splash across the tabloids as if the whole population of England are jazz fanatics. I wonder how many, ordinary, English blokes are that interested in Jazz these days? It is a niche market. I am sad to say he may well be damaged for life. He will certainly never be the man he was. I feel extremely sorry for him." Said the solicitor.

The Barrister said.

"Tailor? What do you mean? This suit was off the peg! Well there have been many musician's who have done things, and they have been arrested, and some have spent time in prison. Who was that singer? About ten years ago? Funny hat, make-up, Boy George, I think he went to prison. I think he actually handcuffed a Norwegian guy, and traumatised him! Ray Charles he was arrested for drug possession. Keith Richards got into a lot of bother. Even, the sainted, Paul McCartney was locked up for a day or two in Japan. George Michael, well he was in heaps of trouble, real sex, drugs, and rock and roll! They all weathered the storms in one way or another. Douglas is certainly not as one of these. Reading all of those case notes, it seems to me that there was a conspiracy against him. He was poorly served by the solicitor, who I think he should answer for his shoddy workmanship. I can tell you after going through all the papers, to my mind, it is criminal the way Douglas has been treated.

Unbelievable! All that would be enough to turn a normal person in to a crazed murderer! At the very least he needs the equity from his house."

The solicitor, had remained quiet during this rant but then said, half in jest.

"Otherwise we might not get paid!" He realised he had been flippant and immediately corrected himself. "Sorry I should not have said that. Douglas sold the rights to the last of his back catalogue, music he had written under a pseudonym, and he has just enough money deposited with my firm to cover our fees, but I know that he has no money left now. He went to see if he could get some benefits, but they would not help him because he owns half a house."

CHAPTER 20
The Housing Crisis

Arwyn had not answered letters regarding the sale of the house she owned with Douglas, she was too afraid, for she knew that she had destroyed Douglas in every possible way, and despite the words of comfort Raymond trolled out, she knew that in the end she could not win this battle.

So here they were in court, nearly a year had gone by. Douglas had scraped by. By selling his old catalogue of music he had enough money to pay the solicitor and barrister, but it took every penny.

When the television portrays barristers, they are dressed in finery with black robes and wigs. In reality they wear business suits and scuttle from room to room in places adjacent to the courtroom. They make deals. Despite his anger, despite all that had happened to him Douglas could not think of himself first. The idea that Arwyn's father had an interest in the ownership of the property was completely dismissed. Douglas knew that Arwyn's parents were frail, and needed a home, so he agreed to let them stay in the property for an agreed period, in exchange for a sum of rent each month. To be paid the first day of each month, Arwyn's choice. The failure to make two successive payments would terminate the agreement and the house would then have to be sold. Of course this deal was done in haste, and the details were noted on the back of an envelope, in making the deal no body thought the whole thing through.

*

Don and Don, Donald and Donna, were some of Douglas's greatest friends. Douglas had done some gigs with Don. Don was the best jazz guitar player he knew. Don, his wife was always with Don, the kind of supportive partner Douglas had always wished for. Don did not miss many of Don's gigs. He was a short man thinning on top of his head, but a man who could easily wear a thick bushy beard. Some times he did, sometimes he did not. He was a heavyset man, he wore beige shirts. Don on the other hand was a tall brunet; they had been married for, just about ever. Like all couples they had some awkward times, but they had learned to take the rough with the smooth, and had survived. They loved each other and as they got older they knew that they needed each other, more, and more. Don was quiet, and he was knowledgeable about many things. He was a very intelligent man. He was kind and careful. Don could get excited, and she could get angry, but she had much in common with her man, whom she adored.

After the court Douglas went straight around to their house to tell them the outcome. If you are sensitive to noise you might like to hold your ears, for the shriek of noise the came out of the tall woman could have knocked over the walls of Jericho.

"YOU AGREED WHAT? ARE YOU STARK RAVING MAD? AFTER WHAT THE BITCH DID TO YOU, WITH HER PONSCY POLICEMAN.

MY GOD YOU MUST BE MENTAL. TO GIVE HER THE GRACE OF LIVING IN YOUR HOUSE. YOU SHOULD HAVE TAKEN THE OPPORTUNITY TO KICK HER ARSE. I AM SPEACHLESS…"

You are too nice for your own good…. You see Don, I told you we should have gone with him, he's not safe on his own, like a child, he always looks for the best in people, he always has to do right by people, even if they smash his life to bits. Unbelievable. I saw her you know, last week in Tesco, she looked like death warmed up, and my god how much weight has she put on? She looked like she could do with a real make over. If she turns up at her school looking like that she'll be out of a job. You see Don, I told you."

Don had the remarkable ability to talk forever without breathing, and to sustain ferocity of delivery, as a machine gun, in some bloody conflict. Her words hit Douglas all over his body; he was bleeding from every limb. Then her husband said.

"Don, lets listen to Douglas, lets see what his thinking was, may be he had good reason."

"I'll need a cup of coffee first, and a sit down, unbelievable. Not safe to be let out alone or open a kindergarten!"

She disappeared into the kitchen. Don looked at Douglas and raised his eyebrows and gave a silent shrug of the shoulders as if to say 'yes I know, and I'm married to her.' When Don's voice screeched through from the kitchen.

"That's enough of that Don, I know exactly what you just did, that raise of the eyebrow and that shrug of the shoulder."

She came back to the two 'boys', who had now shared the details of the deal, both felt that they were on the naughty step. This tall women had them quivering in their boots.

"OK so tell us Douglas." Her voice full of Sarcasm. "Why did you accept such a deal? This had better be good."

Douglas, feeling a bit like a sheep in a vat of dip, paused for a moment, and then said.

"Well it was difficult for me, she may be a bitch, as you put it, she may have harmed me until I am all but clinically dead, but her parents did not. She has to pay me enough rent so I can afford to pay my rent."

Don interrupted. "Yes but the amount you have agreed is only just enough. You will be taxed on that as well, it is an income."

Douglas continued. "Actually I had not realised that, no one mentioned tax…Well the amount is half the rental value. I figure that that is a fair bit of money over the agreed term. I have found a caravan on a farm; I can rent it for less than what she has to give me. The property prices are bound to rise, they always do, so the amount I will earn from that increase over the term will be substantial. Then I can take the money and move away from Cheltenham, may be, may be I could go all the way to Gloucester! Or may be Kathmandu"

They all laughed at the first joke Douglas had made for a long time.

"Somewhere house prices are lower, may be. If I take the money now I am not sure how I can find somewhere around here. I will need a bit of time to organise things. It is very difficult just now the fall out from the newspapers has nearly finished me off. The way that that works today is indelible. May be in time things will level out but it will always be there. So I need time to work things out, my whole life must change, and I have to change with it."

He was welling up and had to pause for a moment or two.

"I have never harmed anyone, I tried to protect her from herself, I believe she has made a catastrophic mistake to get involved with that man. Look at the mess she was in when I started reorganising everything, you say open a kindergarten for me. I will say this, that if she fails to make the payments I will have the house sold."

Don said. "I assume that the rent payments will be back dated to the day you had to move out of the house."

Douglas let out a little bleat. "Actually no, she pleaded poverty and for the sake of not wasting anymore money to the barrister and solicitor, I thought it better not to argue."

Don's mouth dropped open and she turned to look at her husband.

"You know Don it is amazing that murder has not been committed by someone during all of this. There must be many people who would want the Policemen dead. How Douglas has not murdered Aywen, well who knows? The whole thing is awful if you ask me."

CHAPTER 21
Twenty-One: Wendy and Philip

Wendy and Philip Jameston, Wendy also knows as Crystal, the Prostitute, who had been arrested by Raymond nearly a decade before, had spent a miserable nine years. Their children had been damaged, their places at Private School had disappeared, but they had been fortunate in that their grandparents had given them a roof and a home. Nine years is a long time for a child. The wounds were deep.

Neither Wendy or Philip could forgive and forget, and Wendy had become harder whilst in prison, there were few days when she did not plan how she would like to end Raymond's life.

On the day of her release her first thoughts were to reunite with her children, see if she could make some amends with Philip. The next thing that was burning on her to do list was to workout exactly how she could kill Raymond, without having to spend the rest of her life in prison.

CHAPTER 22
Better than the Desert

The caravan was not so bad, at least the space was Douglas's own, and he was no longer in a shared house putting up with the mess, and smell, of other people whom were only together for lack of a better alternative. He paid his rent for the first two months and then to his horror the farmer was at his door asking Douglas why the direct debt payment had not gone through. Douglas fumbled with the banks web site and found that Arwyn had failed to make the deposit for the rent. In the scramble to keep himself afloat Douglas borrowed money from his brother, Matthew, so the payment to him that month might also prove to be a problem, and 'what else?' thought Douglas as he peered into the screen. Two weeks went by and the money from Arwyn arrived. The next payment was also late. Then again the payment was missed and before another month had gone by Douglas realised that Arwyn was two months in arrears.

He called the solicitor and asked what had to happen next, the solicitor said they had to return to the court and obtain permission to sell the house. This upset Douglas for he had understood that that was apart of the agreement already made. He had no idea that more court, more solicitor, and more barrister, had to be purchased, and then he got into other fine print the cost of the sale of the house was to be met equally by Douglas and Arwyn. Douglas was angry and protested that that had not been the agreement that had been agreed was that Arwyn had to bare the cost of the sale, the solicitor said that it was a standard clause, and Douglas said well that was not what was agreed. It was written on the back of that envelope in the courtroom. Then he asked how he was going to pay for this. The solicitor said that Arwyn would have to bear the cost of this part of the action. Of course when it came to it there was another 'standard thing' that Douglas had to pay a part of the costs, about a quarter. There were a number other fiery exchanges over this between Douglas and the solicitor, by this time Douglas was really fed up with the whole thing.

Douglas was sharper during this court hearing, he was firm that Arwyn could have no part in the sale, for fear she might frustrate the process, giving her prolonged occupancy. It was agreed that the sale had to be handled only by the agreed estate agent. In fact Douglas too could have no part in the sales, for apart of the sentence he had received forbade his presence at the property for two complete years. So Douglas was oblivious to the next part of the story.

Of course since Douglas had left the property things had been left untended and things had broken. Generally the house looked grubby. The estate agent said the place looked 'tired', Douglas knew she was being polite. So the value of the property was now lower than estimated. It was summer 2016 the UK had voted to leave the European Union Douglas wondered if that would lower the price even more.

Before the buyer had agreed to the purchase of the house. Arwyn's parent's, Robert and Dorothy died, Dorothy just did not wake up one morning and a day after her cremation Robert did not either. Arwyn tried to put the blame on Douglas. Well that is what she said to her friends and anyone who would listen to her, but they all knew that her mother was oblivious to the world and knew nothing of what had gone on. Robert had completed his mission to care for his wife until she was gone.

Raymond had given up on his idea of taking over Arwyn's house, he felt it was all going to take too long, and it was all going to be too complicated. He had, also, had a bit of luck, a horse he had put a bet on had won a race and given him a couple of thousand pounds, and in the same week a lottery ticket and bought a prize of fifty thousand pounds to his bank account. So he was mortgage free with no longer had need of Arwyn and her incessant moans and groans.

Arwyn did not know what to do, when she talked with Raymond about the situation he told her that it was time for him to move on.

"I have had a nice time with you Arwyn," he said "but I have found another woman to be with, and so I just wanted to say good bye and thanks, it was fun and the sex wasn't too bad either."

What he was really telling her was that now you have no house you are of no more value to me.

They were standing in the kitchen, which Douglas had so lovingly renovated. Douglas thought of everything, so there was a fire extinguisher and a fire blanket. The sink had one of those fancy taps, like a Shepherds Crook with a flexible, pull out, hose, so you could swish water around the bowl and keep it clean. There was a rack for saucepans suspended above the kitchen table. The red and white colour scheme, and under cupboard lighting, gave the whole room a warm glow. On the wall by Arwyn, as she stood looking disbelievingly into Raymond's, oval shaped face, and his deep set eye's, was a magnetic rack for knives. On it were a various knives for cutting small things, and cutting bread, and there was a knife sharpener, and a pallet knife, and a carving folk, and carving knife for the Sunday roast. Potatoes, Beef and Yorkshire Pudding.

The pressure cooker of leading the life Dorothy's had insisted upon was about to burst. Now it was cascading and imploding and exploding out of Arwyn. Raymond's smug mug, and sickly limped words, enraged her as nothing had ever done before. There were noises in her head, coloured explosions in her eyes, as in some Hindu festival, the air about her was full of coloured dust and there was a pungent smell in her nostrils which hit the pit of her stomach. Arwyn reached out her hand. She grabbed the carving knife. There was a lunge and the knife plunged through the white cotton fabric and into Raymond's chest, just left of centre. Raymond had no moment to defend himself; the knife plummeted into his pasty, white, skin, between two ribs, and tore the left ventricle of his heart, and severely damaged his left lung. Blood gushed as the blade was pulled back through the flesh. The wound was neat. There was disquietude in Raymond's eye's, his mouth sucked in, as he felt the sting of the steel blade, the skin of his cheeks was vacuumed into his mouth, and a silver white glint came upon him. This event had not featured on Raymond's list of expectations. His exhale finale; the noise of a mule being branded. Raymond's legs folded beneath his, huge, form and he crumbled. Raymond's was motionless.

Then Arwyn wondered, for a second, if the noise of Raymond's last breath had been overheard, two ears scanned the night air for the sound of neighbour response. There was none. The hand, which had plunged the knife into Raymond, was motionless, whilst the ears listened, then Arwyn's other hand reached across to the tea towel, so conveniently placed, on the hook by the sink, and it was used to wipe the blood from the knife, and then from the hand. These actions were slow and considered, in contrast to the lunge, which had just missed Raymond's rib, the serendipity that had brought Raymond's life to it's end.

Then, silently, Arwyn returned the cloth to the hook. The cloth was red with the evidence of Raymond's demise. Arwyn looked down at the executed corpse, and watched to make sure that Raymond was really, and truly, no longer breathing. The watching continued for a few minutes, and then, when the murderer, Arwyn, had reorganised her thoughts, and had decided what next to do, she reached down to Raymond's body; the wiped hand hesitated a moment, for fear that Raymond might spring back to life, but then the hand was pushed into Raymond's trouser pocket, and it's fingers gripped a set of car keys. The keys to the yellow TR7, Raymond's pride, and his joy, the thing he had loved the most, of all things, that is except himself.

It was murder, the premeditation was but a second, but there was no doubt in Arwyn's mind. The stabbing was a deliberate act. There was no hiding that, but the relief, now that Raymond no longer existed.

If you are a person who believes in heaven, and hell, you know that Raymond was not destined to meet with Saint Peter on that day. In fact nobody really cared, that much, that he was gone. The policemen who had arrested Douglas, and told him that Raymond was a good bloke was lying, as so many people do. A couple of policemen attended his cremation though, but there was no ceremony, no lines of policemen in their ceremonial dress, saluting as the pallbearers carried the coffin into the chapel. There were no friends, or relatives, none of the women he had met on the dating site. Not even his daughter, well there was nobody who could actually be bothered to find out where she was to tell her that her father had passed on, what would be the point? It was decades since that pair had set eyes on each other, and no body even knew her name, or that she existed.

Arwyn went to the hallway of the house and took a jacket from the hook. She put on the jacket and opened the front door. She switched off the light and locked the door behind her. She climbed into the driver's seat of the yellow TR7. She adjusted the seat, she adjusted the rear view mirror, she started the engine, she indicated, she looked over her shoulder, she put the car into gear, released the hand break and drove into the night. The knife, with which she had killed Raymond, was on the passenger seat beside her.

Arwyn was not really crying. She did not really know how to. Darren, Justin and Tracy did not enter her mind, why would they, they had all made it perfectly plain that they had their own lives to lead, and they would whatever Arwyn did with her life. Arwyn's grandchild did appear before her for a moment, she thought 'will the child know it's granny was a murderer?' The collie, who had died sometime before, licked her hand and vanished. She was shrouded in a fog of all the things that had transpired since she put herself on the Internet dating site. She had regrets.

Her favourite CD was in the player, Rod Stewart, *'Every Picture Tells A Story', 'Tomorrow is Such A Long Time', the* Bob Dylan song *'Lonesome would mean nothing to me at all.'* The music filled the gaps in her head the car, on autopilot, came to the M5 motorway; she was headed to the west and to the north, then the motorway veered to the east. Before she got to the M54 she stopped at a motorway services Birmingham, she used the toilet, washed her hands and face. Then bought a cup of coffee from Costa's and she continued her journey.

After Telford the M54 morphed into the A5 to Shrewsbury. Further to Whittingham. She did not falter, she new exactly where she was going.

The A483, it took less than three hours to reach Bersham, and she was in the lands of her Grandmother and Grandfather, and the mines, the pits for, she thought, 'this is where I really came from, this is the land of my forefathers'.

She turned left onto the A525 and it was not long before she was passing through Coedpoeth. Then left again on to the B5426, Minera, she passed the park, and the church, then she came to Maes-Y-Ffynnon Road. Not far now she thought.

Arwyn's destination had not changed in her mind and, although she had been driving for hours, and had had plenty of time to think about it she could see no alternative. She knew what was at the end of this road; she also knew that the end of this road was not the destination she was seeking. The destination she was seeking was not physical, it was mental, what she wanted was relief from that constant call that was always, like a toothache in the lower jaw, 'You are never going to be as good as Susan, but you will be alright with that red hair, you will find a man to pay your bills', Dorothy ringing, tolling, the last bell, *'never send to know for whom the last bell tolls; it tolls for thee'. (John Donne)*

So at last Arwyn had found something she truly wanted. Even though her mother was dead, she was not dead, Dorothy was ever alive in Arwyn's head. Still there, still criticising, still unable to admit that Arwyn had done well in oh so many ways. Arwyn was a murderer now, what would her mother have said about that? Thoughts of her children, grandchild, her sister, her brother still would not enter her head.

The Minera Limeworks, she had visited here with her Uncle, when she had been a girl, it seemed so long ago and then it seemed like yesterday. Thirty years ago she and Douglas had visited here too. The dark from the trees and the night mingled with the green, and suddenly her car burst into the white of the lime where the foliage stopped and the quarry began. It was not so easy to follow the road.

She did not want to involve other people in her death but she thought no matter what I do it will cause some people inconvenience. At this time of the night there will be no one to stop me here in this place.

White dust blow up as the TR7 wheels hit a rock, there were some broken bits of fence, and a large warning sign with 'Redland PLC' written on it. She negotiated a hairpin bend, she was not having second thoughts, but as she accelerated she had not realised that her car was not now facing in the direction of the road, so, although she was fully committed to her own death, the actions which were to cause it came a little before she had expected. She found Raymond's car was flying through the air, for what seemed a century.

She saw the faces of her grandchild, and Darren, Justin, and Tracy. She saw Raymond and the pain warping his oval face, and deep-set eyes, and oval chin and his oval mouth and the blood. She saw Douglas's soft gentle face, and remembered his long black hair the first time that they had kissed. She touched chins with him and said.

"I am sorry Joppy. I did love you. Thank you for the love you gave to me."

Then she wondered what they would do when she did not turn up for work on Monday morning. Would her pupils make life hell for some poor Supply Teacher? Oh she had not written the suicide note, but she had only just thought of that, and it was to late now.

Before she could turn the steering wheel, and head back to the quarry edge, the car, with its petrol tank, had exploded on the quarry floor in a great gush of flames, and a bang, which nobody heard. The flames lit the quarry wall, the car and it's contents burned until there was nothing left to burn. Then it just sat there cooling, until everything had cooled, and everything was cold and gone. The sun rose from the east and when it was high enough in the sky it lit the black coloured wreckage, and a breeze blow, and some white lime dust settled upon the bonnet.

'The Breeze' blowing, though the, now, glassless windscreen whispered. "Arwyn will be glad of the jacket she took from the hallway last evening."

'The Morning' said to 'The Breeze'. "You are absolutely right."

'The Morning' handed over it's duties to 'The Day', and The Day got along with it's business until it was time to hand over to The Evening'.

CHAPTER 23
Douglas

Douglas was, and is still, completely unaware of Arwyn's death. (As was everyone else for quiet a time.) Douglas assumed that Arwyn and Raymond would be living together and getting on with their lives. He wondered how Arwyn's parents were getting along without him, but he realised that he was not the only person in the world who could, or would, be able to care about them. He did not know that they had died, how could he? He had moved away, right away to a place where the News of Cheltenham was never broadcast.

The authorities got involved when Raymond's body was discovered, it was his 'mates', from his own police station began the investigation, but then the murder specialists arrived and they took over, with their fancy overalls and shoe covers. They took their photographs and swabbed and dusted for fingerprints. They spend ages looking for the murder weapon, but that was somewhere in the lime quarry, in the burned out wreck of Raymond's TR7.

The Detective Inspector, who was in charge of the investigation, spoke to her Sergeant. They were standing in the hallway of Raymond's house.

"Have you noticed the camera?"

The Sergeant asked. "What camera?"

"Look there." Said Inspector Lovell, pointing.

"Oh yes, you would never have thought it, hardly noticeable." Replied Sergeant Bowls as she looked down and back at her inspector. "I will get the other rooms searched, may be there are others, maybe there are recordings, somewhere, of what has gone on here."

Indeed there were recordings, many recordings, of Raymond's sexual encounters with various female partners, including Arwyn, from his old house as well as Arwyn's. It seemed that sex on the stairs had been something of a fetish for Raymond. The camera in the kitchen had recorded all that had happened, the picture quality was excellent and so was the sound.

Of course the myriad of 'big brother' cameras and APR, number plate recognition, computers were able to reconstruct Arwyn's final journey, at least until she had past into the windy country places, and on to the dusty lime kiln tracks. There was no recording of the final descent, for although the TR7 had been fitted with a dash cam it had been consumed in the fire, and thank goodness for that. No one would wish to see that final fall, or the expression on Arwyn's face as she hit the reality of her spirit detaching itself from her flesh.

Douglas lived his life, from the moment he won the court battle for his house, probably until now, constantly glancing over his shoulder. Ever worried that Arwyn and Raymond would appear on the horizon. Ever worried that he would slip up and mention something from that dark time. Ever did he wonder if he would bump into one of Arwyn's friends, what if Barbara were to be on a visit to the village near where Douglas now lived, what if they were to meet in the street? He knew that the chances were many, many millions to one, but people do win the lottery, even Raymond had. There had been billions and billions to one against Douglas meeting Arwyn and then falling in love, and all the things that then happened. After all there are billions to one that your life ever started, and that you have been a part of evolution is a miracle.

Douglas did not know that Raymond was dead.

Douglas did not know that Arwyn was dead.

He wondered if one day one of Arwyn's children would appear to take revenge, but actually he thought they, even if the two boys were conjoined, they would not amount to all that much of a force, but young Tracy she would be a force to reckon with, she had all the powers of her grandmother and then some.

The post-traumatic stress disorder never fully left Douglas. There were nights when he dreamed of the terrible experiences. There were nights he dreamed that Arwyn loved him and he would wake and feel wretched.

He tried to put her away, out of his mind, although this was not really easy. Nobody knew him now and he started a new life. As so many people had told him he must do.

Douglas made his new neighbours happy and helped them; he made some new friends and acquaintances. He did his work and scraped up a living. He could not find it in himself to take up with a new woman. He agreed with himself that he had not been successful in this regard and he was not prepared to try again. He thought 'besides at this end of my life bodies, and minds, are more, and more, prone to breakage and malfunction, and I cannot think I would want anybody to have to try and hold my old body and soul together. I am not sure I would have the strength to repair, or care, for a woman who needs caring for'. It was not the thought of a selfish man, it was the thought of a man so badly damaged it was all he could do to get up in the morning, and get through another day. He was lonely, very.

People will tell you that time is a great healer, what they mean is with time you may forget. You can forget the insignificant, and some detail, but not these kinds of events. These kinds of events lurk in dark crevices, and leap out every once in a while; just to make sure you remember them.

They do not wish to be forgotten or they would die. You were told 'don't mess with stories, they are powerful things.'

So Douglas's life began again. He still had his old friends; he had his children, although they were all, now, living many miles from where he lived. He made new friendships, for he was that gregarious sort of person.

He remembered welcoming his first wife to his home, oh so many years ago now.

He remembered asking her. "Have you come here to take away my loneliness?"

She responded

"Yes of course."

She had no real understanding of what she had said, it was just warm breath exhaled after being vibrated by her vocal chords.

So like so many 'older' men, Douglas had memories a plenty, millions of seconds of interesting, worthy, fun happenings. He also had the dark, secret, cupboard of the one true mess he had been caught up in. The cupboard was in a corner of his mind, but padlocks on it were not always enough to keep the doors closed and sealed.

He wanted to share, he wanted someone to be with, someone who, who stopped the loneliness of a single bedroom, and a house with just a little too much space for one, but he was too scared.

He travelled to Rouen and dipped a large croissant in to a huge cup of hot chocolate, it was a wonderful breakfast, far from drab old England, and he knew that he was forty years older than he had been on his last visit to this beautiful city, where once Joan of Arc had been tried. Douglas still held the view 'That the real trouble with the world is that one group of people, with a narrow vision, of what they consider to be right and wrong, imposing their vision on the rest of the population.'

People from one group smash the people from another group, individuals too, for that is what human's do. Oh maybe not you, at least it is hoped that you have never, and will never…Have you ever?

Douglas watched the French, and the way French people do things, and he realised that, for many English people, sex is still an impossible problem. Sex is, after all what this tale was about.

*

"Blimey Craig, that was one hell of a story." Said Dave.

Norman went to the bar and brought back three glasses of Whisky.

"My Granddad, Harry, he would call it evolution."

-Fini-